Now You See It

ALSO BY STUART M. KAMINSKY

TOBY PETERS MYSTERIES
Bullet for a Star
Murder on the Yellow Brick Road
You Bet Your Life
The Howard Hughes Affair
Never Cross a Vampire
High Midnight
Catch a Falling Clown
He Done Her Wrong
The Fala Factor
Down for the Count
The Man Who Shot Lewis Vance
Smart Moves
Think Fast, Mr. Peters
Buried Caesars
Poor Butterfly
The Melting Clock
The Devil Met a Lady
Tomorrow Is Another Day
Dancing in the Dark
A Fatal Glass of Beer
A Few Minutes Past Midnight
To Catch a Spy
Mildred Pierced

ABE LIEBERMAN MYSTERIES
Lieberman's Folly
Lieberman's Choice
Lieberman's Day
Lieberman's Thief
Lieberman's Law
The Big Silence
Not Quite Kosher

LEW FONESCA MYSTERIES
Vengeance
Retribution
Midnight Pass

PORFIRY ROSTNIKOV NOVELS
Death of a Dissident
Black Knight in Red Square
Red Chameleon
A Cold, Red Sunrise
A Fine Red Rain
Rostnikov's Vacation
The Man Who Walked Like a Bear
Death of a Russian Priest
Hard Currency
Blook and Rubles
Tarnished Icons
The Dog Who Bit a Policeman
Fall of a Cosmonaut
Murder on the Trans-Siberian Express

JIM ROCKFORD MYSTERIES
The Green Bottle
Devil on My Doorstep

NON-SERIES NOVELS
When the Dark Man Calls
Exercise in Terror

BIOGRAPHIES
Don Siegel: Director
Clint Eastwood
John Huston, Maker of Magic
Coop: The Life and Legend of Gary Cooper

OTHER NONFICTION
American Film Genres
American Television Genres (with Jeffrey Mahan)
Basic Filmmaking (with Dana Hodgdon)
Writing for Television (with Mark Walker)

Now You See It

A TOBY PETERS MYSTERY

Stuart M. Kaminsky

Carroll & Graf Publishers
New York

NOW YOU SEE IT

Carroll & Graf Publishers
An Imprint of Avalon Publishing Group Inc.
245 West 17th Street
11th Floor
New York, NY 10011

First Carroll & Graf edition 2004

Library of Congress Cataloging-in-Publication Data is available.

ISBN: 0-7867-1423-9

Printed in the United States of America
Distributed by Publishers Group West

To Sheila and Richard Olin for past birthdays
and many more birthdays to come

Lincoln Theatre
Decatur, Illinois
Wednesday 2:16 p.m.
November 17, 1942

A PRETTY YOUNG WOMAN IN sequined tights and a glittering tiara moved onstage and whispered something to Harry Blackstone who nodded and turned to the audience.

"And now," he announced, "I will perform an act of magic so big that this theater will not hold all of its wonders."

Wearing white tie and tails, with a white handkerchief showing out of his left breast pocket, Harry Blackstone looked out at his audience of four hundred people and smiled. Then he winked at a little girl in a seat in the first row on the center aisle. The girl grinned and turned her head toward her mother in embarrassment.

Blackstone was tall and lean; a thin dark mustache and a thick hair of billowing silver hair helped create the illusion that his large ears were not quite so large.

"If you will just follow me into the street in front of the theatre," he said, moving to the steps to his right and down into the audience. "I will reveal to you a secret that, in my many years as a magician, has never before been revealed to an audience."

Blackstone stood now in the center aisle and raised his hands to indicate that the audience should rise.

He reached over to the child he had winked at on the aisle row, took her hand and led her toward the rear of the auditorium where the doors were being opened. He looked over his shoulder, saw that people were standing up, and made another gesture.

"The secret," he said, in a strong tenor voice that everyone could hear, "will be yours as soon as we are all outside."

"Rabbits?" asked the little girl.

Blackstone reached down to the girl with his free hand, touched her blue coat with its large gold buttons and produced a white rabbit, which he handed to the child.

"Much bigger than rabbits," he told her in a confidential whisper moving forward again. "How old are you?"

"Six," she said. "Can I keep him?"

Blackstone looked back at the girl's mother who was a step behind. The woman smiled and nodded.

"You may keep him," said Blackstone. "His name is Dunninger. Can you say that?"

"Dunninger," the girl repeated.

"Carry him gently but firmly," said Blackstone, moving now to use the hand that wasn't holding hers to urge the audience into the chilly Illinois afternoon outside.

Still in costume, people from the show were also exiting the building into the street, stopping traffic in both directions to make room for the people slowly flowing out.

"Can you do that?" the girl asked.

"Stop traffic? I've done it before," he said, moving with the girl and her mother.

"Across the street!" he called out. The audience followed his directions. "On the sidewalk." They began to congregate on the opposite pavement.

There, a woman in tights and a man who looked very much like Blackstone—down to the mustache, silver hair, and large ears, but in a rumpled business suit instead of tie and tails—gently urged people into a semicircle facing the theatre. Blackstone motioned to the woman behind the ticket booth. She pointed at herself, and he nodded that he, indeed, wanted her to join the audience on the street. The woman came out of the booth and crossed the street, where she stood next to a teenage boy.

"There are two of you," the little girl at Blackstone's side said, pointing to the man who looked like her companion.

"There is only one Harry Blackstone," the magician said. "That's my brother Peter."

"Is he magic, too?"

"He has been known to do magic," Blackstone said. "Excuse me."

He took the girl's hand from his and patted it gently. The girl wrapped both hands around the nose-twitching rabbit, and Blackstone said above the afternoon traffic.

"Are you ready?" he said.

"So what's the trick?" called a man from the sidewalk.

"And what's the secret?" came the shrill voice of a woman.

"Behold!" said Blackstone with a sweep of his hand back toward the theater.

Smoke was now coming out of the open door. A shock of red flame could be seen inside the theater beyond the doors. The people on the street began to applaud wildly.

"Hell of a trick," came the voice of the man who had asked the question.

"You said you'd tell us the secret," shouted another man. "How'd you do it?"

"The secret which I could not tell you from the stage, but which I can now reveal," said Harry Blackstone, "is that the theater really is on fire."

Place a drinking glass and a nickel on a table. Light a match. Have someone balance the nickel on the table. Blow out the match. Bend the match and balance it on the nickel. Cover the nickel and balanced match with the glass. Challenge those present to remove the match from the nickel without touching the glass or the table and without the nickel moving. If you wish, you can give the following hint: "You can do it with the help of something you might have in your pocket or purse." The trick: Take a comb. Run it through your hair to create static electricity. Move the comb in a circle around the glass. The match will fall and the nickel will not move.

—*From the* Blackstone, The Magic Detective *radio show,*
which aired from 1948 to 1950 with
Ed Jerome as Blackstone

CHAPTER

1

JUNE 25, 1944

THE PANTAGES THEATER WASN'T ON fire, but Blackstone definitely had a problem. My brother Phil and I had been hired to take care of the problem before it killed the World's Greatest Living Magician.

Inside the Pantages, Phil was sitting in the front row with his sons Dave and Nate. Dave, at fourteen, was two years older than his brother and trying his best to hide his awe. It was what fourteen-year-olds did.

Blackstone had opened the show holding a thin yellow hoop, its center covered by white paper. He turned the hoop to show there was nothing on either side. He then turned its face toward the audience, plunged his hand through the paper with a pop of ripping paper and began to pull objects seemingly from another dimension. He pulled out different color silk scarves and let them drift to the stage floor. Dozens of scarves. The audience applauded. Then he reached through the hole in the paper and began to pull out and deposit onstage a collection of rabbits, ducks, and even a pig. The crowd loved it.

Finally, he reached through the paper and took the hand of a smiling dark-eyed woman in a black dress who stepped through the hoop and stood next to him.

From the slit in the rear curtain where I was standing, I could see the boys and my brother Phil. Phil was applauding, but there was no sign of awe on his broad face.

Phil had seen it all in his more than twenty years as a Los Angeles cop. He had seen it all and had enough. We were partners now, Peters and Pevsner, Confidential Investigations, office in the Farraday Building on Ninth just off Hoover. Clients few. Prospects questionable.

Phil's wife Ruth had died less than a month earlier. She had been sick and going weaker for a long time. When she died, Phil had walked away from the LAPD and taken my offer to join me. I hadn't expected him to accept, but he walked away from the past and took his boys and his four-year-old daughter Lucy with him. While we were at the Pantages, Lucy and Phil's sister-in-law Becky were at the house in North Hollywood.

The space behind the thick blue velvet curtains was dimly lit, but I could see props of all kinds laid out neatly, carefully, around me.

Someone had threatened Blackstone. Someone had said that if Blackstone did not reveal the secrets behind all of his illusions to him, he would appear at this show and, some time during the performance, would demonstrate how serious he was.

"A threat?" Blackstone had asked the man on the phone.

"A threat," he had replied and hung up.

Blackstone had not recognized the voice of his caller.

The magician had contacted the police. They had told Blackstone they were not going to be pulled into some publicity stunt. He had persisted. Eventually he got to Sergeant Steve Seidman, my brother's ex-partner, who suggested that he get in touch with us.

And now I stood behind the thick blue velvet curtain at the rear of the stage peering through a small hole, scanning the audience, turning right and left to look for something or someone unexpected or suspicious backstage.

At the stage door, we had posted Jeremy Butler, the huge, bald, 250-lb former wrestler and present poet who was our landlord at the Farraday Building. Jeremy had been a professional wrestler. He was over sixty now, but I didn't think there were many people on the planet who could get past him without the use of gun or a very large sledgehammer, and even then Jeremy might not go down. I wasn't expecting anyone with a gun or a sledgehammer, but both my brother in the audience and me behind the curtain, wearing a bright blue marching-band uniform complete with white epaulets and big brass buttons, were armed. Phil could shoot. So could I. The difference was that Phil was likely to hit what he was shooting at. History told me that I was most likely to shoot an unarmed bystander or myself.

I was pushing fifty, with a few dollars left in the bank from a job I'd done for Joan Crawford and a nice advance from Blackstone. Since being fired from Warner Brothers six years ago by Harry Warner himself for breaking the nose of a cowboy star who was being less than a prairie knight with a young starlet, I had almost supported myself as a private investigator. Now that my brother had left the Los Angeles Police Department and joined me, we needed enough income to support his family and me. For years my brother and I had carried on a love-hate relationship based on (a) my choice of what he considered a less than reputable profession, (b) my changing my name from Pevsner to Peters, (c) my having been born the night my mother died and a variety of other reasons, most of them more reasonable than a, b, and c. Ruth's death had changed that.

What Phil brought to the partnership was knowledge of the city, its crime and criminals, and a lack of even minimal tolerance for people who engaged in felony. Phil had many virtues. Given time, I can come up with a few beyond his loyalty to his family and friends. Phil also had a few problems, most notably his temper. He did not suffer criminals gladly, nor insults, not even for a fraction of a second. That was before Ruth died. Now he could suffer insult and injury for a second or two, far less than the average criminal lunatic. We were a perfect pair.

Through the slit in the curtain I could see Blackstone pull a handkerchief from his pocket, a plain white handkerchief. He tied a little knot in it and suddenly it came to life, responding or refusing to respond to commands. The handkerchief moved away from the magician who pursued it, and began to dance to its own music. It stopped suddenly when Blackstone asked it to do a minuet. The hankie launched into a can-can instead. The audience laughed. The audience applauded. The handkerchief bowed. Blackstone showed that there were no strings attached to the willful fabric. Finally, seemingly frustrated, Blackstone slapped the handkerchief down to the stage floor only to have it rise and do a belly dance as an encore. The audience laughed while the Ziegfeld of magic played straight man to a piece of cloth.

Behind me, Blackstone's crew silently moved equipment to prepare for the next illusion. I hastily got out of their way and headed toward the right wing, listening to the applause. I heard Blackstone's voice onstage, but the only word I could make out was "ducks."

There was no one new in the crew. The most recent addition had been six months earlier. I eased past boxes, caged birds, doves and rabbits, barrels and people.

A thin boy about ten or twelve, with dark hair and eyes,

wearing knickers and a look of rapt attention stood watching from the wings as the magician pulled live and quacking ducks from what appeared to be an empty tub of water. The boy had been chosen before the show to take part in one of the acts. Phil and I had been told that when Blackstone's ten-year-old son, Harry, Jr., was on the road with them, he would take part in the act. Harry, Jr. was back home in Michigan going to school. But, considering what was happening, that was fine with Blackstone.

The kid in the wings looked nervous.

"You alright?" I asked.

"Fine," he said, his eyes meeting mine, his smile a slight raising of the right side of his mouth that was almost a tic.

"You want to be a magician?" I asked.

"Actor," he said. "Like my father."

Onstage, Blackstone scooped up the ducks and placed them on a table inside of a little duck inn.

Someone tapped me on the shoulder. A young man, no more than nineteen or twenty, with a freckled hometown nose, whispered to me, "We've got a problem."

The little boy in the wings glanced at us as we moved past him and then looked back at the stage where the magician was taking the inn apart plank by plank to show that the ducks had all disappeared. The young man with the freckles, whose name was Jimmy Clark, led the way limping, which I assumed was the reason he was not on some island in the Pacific or pushing back the Germans in Europe, instead of backstage at the Pantages.

Peter, the image of his brother, but without the tux and with his silver hair not billowing, stood in front of a polished cage on a wheeled platform.

"It's gone," Pete Bouton said shaking his head.

"What's gone?"

"The switch on the giant buzz saw," said Pete. "The show stopper, the next act."

"Switch?"

"It's . . . about this size."

He held up his spread-out hands about the width of a cigar box.

"Can't do the illusion without it," he said. "I haven't got time to make another one."

"No backup?"

"It's gone too," said Peter, looking at the curtain. "We can do the illusion without it but. . . ."

"But?"

"There could be a problem," he said. "Not much chance, but . . . I can't ask any of the girls to do it. I'll let Harry know we have to end with something else."

Pete Bouton looked decidedly worried, more worried than a canceled illusion seemed to call for.

"What?" I asked.

"There was a note near the box next to the missing backup switch."

He handed me a folded sheet of paper. I unfolded it and moved back where there was more light.

The note, in neat letters, read:

> Magician, is this the unkindest cut of all? Remember the missing blade? It rests where we can all see it. You found a substitute last time. Not this time. You know what I want. I'll contact you.

There was no signature.

"The trick is safe?" I asked. "I mean, even without the switch?"

"Well," said Bouton. "I've built it with three safety backups, but I don't know what this guy has done."

"Can you check it out?"

"Not without going onstage during the act. It's out there covered by a red silk sheet."

"What's the stuff about the missing blade?"

Pete frowned and pursed his lips.

"Only once before has a major piece of equipment been missing, a saw blade for this act. We have a full 70-foot baggage car wherever we go, and in thirty years we've never lost a major piece of equipment except. . . ."

". . . except for the saw blade."

He nodded and said,

"And that was about twenty years ago."

"I'll do it," I said.

"Do it?"

"The giant buzz saw trick."

"It's supposed to be a beautiful young woman," Bouton said. "The audience doesn't want a beautiful young woman cut in half."

"They'll have to settle for a beat-up middle-aged man."

"I'll have to check with Harry," he said.

"Does he come offstage before the buzz saw?"

"No, but. . . ."

"It's not dangerous, right?"

"Well. . . ."

I didn't like the pause.

"Let's just do it. Tell me what to do."

"Oh god," Bouton said. "Alright. Just go stand in the left wing. When Harry uncovers the buzz saw and it's rolled forward, he'll call for his courageous young assistant to come forth."

"And I come forth."

"You do," he said. "Let's just. . . ."

". . . do it," I said. "The big bald man by the stage door, tell him what's happening and have someone tell my brother, the surly looking guy in the front row with two boys."

"You know what you're doing?" asked Pete.

"Definitely not," I said. "That's the secret of my years of success."

Before he could say more, I moved behind the velvet curtain, past the maze of boxes and animals and headed for the left wing. When I got there, my nephew Nate and the kid in knickers who had been in the wings were standing on the stage next to Blackstone.

"And you are?" Blackstone asked.

"Nathan Pevsner," my nephew said in a quivering voice.

"And you?" the magician asked the other boy.

"Anthony Perkins," the boy said in a high reedy voice.

Blackstone reached into his pocket and plucked out a lightbulb. He held it out in front of him, let it go and stepped back. The lightbulb floated and was suddenly glowing brightly.

Blackstone urged Nate and Anthony to see if there were any strings attached. Nate, wide-eyed, looked down at Phil and then at the bulb. He ran his hand around the bulb. So did the other kid.

"Out," said Blackstone.

The lightbulb went out.

"On," said Blackstone.

The lightbulb went back on and started to float away. Blackstone walked after it, guiding Nate and Anthony by the shoulder as they followed it down the stairs on the right and in front of the orchestra where it hovered about waist high.

The audience applauded, and the magician said to Nate, "It's yours to command. Tell it to turn off."

"Turn off," Nate said.

The bulb obeyed.

"Tell it to move up or down," Blackstone said to the other boy.

"Move up," said the boy.

The bulb obeyed.

I looked across the stage at the other wing. A costumed girl stood smiling. Behind her a figure moved forward, a bearded man in a blue dark suit with a turban on his head. In the middle of the turban was a large green glassy stone.

The man in the turban looked across the stage at me and held up a sign.

The large black letters of the sign read:

Buzz. Buzz.

I started to back up as the turbaned man lowered the sign. Blackstone was returning back to the stage.

"And now," the magician said, holding his right hand out. "If my lovely and courageous young assistant would step out to help me. . . ."

I stepped out on the stage. The audience laughed. I was certainly not lovely, and I wasn't feeling courageous. Blackstone's eyes met mine for a flash. He didn't miss a beat. He grinned as if he were in on the joke.

The red silk sheet was pulled off of the device on the other side of the stage, and four girls in frilly tights began pushing the wheeled platform and buzz saw center stage.

Blackstone approached the device, pulled a lever and the buzz saw, about five feet around, began to buzz and whirl noisily.

"With the help of my assistant," said Blackstone. "We will defy the blade, defy death itself."

Blackstone strode over to me and put a hand on my shoulder speaking without moving his mouth as he smiled, "What is going on?"

I was grinning, too. Jimmy Clark, the freckle-faced kid, had limped down the aisle to where Phil was sitting. He was whispering into my brother's ear.

"Switches are missing," I said.

"Missing?"

"Stolen," I said, as Blackstone guided me to the bench next to the blade, which looked all too hard and solid.

"We'll cancel the act," he whispered between closed teeth. "It's just a show."

"Pete said it's not dangerous," I said.

"Not unless someone's done something else to the mechanism."

I hadn't thought of that.

"We can't let him win," I said, lying on the platform.

"God help us," Blackstone said to me. Then he turned to the audience with a knowing smile and loudly announced, "And now death itself will be defied. Those of you in the first rows, should anything go wrong, we will pay the cleaning bills to have the bloodstains removed. And now. . . ."

He turned and, with the help of three young women, strapped my arms and legs with leather straps. He moved away, and I looked down as the buzz saw began to move toward my body between my spread legs.

The audience gasped. A woman screamed.

Just about then a private detective died.

CHAPTER

Hold out your hand and say, "I have three coins in my hand. One of them isn't a nickel. The three coins total thirty-five cents. What are the three coins?" Solution: The three coins are a quarter and two nickels. Show the coins and say, "One of them isn't a nickel. The one that isn't a nickel is the quarter."

From the Blackstone, The Magician Detective *radio show*

THREE DAYS EARLIER

A LOT OF PEOPLE WERE DYING on continents two oceans apart with America in the middle. In the Pacific, the battle for control of the Coral Sea was going badly, from the Bonin Islands to the Philippine Sea, for Admiral Shigetaro Shimada, His Imperial Majesty's Naval Minister, who had taken personal control of the fleet. Thirty Japanese Royal Navy ships had been sunk, fifty-one seriously damaged, seven hundred and fifty-seven aircraft downed and thirteen landing barges on the way to Saipan destroyed in two weeks. Across the other sea, a week after D-Day, the American army had taken Cherbourg. A Japanese radio report explained that "in France, the Allied Armies are retreating haphazardly inland."

Harry Blackstone, in a dark business suit and blue tie, his hair brushed flat, sat at the round table in the office of Pevsner and Peters on the fourth floor of the Farraday Building.

I sat across from him. The office was large, roomy enough for Phil's desk and mine and the round table with four chairs. It had been the headquarters for the inventor of the aoelean trafingle, a goofy electronic gizmo that made weird almost musical sounds when you touched it, sounds that reminded me of dying plumbing. The echoes of the damned thing still haunted the place.

It was almost ten in the morning. Phil was about to be walking in any second. He was out running down information about a man whose name Blackstone had given us over the phone.

Blackstone had been touring for the U.S.O. since the beginning of the war, with a show almost every day, sometimes two. He had also been able to tuck in some dates of his own at major theaters. His five days at the Pantages, which would begin that afternoon, was the longest booking he had scheduled for one theater since 1939.

One of the latest amenities of the new P & P agency was a hot plate in the corner and an aluminum pot of warming Maxwell House. Blackstone had a cup in front of him. So did I.

He took a sip, paused and waited while I examined the four-by-four card he had sent by messenger the day before.

> The Los Angeles Friends of Magic invite you to attend a
> reception and dinner in honor of HARRY BLACKSTONE
> at the Roosevelt Hotel on Saturday June 28 and 8 p.m.
> Formal Attire. R.S.V.P.
> Marcus Keller

I looked across at the magician who said, "It's a challenge. Marcus Keller is not someone who would be honoring me. He considers himself a rival, and he has both spoken at meetings and written letters to magic magazines attacking me and my show."

"Why?"

Blackstone considered, touched his mustache with a slender

finger, and said, "He is—and this is charitable—a third-rate parlor magician with a family fortune in furniture manufacturing. His real name is Calvin Ott, the name I gave you yesterday when I called. Ott took his stage name from my mentor, the great Keller, claiming that he had given him the secret to all of his illusions. It was nonsense. I made the mistake of saying so to my friend Dunninger, the mentalist. My remarks were overheard by some people and . . ."

"It got back to Keller . . ."

"Ott," Blackstone corrected.

"Ott," I acknowledged.

"That was three years ago," said Blackstone. "The man is more than a little demented, a prankster who has bought, flattered, and muscled his way into the office of Conjuror of Los Angeles Friends of Magic. With determination, money, and a devious personality, Calvin Ott has succeeded in making more enemies than Tojo."

"So why is he honoring you?"

Blackstone shrugged and smiled.

"He most certainly isn't."

"You're going?" I asked.

"I've already accepted. We have no show Saturday night. Ott knows that. The theater has been booked for a Sinatra concert."

"And you want us to . . . ?"

"I have a romantic attitude toward challenges," Blackstone said with a grin. "Normally, I'd just do it and take whatever comes, but the same day I accepted the invitation I received a call at my hotel threatening to sabotage my show if I didn't reveal to him the secret of my illusions. The hint of personal danger was also very much a part of the conversation."

He told me then about the call and the man who'd threatened to show up at the theater to embarrass him unless he agreed to reveal all his secrets.

"How were you supposed to give him this information?"

"He said he would have someone at the theater to get it just before the show."

"You called the police, got to Sergeant Seidman and he suggested that you call us?"

"Correct."

"You think the invitation and the threat are connected?"

"I believe in coincidence," said Blackstone, "but I don't trust in it. No one has ever threatened me before. And Ott's jealous rivalry is at least a bit mad."

I pulled a pad of paper and one of the two sharpened pencils I had placed on the table over to me, took a sip of coffee, and got some background information on Blackstone.

Onre Boughton was born September 27, 1885, in Chicago. One of seven brothers, his father was a Civil War veteran who had fought with the Union Army. His mother was a milliner, and his father made men's hats. Their company, Bouton (the 'gh' removed) and Adams was successful and later became the Adams Hat Company.

"Unfortunately," Blackstone said, "my father could not stand prosperity. He supported the saloons of Chicago's South Side instead of his family. I went, at the age of seven, to live in the Home for the Friendless. My father died when I was fifteen."

Blackstone had apprenticed himself to a Halstead Street cabinetmaker. After seeing a performance by the Great Keller, the young Onre Bouton decided to become a magician. When he was 17, he and his younger brother Peter put together a vaudeville act in which Harry did magic tricks and Pete followed with a comic version of the same trick.

In 1910, at the age of 25, Harry, using his skills at slight of hand and cabinetmaking, created his first big illusion show.

"Pete and I put it together with scrap wood, borrowed props, secondhand costumes and a pile of unwanted handbills for a long-defunct magic act called Fredrik the Great. I remained Fredrik the Great till World War I, when it no longer was a good idea. And the rest is . . ."

". . . history," I said looking up.

"Mystery," he corrected with a smile.

I also learned that Blackstone now made his headquarters, workshop, and home in Colon, Michigan, in St. Joseph County, where he owned 208 acres of woods, fields, and beachfront on Sturgeon Lake. There was more, lots more. I filled four pages before the door opened and Phil stepped in.

I introduced them. My brother shook hands, nodded at the magician, got himself a cup of coffee, and sat at the table.

"Calvin Ott is a nut," Phil said, sitting back and running his right hand over the gray bristle of his military haircut. "Calls himself Marcus Keller. He's got a long list of people he doesn't like. He writes letters, makes speeches, brings lawsuits that go nowhere and spends a lot of his family's money making life miserable for people who have made the mistake of existing on the same planet with him, including a tailor, a magazine editor, three different actors, a producer, an actress, and . . ."

"A magician," Blackstone finished.

"More than one," Phil said, working on his coffee. "But you in particular."

I pushed Blackstone's invitation to the dinner in front of him. Phil had already seen it, but he looked at it again. "I think I should have a talk with Calvin Ott," he said.

Blackstone didn't know, but I did, that "a little talk" to Phil was a few questions and then, if he didn't like the answers, woe to the other guy.

"Why don't I do that?" I said. "You stay with Mr. Blackstone and. . . ."

There was a knock at the door, and a short, pudgy man with thick glasses, very little hair and a half-smoked cigar stepped in without being invited. Shelly Minck was wearing a once-white short smock with small but distinct splotches of blood in a decorative line across his chest.

Shelly was a dentist. At least he had a dental degree. There were those who called him less respectful things than "dentist." His technique was clumsy, his office less than clean, his manner insensitive, and his enthusiasm unbridled. Until a month ago, when my brother joined me, I had rented a small cubbyhole inside Shelly's office down the hall.

Shelly had spent years inventing devices to improve the dental health of the world while, on a personal one-on-one level, he did his best to undermine the mouths of those who mistakenly let themselves be drawn into his chair. One of Shelly's inventions had actually paid off. He had sold it to a medical products manufacturer in Iowa or Nebraska. He wasn't quite rich, but he was close to it. I had tried to persuade him to retire and devote himself to inventing. I had failed and, in so doing, doomed who knows how many innocent and guilty mouths.

"I can't abandon my patients," he had explained. "They count on me. They trust me. My skills are legendary. You know that, Toby."

He was right, but the legend was Sleepy Hollow.

"I'm interrupting?" Shelly asked, looking at Blackstone.

"Yes," said Phil.

"Just take a minute," Shelly said, moving forward, adjusting his glasses on his nose before they slipped off.

"Shelly," I tried.

He held up a hand and said, "Grieg."

"Grieg?" said Phil, turning his body in his chair to look at the dentist.

"Edvard, the composer," said Shelly.

"You've got Grieg in your office?" I asked.

"No, no," Shelly said, sitting down uninvited and glancing at Blackstone.

It was clear Shelly was trying to place the magician. I prayed to whatever gods might be that recognition didn't come.

"I think Grieg is dead," said Shelly. "Good point though. I'll check. Maybe we can go into partnership. Toby, like all great discoveries, the telephone, penicillin, liverwurst, it came to me by accident. Had the radio on. That guy who plays the piano in the afternoon. Had Mrs. Westermanchen in the chair. She just closed her eyes. Music played."

"Grieg," said Blackstone, intrigued by this rotund vision.

"Yep," said Shelly, pointing at Blackstone. "Worked on her cavity. Molar. Deep. Not a peep. Not a scream."

Patients, except for the most stoic and those who enjoyed pain, frequently screamed under Shelly's care.

"Tried it again with three other patients," he said. "Worked. Grieg knocks them out. There's a fortune here somewhere and a medical breakthrough and . . . the possibilities are goddamn staggering and. . . ."

He stopped suddenly and looked at Blackstone.

"Can I trust this guy?"

"Minck, go away," said Phil.

Shelly got up.

"I just told the biggest secret of my life to a stranger," Shelly bleated.

"I'm accustomed to keeping secrets," Blackstone said, obviously amused.

"I can believe this guy?" Shelly asked, looking at me and readjusting his glasses.

"You can."

Shelly turned to the magician, looked at him, and suddenly placed him.

"Blackstone," he said.

Blackstone nodded.

"The magician. Hey, wait a minute. Wait a minute. Maybe we've got something here. Fate. Something. You're here. Fate. I figure out the Grieg stuff. Fate. Juanita says when things like this happen, it means something."

"Juanita?" questioned Blackstone.

Shelly ignored him and said,

"I've got it. Magical dentistry. The Blackstone & Minck secret of painless dentistry. "

"Minck, get the hell out of here," Phil said, rising from his chair.

Phil's face was pink. Soon it would turn red. When it did, it would mean disaster for one babbling dentist.

"Go," I said. "Now, Sheldon."

"But . . ."

"Now," I insisted.

"Fine, fine, fine," he said, moving to the door. "A revolution in dentistry comes through your portals and you turn it away."

Phil was standing and facing him now.

"I'm going," said Shelly, his hand palm out at Phil to hold him back. "Mr. Blackstone, I'm right down the hall. Let's talk."

And Shelly was gone.

"Sorry," I said.

"No," said Blackstone. "That was the funniest performance I've seen since I was on a bill with Raymond Hooey, the comic chiropractor, in Provo, Utah."

Phil refilled his coffee cup and mine and offered Blackstone some. Blackstone declined, lost in thought.

"A dental illusion," he said. "A man, no, a woman strapped into a dental chair. A few people from the audience onstage. A dental drill making that familiar drilling sound. It looks as if I'm drilling. They would swear I was drilling or even removing teeth.

Yes, I remove the teeth, show them, and put them in a small urn. The patient opens his mouth to a few people from the audience who have come onstage. Front teeth are missing. The patient's mouth is closed and when it opens, the teeth are all back, no longer in the urn and then the patient. . . ."

Blackstone stopped, suddenly out of his reverie and said, "That's a ridiculous idea. That dentist is infectious."

"He can be," I said. "I suggest when you leave here you hurry past his door before he convinces you that you need bridgework."

We fixed a fee, forty dollars a day plus expenses plus a two hundred-dollar retainer, shook hands, and Blackstone and Phil headed for the door. As they were about to leave, I said,

"Sure you don't want to just call off Ott's party?"

"I'm looking forward to it," Blackstone said, with more than just a twinkle in his eye.

CHAPTER

3

Place a saucer and a drinking glass 1/4 full of water on a table. Drop a coin in the saucer. Pour 1/2-inch of water from the glass into the saucer. Ask a member of your audience to remove the coin with his or her fingers and not get the fingers wet without lifting the saucer. Solution: Take a piece of paper. Hold it over the empty glass. Strike a match. Drop the burning paper in the glass. As soon as the paper is finished burning, place the inverted glass in the saucer over the coin. The glass will suck up the water. The coin will be dry and can be picked up.

—From the *Blackstone, The Magic Detective* radio show

CALVIN OTT LIVED IN SHERMAN OAKS. I had called him and said I was on Blackstone's staff and wanted to make arrangements for the reception.

He readily agreed to see me and said to come right over. He sounded happy to hear from me.

My cramped Crosley made its constipated and reluctant way up the winding roads, threatening to slip backward into the hillside oblivion when the road was too steep for its refrigerator engine.

I listened to the radio and drove through modern Los Angeles, a mess of architectural styles and convulsive growth. There were survivors of the post-Civil War era with their cupolas and curlicues, brownstones from the 1880s with elaborate ornaments and great bay windows with colored glass, and a never-ending number of frame bungalows and boxlike office buildings from the first two decades of the twentieth century. Not to mention the pseudo-Spanish homes and apartment buildings from the boom back in the '20s that also brought skyscrapers, movie palaces, and bizarre restaurant designs. There was a restaurant shaped like a derby hat, another one shaped like a rabbit, a third like an old shoe, another like a fish and one like a hot dog sandwich. There were also modern houses and steel, concrete and glass buildings. The landscape was also dotted in much of the County of Los Angeles by huge gas tanks, gaunt and grimy oil derricks, and silver power lines.

KMTR radio news told me the Chinese had stormed the Japanese North Burma base of Mogaung. The Soviets were closing in on Minsk. French patriots had killed the Vichy Minister of Information and Propaganda, Phillipe Henriot, in his bed in Paris, and the Chicago Cubs were at the bottom of the National League standings with an 18-34 record.

I passed houses with wrapped bundles of scrap paper pilled on the narrow sidewalks for pickup. The day was clear. Wet paper wasn't accepted. I didn't know why.

Near the top of the hillside, the baritone voice on the radio told me that a Mrs. Elizabeth Koby of Whiting, Indiana, a $24-a-week Standard Oil employee, had received her two-week check. It was for $99,999.52. She returned it.

In Augusta, Maine, Ralph E. Mosher, who'd won the nomination for state senator on both party tickets, reported his total campaign expenses as eighteen cents including ten cents for a beer to "relax tension."

In Los Angeles, a few miles down from where I was driving to the domicile of Calvin Ott, the police were investigating the robbery of $251 from Jim Dandy's Market. The robber left one clue, his heel prints.

Now well informed, I pulled onto the cobblestone driveway I

was looking for and parked alongside a heavy blue four-door Pontiac.

The house wasn't big, not for this neighborhood, but I didn't think there were many to match it in the neighborhood. Stone gargoyles stood on either side of the entrance. Their heads were turned so their blank eyes would meet approaching guests. The high doorway itself was made of dark wood. Cut deeply into the wood was the figure of another gargoyle. There was no handle that I could see. No knocker and no bell.

I raised my hand to knock, but before I could, a deep voice from above the door said,

"Your name?"

"Toby Peters."

"Say the magic words that opens the door of the cave."

"Open sesame," I tried.

"No," came the voice.

"Give me a hint."

"It's 'abracadabra,'" came the voice.

"Abracadabra," I said.

The door opened. A thin man in a white suit, white shirt, white shoes, and black tie stood in front of me. He had a glass of clear liquid in his left hand. His face was smooth and pink, his hair receding. He was about forty.

"Calvin Ott?" I asked.

"Maurice Keller," he said, with a shake of his finger to suggest that I was being intentionally naughty. "Come in."

The brightly lit wood paneled hallway was covered with large, colorful eye-level posters, evenly spaced.

"That one," Ott said beaming as he closed the door behind me, "is my favorite."

The poster showed a nearly bald man sitting in a wooden chair. The man's head was floating away from him. The words on the poster read: Keller In His Latest Mystery. Self-Decapitation.

"A favorite," Ott said, pointing to the poster. "The master. A brilliant illusion."

"Impressive," I said as he led me down the hallway past more posters.

On my left was the wide-eyed face of a man wearing a large turban with a bright emerald green stone in the middle of it. The words on the sign read: *Alexander. The Man Who Knows.*

On the right was a poster of a smiling man with cartoonlike ghosts floating around him: *Do Spirits Return? Houdini Says No And Proves It.*

We moved past colorful posters of Brush the Mystic and His Hindu Box; Carter The Great Beats The Devil; Floyd, King of Magic; Dante; Levante, Long Tak Sam.

Ott stopped and faced the last one on the left at the end of the hallway.

"Probably my favorite of all."

It was a color illustration, depicting a clean-shaven smiling man in a tux with a white flower in his buttonhole walking next to a white shrouded skeleton looking at him. A pot of fire sat next to them with little drawings of someone in an electric chair, a guillotine, and a man about to be lowered into a glass vat of water. The name Steen ran across the top of the poster, and there a phrase in French on the bottom.

"The man who is amused by death," Ott translated, stepping into a large white-carpeted living room with ceiling-to-floor windows at the end.

The matching plush furniture included two armchairs and a sofa, with a large low round table between them. On the table was a skull nestled on a well-polished dark wooden base. The room was lined with shelves filled with gadgets.

Ott pointed to one of the chairs. I sat. It was comfortable. He clapped his hands and the chair began to shake. I held onto the arms to keep from falling.

"Spirits?" he asked, eyes widening.

He clapped again and the shaking stopped.

"Spirits?" he repeated. "Sherry? Something stronger? A beer?"

"Pepsi," I said. "If you have it."

The skull had turned slightly and was looking at me.

"That's the skull of Bombay The Great," Ott said, a small smile on his face. "Bombay perfected the flying carpet illusion. He lost his head in a train wreck outside of Turin in 1883. I gained his head forty years later. Pepsi?"

"Yeah," I said, meeting Bombay the Great's hollow gaze.

"Be right back," Ott said, his grin growing, his eyebrows raised. "Amuse yourself, but don't touch."

When he left I got up and looked at the gizmos on shelves. There were glasses—both the kind you drink from and the kind you wear—books, lamps, an open straight razor, a package of gum, a long knife with a fancy ivory handle and a curved blade, matchboxes, a typewriter, cigar boxes, small statues of African figures and Greek warriors. A glassed-in cabinet held neatly arranged pistols and knives.

I was looking at a compact wooden radio when Ott returned with my Pepsi glass and a glass of something amber for himself.

"That's the Anderson Surprise Radio," he said, sitting and crossing his legs. "You turn it on and it works. You turn the dial and the top pops open with a loud electrical sizzle and a shower of spring-activated colorful balls. The company went out of business two years ago. An old man tried to get H.V. Kaltenborn on that radio, had a heart attack instead of the news."

"Fascinating," I said, raising my glass.

"Isn't it?" he said, raising his.

"And the guns?"

"Cigarette lighters, flares, guns for making loud noise and lots of smoke. That's what audiences like. The smell of smoke. The noise. The danger they know isn't really danger and yet can think,

'What if something goes wrong?' Something could always go wrong. And sometimes it actually does."

I drank and felt something on my chin. The glass was leaking. Ott beamed and grinned. I put the glass down in front of Bombay the Great.

"Dribble glass," Ott said. "Can't resist it. Sorry."

He didn't look sorry. I wiped my chin and neck with my sleeve, trying to show nothing.

"Get you another one?" he asked, starting to rise.

"No thanks," I said.

He looked around the room with satisfaction.

"World's largest collection of practical jokes," he said with a sweep of his hand.

"Practical?"

"Yes, I've always wondered why they were called practical jokes too," he said. "But I've learned to accept life's small mysteries. You?"

"I try to solve them," I said. "Unanswered questions give me stomach cramps. Why are you hosting a dinner in honor of Harry Blackstone?"

He nodded, reached into his pocket and pulled out a silver cigarette case and a small matching lighter. He took a cigarette from the case, put it in his mouth, and flicked on the lighter. A tiny pink umbrella popped up from the lighter.

"Funny?" he said with a grin.

"Hilarious," I said.

He put the lighter and case back in his pocket, played with the cigarette for a second and offered it to me.

"Don't smoke," I said.

"Just as well," said Ott with a wide toothy grin. "It would have exploded."

"Blackstone," I reminded him.

"Bygones are bygones," he said, leaning back and looking at

the ceiling. "He insulted me. I've learned to accept insults. Grudges are useless. Blackstone is a fine magician."

"I didn't see any Blackstone posters in the hall."

"I respect him. I don't admire him. My moods, my opinions change constantly. I can be laughing one minute, crying the next. Would you like some peanuts?"

"No. I'd like some answers."

He let out an enormous sigh and stood up, taking a long drink from his glass and then placing the glass on the table.

"What do you see before you?" he asked.

I saw a slightly looney man with a lot of money and time.

"Calvin Ott," I said.

"No," he shouted, his face turning red. I think I jumped in my seat. "No," he repeated calmly. "You see Maurice Keller, Illusionist Extraordinaire."

"When's the next show?" I said, forcing myself to grin and sit back.

"I don't perform in public," he said. "I may have something special in honor of Blackstone, however."

"Mind if my brother and I show up?"

"No," he said, happy again. "You'll be welcome. In fact, I insist."

I got up, looked at Bombay the Skull, who turned away from me. Ott was grinning.

"Would you like to see the rest of the house?"

"No, thanks," I said.

"Your loss," he said as I turned toward the hallway. "You can show yourself out?"

"I can."

"There's no door handle," he called as I walked down the hallway of posters. "Just say the magic words."

"Abracadabra," I said standing in front of the door.

"No," called Ott. "That's for getting in. The other words."

"Open Sesame," I said.

The door swung open suddenly, missing me by a few inches.

Behind me Ott said, "I've been meaning to get that fixed before someone got hurt.

I went outside. The door closed. The stone gargoyles watched me leave.

I drove home, Mrs. Irene Plaut's boarding house on Heliotrope in Hollywood. I hadn't let onto Ott, but the dribble glass had done more damage than I let show. My shirt was soaked with sticky Pepsi. I had to change.

I found a Bill Stern sports report on the radio. Bucky Walters of the Reds was on his way to winning 30 games. A bunch of pitchers looked like they were going to win 20 including George Munger of the Cards, Bill Voiselle of the Giants, Rip Sewell of the Pirates, Ted Hughson of the Red Sox, Hank Borowy of the Yankees, Hal Newhouser of the Tigers, and Bill Detrich of the White Sox. It was a pitcher's season.

There was a parking space right in front of Mrs. Plaut's. It was small, but so was the Crosley. I hadn't picked up a parking ticket in almost two years, which is quite an accomplishment given the Los Angeles traffic regulations that seemed to be designed to guarantee an unlimited source of revenue from drivers who couldn't keep it all straight.

The Los Angeles speed limit was twenty miles an hour in business districts, twenty-five miles an hour in residential districts. Right turns were permitted against the red from the right-hand lane after a full stop, but pedestrians and vehicles proceeding with a signal had the right of way. There was no parking along red or yellow curbs, three-minute parking along white curbs, fifteen-minute parking at green curbs. Along unmarked curbs, you could park for forty-five minutes in the Central Traffic District from seven in the morning till four-thirty in the afternoon, but there was no parking in the district from four-thirty to six p.m. Parking was unlimited from six p.m. till two a.m. From two to four a.m. there was a thirty-minute parking limit, but parking was unlimited from four till seven a.m.

Having parked legally, I plucked at my moist shirt as I walked up the sidewalk to the porch where Mrs. Plaut, tiny, thin, ancient and determined, sat on the porch swing, a pencil in one hand, and a pad of lined paper in the other. That meant one of two things, neither of which boded well for me. She was either working on her family history, which was now several thousand pages long or she was doing a grocery list.

If it were the history, I would soon be getting a pile of neatly written pages to read and approve. Mrs. Plaut, more than a little hard of hearing and often in audio contact with a world the rest of us couldn't hear, believed that I was two things, a book editor and an exterminator. She did not think the combination odd and had once told me that the long-gone Mr. Plaut had once been a prospector, stagecoach driver, and tree surgeon at the same time.

If she were working on her grocery list, it would mean a trip to the nearest Ralph's, which I didn't mind. What I minded was the mind-numbing explanation of the rationing system, which Mrs. Plaut had mastered and I was expected to remember.

"Mr. Peelers," she said, looking up at me.

I had long ago decided not to correct her.

"It is I," I said.

"I was going to give you this list this evening, but as luck would have it, here you are."

"Here I am, as luck would have it," I said. "I need a shower and a change of clothes."

She looked at me and said,

"You need a shower and a change of clothes."

"I'll do that."

"Shopping list," she said, handing me the sheet she had been working on. I didn't look at it.

"We're having beef heart stew tonight, if you can do the shopping this afternoon."

"I'll do the shopping this afternoon," I said.

She reached into the crocheted purse next to the wooden chair and came up with three one-dollar bills, which she handed to me along with the dreaded ration coupon book.

I looked at the list:

Beef hearts, two lbs.	40 cents
20 oz. loaf, bread	10 cents
Hot dogs, one lb.	19 cents
Ritz crackers, one lb.	19 cents
Armour's Treet, 12-oz. can	27 cents
Super Suds, large	23 cents
Cuticura skin ointment	37 cents
Squibb Aspirin (200)	69 cents
Miracle Whip 16 oz.	19 cents

"The Cuticura is a necessity," she said. "My hands."

"I'm sure," I agreed.

In truth, Mrs. Plaut did have delicate hands and long fingers.

"The ration calendar," she said.

The dreaded ration calendar. There was no escape so I simply listened, mind growing numb.

"Processed food," she said, without reference to notes. "Blue A8 through V8, book 4, is now valid at 10 points each for use with tokens. You understand?"

"Perfectly," I said.

"W8, X8, Y8, Z8, and A5 became good July 2."

"Got it," I said. "Anything else?"

"Meats and fats," she said. "Red A8 through W8, book 4, are now valid at 10 points each for use with tokens, of course."

"Of course," I agreed.

"And you should know, Mr. Peelers, that A-10 coupons are now valid for gasoline. Rationing rules now require every car owner to write his license number and state on all gas coupons in his possession as soon as they are issued to him. And here."

She handed me about thirty additional sheets of lined paper.

"A chapter about Wooley in England," she said.

"Wooley?"

"My second eldest brother, now deceased," she said, with a shake of her head to indicate that this was information I should have possessed. "I would appreciate your reading it this night."

"May I take a shower and change now?" I asked.

"You won't need any change," she said. "The three dollars will be quite enough."

I didn't answer. I went inside and headed for the steps. On my left were Mrs. Plaut's rooms. Inside, her caged bird was screeching. She changed the name of the bird with cycles of the planets, the changing of the tides, the fortunes of war, the sudden emergence of long-forgotten friends. The current name of the bird, she had informed us at dinner the night before, was Admiral Nelson. It was as certain to change by breakfast tomorrow, as it was that Dewey would get the Republican nomination for president.

On my left was the parlor, decorated in the latest furniture and fashion of the year right after the Civil War.

I went up the steps and to my room where I put Mrs. Plaut's grocery list, coupons, and the chapter of her book on the small table near the window. Then I took off my shirt, selected another one that seemed to have no missing buttons and was reasonably clean, and headed for the bathroom down the hall. Stripped, door secured by the flimsy hook and little eye, I showered and sang *A Little On The Lonely Side*, at least the words I could remember.

When I finished, I headed back toward my room pausing at the door of Gunther Wherthman, my closest friend, who stood less than four feet tall and carried himself with a dignity that should have been the envy of every slouching congressman.

I knocked. Gunther called for me to come in. The door wasn't locked. No doors at Mrs. Plaut's were allowed to be locked. Privacy, she believed, nurtured the possibility of perversion.

Gunther's room was the same size as mine, but that's where the comparison ended. My room looked like a messy college freshman's dorm closet. A worn sofa against one wall, a dresser near the door, a small table with two chairs. A box of a refrigerator the size of a peach crate, and a mattress against the wall. The mattress plopped down on the floor at night and so did I. My back is ever on the verge of rebellion and needs a firm thin mattress and the promise that I will never sleep on my stomach or side.

Gunther's room had a neatly made-up single bed in the corner with a muted multicolored Indian blanket over it and matching pillows on top. There was a single soft brown leather armchair, a dark Persian throw rug on the floor, dark wooden bookshelves against the walls, and a desk near the window with neat piles of paper, magazines, reports, and books. In the swivel chair by the desk, Gunther sat wearing, as he always did, a three-piece suit and tie. Gunther worked in his room as a translator for industry and the government. He always dressed for work.

"You think Grieg's music can cause someone to feel no pain?" I asked, standing in the open doorway.

"He was of a dour Norwegian bent," Gunther said seriously, with his slight Swiss accent, "and it has been said that even his *Peer Gynt Suite* might incline those less than devoted to his work to escape the performance by a protective self trance."

"Meaning?"

"When bored by Grieg, people have been known to fall asleep, sometimes with their eyes open," he explained. "May I ask why you present this question?"

"Shelly," I said.

Gunther shook his head. The dentist's name was explanation enough.

"What do you know about magicians?" I asked.

"When I was with the circus," Gunther said, tapping the tiny fingers of his right hand on his desk, "I encountered several. At one point I was even employed by Spengler Aroyo, Spengler the Magnificent. Magicians like to have little people in their acts. He billed me as Hugo the Dwarf. I objected. I am not a dwarf. I quit. Magicians are often dual of visage—open, gregarious in public, intense and brooding in private."

"Phil and I are working for Harry Blackstone," I said.

"It is my understanding that he is an amiable gentleman of his word," said Gunther. "Can I be of service?"

"I'll let you know," I said. "What are you working on?"

"This?" he said, putting his palm on a yellow folder. "This is a fascinating technical report in Danish of a process for the ultra-refinement of crude oil."

"Fascinating."

"You jest," said Gunther with a smile.

"See you at dinner," I said. "Beef heart stew."

I left the room closing the door behind me as the phone at the end of the hall rang. I moved to get it.

"Hello," I said.

"Tobias," said Phil. "Our client got another call. "Tomorrow night's performance at the Pantages. The son-of-a-bitch said it would be Blackstone's last unless he turned over his secrets to someone who would come to him at the theater before the show."

"You talk to the caller?"

"Yeah," said Phil. "I told him we would be waiting for him. He laughed and called me a blustering stooge."

"What did you do?"

"Tore the damn phone off the wall."

CHAPTER

4

Write something on a sheet of paper, fold it, and tell the other person to place it in his pocket. Lay out two small piles of cards. Make it clear that the piles do not have the same number of cards. Tell the other person that you have predicted which pile he will point to. Have him point to a pile. Tell him to open the sheet of paper you have written on. The number 7 is written on the paper. Pick up the pile and count. There are seven cards in the pile. Solution: If the other person had picked the pile with four cards, you turn the cards over. They are all sevens.

From the Blackstone, The Magic Detective *radio show*

AND THEN IT WAS WEDNESDAY, the 25th, and I was on the platform on my back about to be buzz-sawed up the middle, while dressed in a blue uniform with epaulets and big brass buttons.

I don't know what happened. I don't know how it happened. I do know that the blade was real and spinning noisily very close to the last place I wanted it to be. Then darkness. I felt myself turning over, rolling to my right. Then I was lying on a mattress looking up at Jeremy Butler who reached down, took my arm, and lifted me up. Jimmy Clark, the freckled kid with the limp, stood next to him.

I reached down to be sure I was intact and dry. I was.

"Come," said Jeremy, turning and leading me away. Beyond the curtain, from where I had tumbled onto the mattress, the crowd was applauding.

"What happened?"

"Blackstone turned you into a lion," Jimmy said. "We've got to hurry so he can turn the lion back into you."

The three of us dodged props, went through a small pack of heavily made-up girls with spangled blue swimsuits, evaded two men in Babes in Toyland uniforms like mine and headed up a steel staircase. The kid was in the lead, then Jeremy, then me.

The staircase rattled. Someone in the wings below gave a loud "shush," which could probably be heard in the first half dozen rows of the theater.

At the top of the stairs, the kid went to a door, opened it and stepped back. I entered a large dressing room lined with mirrored dressing tables.

There was only one person in the bulb-lit room, a man at the third table on my left. He was leaning forward, his face pressed against the mirror, eyes open as if he were astonished by his own image and trying to get a closer look.

He was dead. No doubt. The giveaway was not just the open eyes and mouth, but the hole in the side of his head and the thick stream of blood making its way down his cheek.

"Who found him?" I asked.

"Marie," said Jimmy.

"Marie?"

"This is her dressing room and the other girls'," the kid said, unable to take his eyes off of the dead man. "She came back for . . . and she found him."

I moved forward toward the body.

"Get Marie," I said.

"She won't come in here," said Jimmy. "I know her. She'll start screaming and all. He's dead, right?"

People were gathering in the open doorway.

"Most sincerely dead," I said, leaning over to look at the dead man's face in the mirror. "And call the police."

Outside the open door, people were gathering, looking, not quite taking in what was happening.

"Jeremy, close the door."

Before he could close the door, my brother Phil and Pete Bouton stepped in. Phil looked at the body. He'd seen dozens before, but this one he recognized.

"Robert R. Cunningham," he said.

"Who?"

"Blackmailer, con man, blackmail, posed as a cop sometimes, or an insurance investigator," said Phil, moving in for a closer look at the dead man. "Had a private detective license. We took it away."

Phil touched Cunningham's cheek.

"Couldn't have gotten it more than a few minutes ago. Who heard the shot? Saw someone?"

"The buzz saw," said Pete Bouton. "The sound of the buzz saw probably drowned out the shot."

"Which means," I said. "The killer waited for the saw to start making noise."

"Or he . . . ," Phil began.

"Or she," I amended, "just got lucky."

A knock. The door opened, and Jimmy Clark stuck his head in.

"Called the cops," he said. "Marie's out here."

"Thanks," I said, and then to Phil. "She found the body."

Phil and Bouton stayed with the dead man. The kid and I went out onto the landing and through a small crowd of people. Voices in the crowd asked, "What happened? Someone hurt? Shouldn't we call an ambulance? Who . . . ?"

Jimmy guided me into a room three or four doors down. The room was crowded with boxes of rabbits, quacking ducks, fluttering and frightened cooing doves. Sitting with her back to a mirror was a pretty girl with short dark hair in bangs, very red lips and one-piece green bathing suit covered with glitter that caught the light and shimmered with each sob.

I ushered Jimmy outside, closed the door and turned to the girl.

"Marie," I said.

No response.

"Marie," I repeated.

This time her head jerked and she looked at or through me.

"You found the body."

It wasn't a question, but she answered with a nod.

"You hear a shot?"

This time, the nod was a negative shake of the head.

"You see anyone near the dressing room?"

Positive nod this time.

"Who?"

She tried to speak, caught her breath and said, "A man. Came running out. I was going in to get . . ."

"What did he look like?"

"Suit, tie I think. Had a beard like the devil always has in pictures and movies you know?"

"I know."

"And he was wearing a what-do-you-call it? Thing you wrap around your head?"

"Turban," I said.

"Yeah, with this green piece of glass right in the middle, here." She pointed to a spot just over his forehead, and added, "He's dead. Cunningham. I could tell, right?"

"He is," I confirmed. "You know why he was in the women's dressing room?"

"Gwen's boyfriend," she said.

"Gwen?"

"She's the tiger lady, the one in the tiger costume," Marie said.

I remembered her. She was very pretty and very young.

"Dead man is about forty-five, overweight, and looks a lot like Charles Laughton," I said.

"He's also rich," she said. "Gives . . . gave her lots of stuff, you know?"

That explained a few things. Cunningham was seeing a girl in the show. Cunningham used a false name. Cunningham pretended he was wealthy. Now Cunningham was dead. The police were on the way. I wanted to find Gwen.

"Police will be here soon," I said. "Stay here. You want company?"

The "yes" nod.

"I'll send someone in."

I went out the door. The pack was waiting for me. Jeremy was on the landing now, protecting the door of the dressing room where Phil was looking for whatever he could find.

I motioned for Jeremy. He pressed his way through the crowd on the narrow landing, and I told him to sit inside with Marie till the police came. He went through the door and I asked, "Which of you is Gwen?"

No one answered. People looked around at each other.

"The girl in the tiger costume?" I tried.

"Gone," came a voice from the stage level below.

I looked over the railing and down at an old man with an open white shirt and a pair of wide suspenders.

"Gone? Where?"

"Out there," said the man, pointing a pipe toward the stage door. "You went up the stairs," he said, pointing the pipe at the stairs, "and she went flying out, running like a banshee was snapping at her heels." He was pointing toward the stage door again.

On cue, the stage door opened and two uniformed cops came in.

"What is going on?" said Blackstone, stepping off the stage and looking at the cops and then up at me. "I need Peters back on the roller right now. I have a very impatient lion and more impatient audience, and I need something that resembles silence."

"Man's been murdered," I said to the cops and Blackstone.

The backstage crowd went silent.

Blackstone said, "Who?"

One of the cops said, "Where's the body?"

"In there," I said, pointing at the dressing room door and then to Blackstone, "A man named Cunningham."

"Why? Who did it?"

The cops were hurrying up the clanging stairs, muscling past performers and stagehands. The cop in the lead was florid and heavy, one of the wartime retreads. The kid behind him looked like my fourteen-year-old nephew.

Blackstone's questions were good ones.

I didn't have the answers.

"Did anyone see a guy with a beard wearing a turban with a green stone in it?" I asked.

"I did," said Jimmy Clark. "He was up on the landing next to the dressing rooms right before the buzz saw act."

"Went out that door," said the old man with the pipe, pointing once again at the stage door. "Couple of minutes ago right behind the tiger lady."

"Sara," Blackstone called in a loud whisper and pointed to a blonde girl in a Little Bow Peep costume. "You'll appear instead of Mr. Peters. Now all I need is some new patter."

"The double whoops," Pete said, leaning over the rail.

Blackstone raised a finger, nodded, motioned for Little Bow Peep to move behind the curtains, and went back onstage.

CHAPTER

5

Hand half a pack of playing cards to two people with the cards faced down after you have dealt out two piles. Have each person take a card from his or her deck, look at it, and place it in the other person's pile. Have each person shuffle the half deck he or she has. Place on pile on top of the other. Look at the cards. Pull out two. Lay them facedown. Have the two people turn over the cards. It will be the two cards they have selected. Put the packs together, shuffle them, and then spread them out to show that it is a regular deck. How it's done: Take a normal pack of cards. Alternate a red card with a black card. When you deal out the two packs, one will be all black and the other all red. When each person puts the card he or she has chosen into the other pack, there will be one red card in the black pack and one black card in the red. Look through the pack and pick the two cards.

—*From the* Blackstone, The Magic Detective *radio show*

A THIRD COP I HADN'T SEEN was stationed at the stage door. I knew the routine. No one in, no one out, till the detectives came and said otherwise.

"I need Gwen Knight's address fast," I told Peter Bouton, looking down at the cop at the door and hearing the other two cops going into the dressing room where Phil was waiting with Cunningham's body.

The cop at the door was familiar to me. I didn't remember his name. He had been transferred to the Wilshire District when the Hollywood force had been juggled after a hush-hush about uniforms on the take from bookies that hung around Columbia Pictures studio. He looked up at me. Recognition.

"Downstairs," said Bouton.

I followed him down the wobbling metal steps and into a small office lined with rusting file cabinets surrounding a small banged-up wooden desk.

"I leave my stuff in my briefcase whenever we . . ." Pete began as he shuffled through a pile of papers reaching behind the desk. "Here."

He pulled a battered briefcase from behind the small desk and opened it. He found the sheet he was looking for.

"Not what I thought," he said. "The other girls are staying at the Arlington Arms. Gwen is staying with someone . . . her sister . . . on Beverly, the Bluedorn Apartments."

He found a pencil and a small pad of paper and wrote the sister's name, address, and phone number on it. He handed it to me. I glanced at it, pocketed the sheet and said, "Thanks."

I left the small office, ignoring the eyes of the cop at the door, and headed for the stage. Blackstone was pointing a wand at some black enamel boxes. The buzz saw trick was over. I could only see the sides. I moved behind the curtains and down the stairs into the audience. People were looking at me. I glanced back. Blackstone saw me and said with a wave of his hand, "Ladies and gentleman. The man who was cut in half by the buzz saw."

The audience applauded. I bowed as I went up the aisle.

"Uncle Toby," Nate called out.

I waved at my nephews, grinned at the audience, hurried through the doors and into the lobby. No cops on guard. I almost bumped into Calvin Ott, who was entering the theater. He was dark-blue suited and grinning.

"Mr. Peters," he said. "How is the show?"

"You missed the best part," I said.

He looked at my uniform and shook his head.

"Welcome to show business," he said.

He moved around me and went inside. I wondered what the hell he was doing there, but I didn't have time to ask. I went around the corner to my car and squeezed in.

Changing out of the Chocolate Soldier costume would have been nice, but I didn't have the time. I made it to the address on Beverly in eleven minutes. It was an apartment building, The Bluedorn, six stories, white brick, nice bushes and front lawn, slightly on the classy side, which meant there was a doorman.

He was lean, blue uniformed, no cap, thin white hair brushed against his scalp to the right.

"I'm here to see Gwen Knight. She's staying with her sister, Evelyn."

"You working an apartment door around here?" he asked looking at my uniform.

"Yeah," I said. "Boyleton Arms."

He shook his head.

"What's it about?"

"Miss Knight was at the Boyleton a little while ago," I said. "She left her keys."

I took out my own keys and jiggled them. He held out his hand.

"I'll give 'em to her."

"Got to do it myself," I said. "No offense. Manager told me I had to give them to her myself. You know how it is?"

"She in a show there or something?" the doorman asked. "She came runnin' in maybe a minute ago wearing one of those . . . a tiger costume or something." He ran both hands up in front of him fluttering, as if that would create a clear picture for me of what she was wearing.

"Right," I said. "She's in a show. Blackstone the Magician at the Pantages."

He put down his hand, shrugged, and said, "Four-twelve. Elevator's on the left."

"Anyone else come in here from the show in the last ten minutes or so?" I asked.

"Why?" he asked suspiciously.

"She was with a guy with a beard, turban," I said.

"No guy like that," he said. "I don't see why. . . ."

I pocketed the keys, went through the lobby door, and headed for the elevator. There was no one in the small lobby. The elevator doors were closed. I pushed the button and watched the brass arrow move down 4-3-2-1. There was a ding and the doors slid open.

She was sitting on the floor, her back against the rear wall, sleek in an almost skin-tight stripped costume. Both of her hands were pressed against her stomach.

"He shot me," she said, eyes open wide in surprise.

Blood was beginning to seep through her fingers. She looked down, saw it, and then looked back at me.

"I think maybe he killed me," she said.

The elevator door started to close. I held it back with both hands and reached for the switch to turn it off.

"I'll be right back," I said and ran to the doorman.

"Call an ambulance, quick," I said.

"What?"

"She's been shot."

"Who?"

"Just call an ambulance. Hurry." I turned and called back, "Elevator."

Gwen Knight had gone pale. There was more blood. I've seen plenty of blood, much of it my own. I knelt next to her and gently moved her hands.

"I'm dying right?" she asked.

"No," I said.

"You're just sayin'," she said.

"No, I can see the bullet. It didn't even break your rib. Just keep your hands on it to stop the bleeding."

"It was a little gun, you know?"

"A little gun."

"Like . . . ," and she moved her hands, bloody palms facing each other to show how little the gun was that shot her.

I placed her hands back on the wound.

"Like they use in the show. Pellets," she said. Her eyes rolled back. "I think I'm going to throw up."

"Why did he shoot you?" I asked.

"I saw him coming out of my dressing room," she said. "I went into the dressing room and there was poor Robert."

"Dead?"

"Almost," she said. "You're sure I'm not dying?"

"Positive," I said, though I was thinking more along the lines of ninety-five percent that she would be all right. "He say anything?"

She closed her eyes and said, "The guy with the turban?"

"No, Robert."

"Yeah, but it didn't make any sense."

"What did he say?"

"Wild on Thursday."

"Wild on Thursday?"

"What did he mean?"

"Search me," she said.

She tried to shrug, but it sent a twitch of pain through her.

The doorman came running up and looked down at Gwen, whose eyes moved back in focus. She had great, even white teeth.

"They're comin'," he said. "Ambulance. And the cops."

"Thanks," I said, and then to Gwen, "The one who shot you?"

"Same guy who shot Robert," she said. "Sure I'm not dyin'?"

"Sure, cross my heart," I said.

"That guy I told you about with the beard and turban," I said to the doorman.

"Nobody like that came in in the last four hours," said the doorman. "I'd have remembered."

"Forget the turban and beard," I said. "Anyone come in who didn't live here?"

"Yeah."

"Who?"

"You."

"Besides me."

It was faraway and beyond the lobby doors, but I heard a siren on the way.

"No. Yes," he said. "A doctor, just a few minutes before you. On his way to make a house call on Mr. Collins. Hey maybe I should call up there and he can come down and. . . ."

"You check with Collins before you let him in?"

"No, the guy looked like a doctor, gray hair, glasses, nice suit, one of those pebble leather doctor bags."

"He asked for Mr. Collins?"

"Yeah, well I thought he said Cowens, but I asked him did he say 'Collins' and he . . . I let the shooter in, didn't I?"

"Looks that way," I said.

"Shit."

He stepped back and shook his head.

"And I'll bet you're not a doorman," he said.

"No, I'm not," I confirmed. "I'm a private detective."

"Shit."

His hands were on his hips now, and I figured he was wondering how he would look without his uniform and without a job.

"Hey," said Gwen. "Remember me? I'm the one was shot."

"Let's get your sister," I said.

"Not home."

The siren was close, very close now. It whined down, and the lobby door rattled. It was two uniformed cops and Detective John Cawelti of the Wilshire District. I put it together fast as the doorman ran back to let them in. I had asked Pete Bouton at the Pantages where Gwen lived. He had told the cops. I hadn't asked him not to. They had come after me. Wounded woman. Hated private detective.

I got into the elevator, flicked the switch, and pressed the button for the fourth floor. As the doors closed, I could hear the sound of at least three sets of feet clapping against the tile floor.

"What're you doin'?" Gwen screamed.

I held out my hand to calm her.

"Getting out at four, sending you back down to the lobby. "You'll be alright." The elevator started up. "You never saw the guy who shot you and Cunningham?"

She closed her eyes tightly.

"Hurts?" I asked.

"No, I'm trying to think. There was something familiar about him, but . . . I don't know. I'm gonna live, right?"

"I don't know if you're going to live *right*, but you're going to live."

The elevator stopped, and the doors lazily opened. I reached back in and pushed the lobby button.

"You'll be fine," I said as the doors started to close.

I smiled and gave her a thumbs up. Then the doors were closed and she was gone and I looked for a way to get out of the building.

I ran past the steps next to the elevators. No point in going down. The police would see me when I hit the lobby. The hallway was wide with worn-out but reasonably clean green carpet. Someone was blaring a radio behind a door on my right. Johnny Mercer was singing *Ac-cen-tuate The Positive.*

"What did they do just when everything looked so dark?" Mercer sang.

In my case, when everything looked dark, I ran for the window at the end of the hall. Beyond the window was a fire escape. The window went up easily and I stepped out, closing it behind me.

Down or up? I looked down. Narrow driveway. No one in sight. I started down, heard something below, looked and saw someone on foot turning the corner into the driveway. A cop. I started up. Too noisy. I took off my shoes and climbed. I didn't look back till I was on the roof.

I saw someone dart from behind a whirling metal air vent I was more surprised than I had been by Blackstone's floating lightbulb. The shooter had gone up, too.

He was lean and fast and about thirty feet away. I couldn't see his face, but I could see that he was carrying something in one hand. I had no gun, but he did, a very little one that shot pellets, but enough of a weapon to make a hole in Gwen's chest and, with a lucky or accurate shot, take out an eye and lodge in whatever small brain I may have had.

He dashed. I followed. And then he was gone. I stopped and looked around, panting. A chimney a few feet from a square brick seven-foot-high block with a door. The door was closed. I was pretty sure it hadn't been opened.

I stood waiting, still panting.

"Come out," I said. "Hands out and empty."

Nothing. I took a step forward.

"There are two guns up here," I said. "Mine, which shoots real bullets, and yours which shoots little balls. If I find you with a gun in your hand. . . ."

He stepped out from behind the wall next to the door, gun at arm's length and fired. He was a damned good shot. The pellet thudded into my left shoulder. I spun around. The door opened. Yellow light beamed out. I had a clear shot at his back, if I had a gun. With an electric ache in my shoulder slowing me down, I headed for the open door looking around for a weapon, a brick, a stick, something, anything. I came up with nothing.

A few feet from the door, I suddenly felt like I was going to lose my last meal, a couple of tacos, and a Pepsi at Manny's on Hoover.

I stopped and leaned over. By the light of the open door, I watched blood dropping lazily from the wound in my shoulder.

There was no point in chasing him. I hoped the cops downstairs would stop him.

I stood up and moved toward the open door. Three steps below me was the turban, its green stone catching the yellow light. A few steps further down were the beard and mustache. I had seen a collection of guns in Ott's house. I had seen a poster of a man with a beard and mustache in a turban on his wall. And the turban, right down to the green piece of glass, looked just like the one on the steps. Not proof, but I didn't need proof. I was a private investigator, not a cop. I went down, slowly picking up the evidence.

When I reached down to pick up the turban, a young cop, with very pink cheeks, the visor of his cap perfectly balanced over his eyes, stepped out and leveled his gun at me.

"Don't move," he said.

I froze.

"Arms up and come down slowly," he said.

I got my right arm up. My left throbbed with pellet pain, but I managed to get it almost to shoulder level.

"You're bleeding," he said as I came down the last few steps.

"I've been shot. Did someone come past you on the way up?"

"No," he said.

"I need a doctor," I said.

"There's one downstairs with the woman you shot," he said backing away, gun leveled at my chest.

"I didn't shoot her," I said.

"Tell the detectives," he said.

He moved behind me and picked up the turban, beard, and mustache.

It didn't look great for me, but I was reasonably sure I could talk my way out of it. This time, I'd just tell the truth. With about three quarters of the detectives in the Los Angeles Police Department, it would have worked.

But it was John Cawelti waiting for me in the lobby of the Bluedorn Apartments.

CHAPTER

5

Lay a pencil, telephone, hat, watch, glasses, lipstick, and a book on a table. Seven objects. Ask someone to pick an object, but not tell you what it is. Turn your back and tell them to arrange the objects any way they wish. Tell them to think of the first letter of the object shown. Tell them to then spell the object silently and slowly as you touch the objects saying one at a time, "First letter," etc. When the person finishes spelling, your hand will be on the object they chose. Solution: Each object has a different number of letters in it. It doesn't matter what the first two objects you touch are. There are no objects with only one or two letters. One of the first two objects you touch might even be the one the person thought of which will make the trick even better because they'll think you have missed the chosen object. If the person selecting the object says "stop" at the number three, your hand will be on the hat. At four it will be on the book, etc. Thinking of the first letter is a meaningless red herring.

—*From the* Blackstone, the Magic Detective *radio show*

AT THE L.A. COUNTY HOSPITAL emergency room, a kid doctor plucked the pellet from Gwen's chest and said she would have to stay overnight. Then he took the pellet from my shoulder and patched me up.

"I've never seen so many scars on a living human," the kid said.

"And each one has a story," I said.

"War?"

"No, mostly mistakes, bad timing, stupidity," I said.

The pellet had barely penetrated the flesh. At the distance I had been shot, that was about the best the shooter could have hoped for other than hitting my eye.

"You'll be fine," said the kid doctor dressed in crumpled whites who looked as if he hadn't slept in a week. "In Casino if that had been a bullet, we would have pulled it out, splashed on some iodine and a bandage and handed you your rifle." No overnight for me.

Two waiting uniformed cops took me to the Wilshire Station.

I knew the Wilshire Station. My brother had been a captain there. That was right after he had been a lieutenant and right before he had been busted back to lieutenant again.

Lieutenant John Cawelti, he of the pocked face, red hair parted in the middle, and perpetual look of badly concealed hatred for all things Pevsner or Peters, sat behind a desk in a small office.

He pointed to the chair on the other side of the desk and got up to close the door and stepped over to me.

"Where do we start?" Cawelti said standing over me.

The office hadn't changed much since Phil had left it less than a month before. Same desk with a murky window behind in and a view of a brick wall. Same three chairs, one behind the desk, two in front of it. The top of the desk had a full in-box in the left corner and a full out-box in the right, with a few files laid out unevenly between them. A coffee-mug stain marked the top file. The only change I could see was the plaque on the wall across from the desk.

I turned my head to look at the plaque, ignoring Cawelti who hovered over me with Listerine breath. The plaque read: To John Merwin Cawelti, in recognition of his efforts on behalf of the Los Angeles Police Department's annual picnic for the widows and orphans of our comrades who have fallen in the line of duty. Both the Mayor and the Chief of Police had signed it. About half the members of the department had the same plaque.

"Where do we start?" Cawelti insisted.

"Merwin?" I said turning my head and looking up at him.

He pointed a finger at me and jabbed it into the spot where the pellet had struck. I did more than wince. I clamped my teeth together and almost passed out.

"I want my lawyer," I said.

"Why?" he asked. "You haven't been accused of anything yet?"

"Then I want to leave," I said, starting to get up.

I leaned quickly to my right to avoid the jabbing finger.

"You shot Birmingham," he said.

"Cunningham, and I didn't shoot him."

"You shot him and went after the girl because she saw you shoot him. Then you shot her."

"And then I shot myself," I said.

"Yeah. And pitched the gun. We're looking for it."

"Ask the girl," I said. "She'll tell you I didn't shoot her."

"And she'll tell me you didn't shoot Cunningham, right?"

"The girl saw the shooter. She'll give you a description."

"Yeah," he said. "Beard, turban, bullshit. We've got the beard and turban where you dropped them on the steps."

"I was onstage about to be sawed in half by a buzz saw when Cunningham was shot," I said.

"We don't know exactly when he was shot."

"Check with the doorman. Check with Gwen. They'll tell you I couldn't . . ."

"And I'll tell you you could," he said. "You're working for the magician. Cunningham was trying to blackmail him. You shot him. Then you went after the witness."

"I helped her, and who do you think shot me?"

"Shot yourself," said Cawelti, face inches from mine.

"And threw the pellet gun away? Did you find it?"

"Not yet," he said.

"You've got the other gun?" I asked.

"What other gun?"

"The one that was used to kill Cunningham," I said. "That was no pellet hole."

"You had plenty of time to dump it," he said, finger hovering over my arm.

"Time for my lawyer, Merwin. Martin Raymond Leib," I said.

Cawelti's face was bright crimson. He reached out for my wounded shoulder, and I shuffled my chair backward. He took a step toward me.

The door behind him opened. I couldn't see who it was. Cawelti was between me and the door. He stopped, turned his head, and came flying past me, hitting the wall.

Phil stood there, door open behind him.

A couple of detectives I recognized were in the doorway.

"You're under arrest," Cawelti shouted at my brother.

"For what?" Phil said.

"Assaulting a police officer," Cawelti said, pushing himself away from the wall.

"You fell," I said.

"Looked that way to me," said one of the detectives in the door, a big bald sergeant named Pepperman, who had been mustered out of the army in 1919, the same year as my brother.

"Didn't see it," said the man next to him, Bill O'Keefe, who Phil had once pushed out of the way of the knife of a drugged-out Mexican kid named Orlejo Sanchez.

"Get the hell out of my office," Cawelti said, taking a step toward Phil and then thinking better of it.

"You alright?" Phil said, ignoring Cawelti and looking at me.

"Lovely," I said.

"Your brother killed a man tonight and shot a woman," Cawelti said. "You don't get out, you're under arrest for interfering with a murder investigation."

Phil turned his unblinking eyes on him.

"You've got nothing," Phil said.

"At the least," Cawelti said. "At the goddamn least, I've got him for leaving the scene of a crime, two crimes."

"I was chasing the killer," I said.

"Chasing yourself?" Cawelti asked.

"We're going," said Phil, motioning to me to follow him.

"Hold it," said Cawelti. "You're not a police officer anymore. I'm in charge here. I'm the law. You do what I goddamn tell you."

"Ask nicely," Phil said.

I knew the look. So did Cawelti. So did the two detectives standing in the doorway. Phil might be arrested. He might even be shot, but, if he lost his temper, John Merwin Cawelti would be in need of a very long period of recuperation.

Cawelti was breathing hard now as he said between his teeth,

"Please get the hell out of here."

"Not without Tobias."

"He's now officially under arrest for murder," said Cawelti. "You want to help him escape?"

Phil's fists were clenched. He stepped toward Cawelti again. Cawelti retreated back, but this time he didn't back down.

"He's under arrest," he said.

Phil stopped and said,

"He'll be out of here in an hour."

"Maybe," said Cawelti.

"I'll be outside," Phil said. "Right outside."

The two detectives in the doorway made way for him to leave. Cawelti strode across the room and closed the door. Then he turned to me.

"Tell me a story," he said.

I told him about Calvin Ott, otherwise known as Maurice Keller. He wasn't impressed. I told him about the missing buzz saw blade. He was even less impressed. I told him I wanted my lawyer. Twenty minutes later, Martin Raymond Leib, decked out in a perfectly pressed blue suit and a red-and-blue striped tie—all 300 lbs of him—entered the small office with a small smile of satisfaction. He was thinking of what he was going to bill Peters and Pevsner for his legal services.

I was thinking about my aching shoulder.

Marty told me to step out of the office. I did. Phil was there.

We waited while Marty—slowly, I was sure, and with a patient smile—earned his fee.

Marty Leib could afford to be slow and patient. He got paid by the hour. Pepperman brought us cups of coffee in nonmatching diner mugs and asked me about my shoulder, and asked Phil how things were going.

About fifteen minutes later, the door opened and Marty, hand still on the knob, said, "Come on."

We followed him through the squad room past working cops and empty desks. Marty, the size of a small rhino, cleared the way.

On the landing outside the squad room, Marty turned to us and said, "Lord, I so enjoy sending dear old John C.'s blood pressure into the stratosphere. He is so easy to intimidate. I would almost do it for nothing."

"It's a deal," I said. "Nothing, and I promise to get in as much trouble with Cawelti as I can to bring a little entertainment into your busy life."

"I said 'almost,'" Marty reminded me. "We are almost finished with the war. We are almost a neighbor of the planet Mars. It is almost midcentury. It all depends on the definition of 'almost.'"

"What did you do?" I asked.

"Poor J. C. has no evidence, no witness, and no weapon to connect you to the Cunningham shooting. I suggested that we all visit the young lady in the hospital and ask her if you were the one who shot her. I suggested strongly that if she did not so identify you as the person who shot her or the man who came out of the dressing room where Robert Cunningham was shot, I would immediately bring suit for false arrest. Detective Cawelti went from combative to surly to reluctantly and grudgingly cooperative."

"Send us the bill," said Phil, unfolding his arms.

Marty nodded, patted me on the shoulder, the one that just had the pellet removed from it. He didn't know. I tried not to pass out and succeeded.

Marty moved down the stairs. At the bottom of the stairs, out of sight, he sang, "The things that you're liable to read in the bible, they ain't necessarily so."

"Lousy voice," I said.

"Don't have fun," Phil said, unfolding his arms.

"What?"

"You're enjoying this," he said. "You've been shot, almost cut in half by a buzz saw and arrested for murder. A man's been murdered. A girl was shot, and we just ran up a lawyer's bill."

"You're right," I told my brother, but I thought he was dead wrong. "Except I wasn't almost cut in half by the buzz saw. That was an illusion. And we can bill Blackstone for Marty's services."

"Let's go," Phil said with a sigh that suggests a lot of things to a brother. It meant "Why did I decide to go into partnership with my infantile brother?"

I didn't have to ask where we were going. We both knew.

Twenty minutes later, we were standing between the two stone gargoyles under the light of the almost full moon. It was about one fifteen in the morning.

Phil held up his fist to knock. I put my hand on his arm and lowered it.

"Magic," I explained and said, "Abracadabra."

The door opened. In front of us stood a bearded man in a white suit, wearing a turban with an emerald green stone in the middle.

"You're late," the man said.

The turbaned man turned and started down the corridor. Phil reached out and grabbed his arm spinning him around.

"Look Ott," Phil said softly. "I . . ."

"He's not Ott," I said.

He was too short and heavy to be Calvin Ott.

"I don't give a damn who he is," Phil said, nose to nose with the now wide-eyed man. "I want to know where he was all night, every goddamn minute."

The man looked at me hopefully.

"Phil, whoever shot Gwen and me dropped the turban and whiskers. Cawelti's got them."

"There could be a second set," said Phil.

"There are seven sets," the man said, his voice rising. "And I don't know any Gwen and . . ."

"Leo, who was at the . . . ?"

A man stood at the end of the corridor, a drink in one hand, a cigarette in the other.

"That's Ott," I said.

"Keller," Ott corrected. "The name is Marcus Keller."

Keller or Ott wasn't wearing a turban or a beard. We weren't looking for a man dressed like the one who had shot Gwen. We were looking for someone who had lost the disguise.

"Would your friend please release my guest," Ott said, pointing his drink at Phil whose right hand was now firmly around the turbaned man's neck.

"He's my brother," I said. "And my partner. And he has a very bad temper."

"And a voice of his own," said Phil, letting the man go. "What the hell is going on here?"

"I understand you were a policeman," said Ott, emphasizing the word "were."

The man Ott had called "Leo" staggered back. It was not a magic moment for him.

"I could call a real policeman and have him take you away," said Ott, sweeping his cigarette-bearing hand in a broad arc.

"Not before I convince you to tell us what the hell is going on here," Phil said, taking a menacing step toward Ott who stood his ground.

"It's the anniversary of the death of Dranabadur," Ott said, looking at a poster on his left.

I remembered it now from the last time I had been here. The turbaned man, the emerald, the whiskers. I looked at it again. Dranabadur's dark face filled the poster with the words: **Dranabadur, the Orient's Master of the Singing Blade of Death.**

"Leo, are you alright?" Ott asked casually.

"Yes," Leo gasped, moving past Ott.

"Come," Ott said with a smile I didn't like as he turned his back on us and began to walk. "Dranabadur was a little known genius. Died twenty-seven years ago at exactly one-fifty-three in the morning, if the hospital report is to be believed."

We followed him as he talked.

"Dranabadur's real name was Irving Frankel," Ott said. "Born in Brookline, Massachusetts, of less than noble or Oriental origin. He was a genius and went to his death without revealing the secret of his most famous trick, the singing blade."

"What killed him?" I asked.

"The blade, of course," said Ott, stepping into the living room that looked the same as when I'd last seen it, except it was now full of people. There were seven of them, all men, or, at least, I thought they were all men. They were all wearing white suits, beards, and turbans with a green stone. They were also all standing and facing us. Some of them had drinks in their hand.

The little chubby one called Leo, who had greeted us at the door, moved to join the others.

"Where's your costume?" Phil asked Ott.

"I never wear one for these events," he said. "I lead the service.

And I provide the reward of fifty thousand dollars to the one who solves Dranabadur's illusion of the singing blade, solves it and gives me exclusive and binding rights to it."

He looked at his watch.

"Hey," Phil said, stepping in front of Ott who smiled more broadly, a mistake when dealing with my brother.

I could see that Phil was giving serious consideration to committing mayhem.

"We can talk after the memorial service," said Ott, taking a step to his right so that he could see past Phil.

I touched Phil's arm, realizing too late that instead of restraining him, it might turn him on me.

"We're about to begin," Ott announced.

"Oh Christ," sighed Phil. "This is bullshit, Tobias."

I shrugged. One of the Dranabadurs standing near the wall on our right reached up and flicked a switch. The room went dark. Then a dim green glow came from the ceiling. Light danced green on the well-polished head of the dark skull of Bombay, still sitting in the same place he had last faced me.

"Magic," said Ott, his face green, his smile more than a little nuts. "We live to perform, to dazzle, to mystify. We honor at the anniversary of their moment of departure those who have come before us, those who have achieved. . . ." He hesitated trying to find the right words.

"The highest plateau of deception," one of the whiskered group supplied.

"Yes, thank you," Ott said. "The highest plateau of deception. Dranabadur's singing blade remains among the list of eighteen illusions of magic that have never been duplicated, the secrets of which have never been revealed and have gone to the grave with their creators."

There was a pause during which Ott took a long drink, looked at Phil and me and then back at the group of costumed guests.

"Another year," said Ott. "Has anyone solved the mystery? Can anyone claim the reward?"

"Yes," came a voice from the corridor behind us.

A startled Ott swung around, the remains of his drink spraying me. In the green glow, a figure stepped out of the corridor and into the room.

"Stephen, the lights," Ott called.

The green glow disappeared. There was an instant of darkness and then light.

The man who had stepped out of the corridor was Blackstone.

"I didn't invite you," said Ott, clearly shaken, his voice rising.

Blackstone was wearing his tux and tails from the show. His white hair billowed. His mustache caught the light.

"The singing blade," Blackstone said.

"You don't know how it was done," Ott said.

"But I do," said Blackstone. "And it is not for sale, nor do I ever intend to perform it. There are some secrets which are better not revealed. The legend of Dranabadur would be gone."

"You lie," Ott challenged, his voice quivering.

"No," said Blackstone calmly, facing the frozen costumed group in front of him and looking at them as he named "Wayne, Paul, Walter, Milton, Steven, Bill, Richard, Leo."

"What do you want?" Ott demanded.

"What do I want? A man of questionable motive and character was murdered at the theater tonight during my performance. A young woman in my troupe was shot tonight by a man dressed as . . ."

He pointed dramatically at each of the people in front of him.

". . . Dranabadur. Knowing of this annual party, it seemed a reasonable place to come for answers."

I watched Ott's face. Tension. Then a series of quick contortions and decisions. Throw the magician out of his house? This was Blackstone. The eight men in costume behind him might not want to take part of the blame from throwing Blackstone out. They might even go with him. Ott's face loosened a little. Phil and I had been hired to find out why Ott had set up the testimonial dinner for Blackstone. How would it look if he threw out of his home the man he was going to honor on Wednesday?

"Forgive me," Ott said. "I was . . . of course you are welcome, anytime."

"Mr. Pevsner, Mr. Peters," said Blackstone. "I assume you are here seeking the same answers. Please."

Ott moved to the side to sulk and pour himself another drink. The stage had been taken from him. I think he was shaking.

"How long have you been here?" I asked the group.

They looked at each other and one, the one named Stephen who had operated the lights, said,

"Since about eleven. I mean most of us started to arrive about eleven. I came about ten minutes earlier. Marcus wanted to go over my handling the lights."

No help there. Anyone in the room could have shot Cunningham and Gwen and been here by eleven.

"I'd like to talk to everyone here alone, one at a time in some nice quiet room," said Phil.

"No," said Ott, regaining a touch of courage. "This is my house. You are not the police. These are my colleagues. The gathering is over. The mood is destroyed. I am feeling decidedly drained. Please leave, depart, go, and I shall see you all on Wednesday night."

Slowly, led by the little chubby one called Leo, they moved past us giving good-byes, exchanging a word or two with Blackstone. Phil didn't try to stop them though he gave each one his look that said, 'I know you're guilty.'

When they had all left, Ott faced us and said, "Anything else?"

He was very calm again. I didn't like the latest smile. He had something up his sleeve, probably an ace of spades.

"Why did you come to the Pantages tonight?" I asked. "The show was almost over."

"A whim, to see a little of the master at work," he said with a thick layer of sarcasm.

"Just happened to be the night someone was murdered," said Phil.

"Didn't discover that till I entered the theater and was stopped by a police officer," said Ott.

"Didn't know the dead man, Cunningham?" I tried.

"That's what the police asked me. I'll give you the same answer I gave them, no. More questions?"

"Someone was supposed to be at the theater, someone who had threatened to ruin my show if I didn't turn over my secrets," said Blackstone.

"You think it was me?" asked Ott, pointing to himself.

"Yes," Blackstone said.

"Why not the man who was shot? Or the one who shot him?" asked Ott smugly.

"Pieces of the puzzle," said Blackstone.

"Well," said Ott with an overdone sarcasm, "if anyone can put the pieces together, it's the great Blackstone. I am, as I said, drained. I will see you all on Wednesday night," Ott said, holding his glass up in a toast to Blackstone.

We went to the front door. I was about to say "Open Sesame" when Blackstone simply clapped his hands and the door opened. We stepped out into the night past the gargoyles. The doors closed.

"I hate to say it," said Blackstone, "considering the murder and Gwen's shooting, but I enjoyed that."

We moved to the street. The cars that had filled the driveway when we arrived were gone. There was one, lone dark Buick parked in front of Phil's Ford. Pete Bouton stood next to it.

"Alright?" he asked.

"Fine," said Blackstone.

"A question," I said. "Do you really know how to do the singing blade trick?"

"Ah," said Blackstone looking at his brother. "Pete?"

"I'd say there are maybe eight or nine people here in the United States, four in Europe, one in Australia and who knows how many in China who could do it," said Pete.

"Then why don't they?" Phil asked.

"It's not much of a trick," said Blackstone, looking back at Ott's house. "Any really competent illusionist could figure out how it was done. The technology has come a long way since Dranabadur. But, that said, there are still brilliant illusions, which have endured for centuries. The singing blade, however, is not one of them."

"Ott's an idiot?" Phil asked.

"Mr. Ott is a wealthy amateur in the worst sense of the word," said Blackstone. "Given the opportunity, he would reveal every one of Peter's and my illusions."

"So he's just jealous," I said.

"Not just of me, but I do seem to have become his obsession. I did not like the way he recovered in there."

Blackstone looked back at the house.

"Wednesday night," he said. "Gentlemen, you have work to do."

"You knew all those people who were here tonight?" said Phil.

"Yes," said Blackstone. "Local magicians, not professionals."

"Can you give us their names? Full names?" asked Phil.

"I'll have a list in your office in the morning."

Blackstone got in the car with his brother and they drove off. Phil and I did the same. We didn't talk. There was nothing to say except good night when he took me back to my car parked behind the Bluedorn Apartments.

I got back to Heliotrope and parked half a block down from Mrs. Plaut's at a little after two. There was one more surprise waiting for me before I got to bed.

CHAPTER

Announce that you are about to demonstrate a magic detector. Take a quarter. Place it on table. Turn your back. Tell the person to pick up the coin with either hand. Have them hold the hand to their forehead for about fifteen seconds while you concentrate. Tell the person to put the coin back on the table. Turn and have them place their hands on the table. Look into the person's eyes and then point to the hand that held the coin. Tell them you can repeat the trick and do so a few times. Solution: Before looking into the person's eyes, look at their hands. The whiter hand will be the one that held the coin. Being held to the person's forehead causes the blood to drain enough from the hand to make it whiter than the other. Be sure to glance at the hands the instant you turn around. Take as long as you like looking into the other person's eyes. You already know which hand held the coin.

—*From the* Blackstone, The Magic Detective *radio show*

I GOT UP THE PORCH STAIRS, through the door, and past Mrs. Plaut's door. No problem. I got to my room. Still no problem. I turned on the light. Problem.

I saw it on the small table near the open window. Dash, the orange cat who sometimes permitted me to share the room with him, was sitting on it. The black cardboard covered composition book lay next to the salt and pepper shakers. A sheet of cardboard stood propped between the shakers. On the cardboard was written, **Please read before morning. Breakfast at eight.** It was signed, Irene Plaut.

"No way out of it," I told Dash, who licked his left front paw.

I undressed down to my underwear, felt the stubble on my chin, filled a bowl with milk for Dash, and poured myself a big helping of Wheaties and milk.

Then I sat to eat, read, and wonder about the latest addition to Mrs. Plaut's family history.

Wooley and The Bear

Brother Wooley was not one to shrink from his duty or a battle with fists or bottles or anything that was helpless. Wooley toward the end of the days the good lord had given him on this orb of woes and frequent joy did shrink a bit but that was because of lumbago.

Be that as it may my brother Wooley who was as skinny as a dandelion stem was at the London Zoo. In truth Wooley had yellow hair and looked much like a dandelion if one applied one's imagination. This may account for why my aunt Evangeline called Wooley "the wilted flower of the family." Aunt Evangeline was a tsk-tsker. To Aunt Evangeline everything was a shame or a sin or both. Aunt Evangeline simply called me "Poor Irene." Then she would shake her head and tsk-tsk. Aunt Evangeline was loath to explain. Aunt Evangeline would not say. This concerned me for many a year but a distant cousin named Sarah Free-homver from Sandusky Ohio did later tell me that Aunt Evangeline had met her but once and said to her upon taking her hand, "I'm so sorry." Sarah Freemhover was not at all sure what Aunt Evangeline was sorry about and she never did explain.

Wooley had a greasy order of fish and chips wrapped in newspaper that he ate as he ambulated around the zoo. He ate the fish and chips not the newspaper. Do not misunderstand. Wooley was thin and bemused but he was not a simpleton.

He stopped before a cage behind whose bars sat a very large brown bear. People passed pausing only to glance upon the poor creature. It was a hot summer day. The bear just sat. When no one was about Wooley said, "Like some fish and chips?"

The bear looked at Wooley and Wooley threw him the wrapped-up newspaper containing one reasonably sized piece of cod and some fried potatoes. The bear picked up the newspaper and said "Thank you."

"You're welcome," said Wooley and walked away so the bear could eat with some privacy. It was only after he had walked approximately forty paces and was looking at nervous wolf that Wooley realized that the bear had spoken.

Wooley turned and went back to the bear's cage. The creature had finished the fish and chips and the newspaper it had been wrapped in was nowhere in sight which led Wooley to the immediate conclusion that this talking bear had eaten the newspaper as Wooley had not done.

"You spoke," said Wooley.

Three people in addition to my second eldest brother were now standing in front of the cage. The three people were a man and a woman and their small daughter. It might have been their granddaughter. Wooley was not concentrating on them. They were concentrating upon him after he had addressed the bear.

The bear looked at Wooley and licked its paw.

Wooley looked at the three other people before the cage and said "He talked. I gave him fish and chips and he talked. He said 'thank you.'"

"Polite bear," said the man ushering wife and daughter or

granddaughter away. The child may in fact have been a niece or a neighbor's child or even a foundling they had taken in but that is no matter.

When they were gone Wooley again addressed the bear. "You can talk?"

The bear looked at the roof of his cage.

Wooley urged the bear to talk again, even promised him more fish and chips. Wooley believed the bear was considering the offer. Wooley pleaded.

"If you don't talk I'll spend my life thinking I am a lunatic."

The bear didn't answer.

Wooley believes he raised his voice to the creature. So intent was he that he would not have noticed the three men in blue zoo uniforms running toward him. He turned only because the bear said, "Look out," and looked toward the men in blue zoo uniforms who now took hold of Wooley's arms.

"Did you hear that?" Wooley asked the men, one of whom smelled of something vile, perhaps a Dromedary, which I understand is one of the most vile smelling of God's creatures.

"Heard what?" asked the man with bad breath.

"The bear spoke," said Wooley. "He told me you were coming."

"And here we are" said the man with bad breath. "Let's go to the office and discuss this curious phenomenon."

Wooley was taken to the office of the keeper of the London zoo who was fat and sassy and grumpy. Wooley was a man of great conviction and determination and given to the truth that our mother had told us would keep us in good stead with the Lord and with our fellow man because once you started lying it was close to impossible to remember all of your lies.

Only a part of an hour earlier Wooley had been thinking of getting to a job interview. Wooley was an accomplished mandolin player. He could play the banjo too and was known in the family and beyond for his fast moving version of Waiting For The Robert E. Lee alternating between instruments.

"The bear spoke to me," said Wooley.

"She spoke to you," said the zookeeper.

"Yes," said Wooley.

"No, I mean the bear is female," said the zoo director.

"She spoke to me," Wooley repeated reaching up to adjust his hat, which had been jostled by the three men in blue zoo uniforms.

"She did not speak," said the zoo director turning red.

Wooley said nothing. Stubborn ignorance cannot be overcome by the word of even the most truthful of men.

"The bear has been with us for two years and has never spoken," the zoo director said trying to appear calm in the face of honest certainty.

"There was the little lad about two months back who said the bear said Thank you."

"Yes," said Wooley. "That is what the bear said to me."

"The little boy also said that one of the elephants threw a clump of dung at him" said the zoo director who glared at his employee. "You may either leave now and never return to the zoo or we will call the authorities and have you taken to the hospital."

"I am not ill."

"You are deluded, sir. Perhaps you have been drinking."

Well Wooley had successfully imbibed a wide swath of spirits over the course of his adulthood and perhaps even a bit before that but that morning he was sober and had drunk nothing but very ill-tasting English coffee.

Wooley chose to go to the hospital rather than be banished from the zoo though as it turned out the zookeeper had not given him a choice at all because he still ordered that Wooley was not to enter the zoo again.

Wooley passed three weeks in the hospital proving to the doctors and nurses and alienists that he was of sound mind if fragile body except for his insistence that he had heard the bear speak. They allowed him to leave. The job with the dance band no longer existed. Wooley could have come home but he got a job waiting tables at a restaurant called the Chicago Bar & Grill.

When he was not working Wooley would attempt to get back in the zoo and talk to the bear. He climbed fences, crawled under bushes, took to wearing disguises including that of a Zooave and a pregnant woman, but it was all to no avail. He would always get within approach to the bear cage and be apprehended by one of the guards who had been assigned on a rotating basis to watch for him.

Twice his eyes met those of the bear but the creature did not speak. One time the bear had a paw over his eyes as if trying to keep out the sight of Wooley being caught.

Wooley was never the same. The same as what you may ask. The same as he had been before being spoken to by a bear.

Eventually my brother Ezra and my cousin Matthew went to England at the expense of the London zoo to escort a recalcitrant Wooley back to the shores of our great land.

Wooley moved to Denver, obtained employment at a restaurant, saved his money, and bought a very old bear from a traveling carnival. He shared a one-room house with the bear and ended his days attempting to teach the bear to speak. He failed but he did learn to love the bear who had come to him with the name Bruno but which he changed to Ernest.

Love comes to us in strange and mysterious ways. Amen.

The night was filled with dreams of talking bears, bears in tuxedoes performing magic tricks, bears sawing other bears in skirts in half to an audience of bears applauding almost silently with their padded paws. Bears wearing turbans with green stones. And there I was onstage, the only human—if indeed human I be—waiting my turn in a line of bears to be sawed in half, evaporated, decapitated, eviscerated, levitated or, if they figured out I wasn't a bear, masticated.

"Your first time?" asked the bear in front of me in line offstage.

"Yes," I said.

"Just don't let them shoot you," the bear said. "Blackstone the Bear can shoot straight. Killed more bears last year than all the hunters west of the Mississippi. Bear that in mind."

The other bears laughed, and then I was in bed sleeping. The three bears came up to me. Papa Bear leaned over and I felt a dry tongue on my face. I opened my eyes. Dash was looking down at me with his round green eyes. The sun was coming through the window. My Beech-Nut Gum wall clock said it was almost seven-thirty.

I rolled over, got to my knees, stiff, sore, and wounded, stood and said to Dash, "So far so good."

Then I rolled up the thin mattress on the floor, put it in the corner, dressed quickly, pants not terribly in need of pressing, fresh white shirt, and rewarded Dash with a bowl of corn flakes and milk.

At seven-thirty, the door to my room flew open. I was ready. Mrs. Plaut, broom in hand, looked down at where I would normally be lying on my back, eyes closed.

"Good morning," I said cheerfully.

She turned her eyes to where I sat at the small table near the window.

"You are fully awake," she said with a hint of suspicion.

"That I am," I said.

"Have you been carousing all night instead of reading my pages?"

"I have not been carousing," I said. "I've been getting shot, but I read your pages. Fascinating."

She adjusted her glasses.

"Wooley is an interesting character," I said.

"Breakfast in twenty-two minutes," she said. She seemed maybe a little disgruntled at not having her ritual morning moment of terrorizing me into wakefulness. Then she stopped and faced me again, supporting herself with the broom, which was only a little narrower than she was.

"Wooley was not interesting," she said. "He spent his life in family exile in Americus, Georgia, serving as assistant to a half-mad pharmacist named Spaulding."

"But the bear, England?" I said.

"Wooley never was in England," she said.

"You made it up?"

"Invention is the parent of truth," she said.

"Who said that?"

"I just did," said Mrs. Plaut.

I looked at Dash. He turned his head away and leaped onto the window ledge and leapt to the tree. Stiff, sore, and shoulder aching, I had neither the agility nor opportunity for such an escape.

"So none of the business about Wooley and the bear is true?"

"Not a lick," she said.

"What about all the other stories about your family?"

"All true," she said with indignation. "Every last word. What do you take me for Mr. Peelers?"

"But Wooley?"

"I felt the tome needed spicing up," she said. "My imagination is futile."

"Fertile," I corrected.

"Breakfast this a.m. is Treet omelets accompanied by margarine-fried diced carrots gently mixed in," she said. "There will also be an announcement of consequence."

And she was gone.

That gave me time to shave, rub some Kreml in my hair, change the Band-Aid covering the pellet hole in my shoulder, wince a few times, wash, avoid my battered image in the mirror, and knock at Gunther's door.

"Enter Toby," he said.

"You know my knock," I said, opening the door.

"I know that it is nearly eight and that Mrs. Plaut does not knock," he said.

He was dressed in his usual three-piece, perfectly pressed custom-made suit. Since he was a little over three and a half feet tall, all his clothes had to be custom made, right down to his silk ties and leather shoes.

"Treet omelets this a.m.," I said.

"Such a culinary delight is not to be missed," Gunther said.

"And Mrs. Plaut says she has an announcement of consequence."

"Then we should be at the table at the stroke of the hour," said Gunther, rising from the chair at his desk and putting aside the book he had been holding.

At Mrs. Plaut's dining-room table sat Ben Bidwell, the one-armed fortyish automobile salesman, and Emma Simcox, a light-skinned, shy pretty Negro who Mrs. Plaut said was her niece. I never asked about this relationship. I had the feeling that one night I would come home to an explanation of the Simcox connection in a chapter of Mrs. Plaut's never-ending, and now fictionalized, memoirs.

Gunther and I sat. Bidwell and Emma were next to each other. He wore a grin. She wore a smile. Coffee was on the table.

"War'll be over soon," said Bidwell.

"Looks that way," I said.

"Then we'll have to deal with the national debt," said Bidwell. "Two hundred and sixty billion dollars. How are we going to deal with that, I ask you?"

"There has been a meeting of forty-four nations at the Mt. Washington Hotel in Bretton Woods, New Hampshire," said Gunther. "A World Bank has been established. National debts are on the agenda."

"That a fact?" said Bidwell with admiration.

"It is," said Gunther solemnly.

Mrs. Plaut came in with omelet plates, placing one in front of each of us. It rated "A" for smell and something murky down the alphabet for looks. The omelets were a rainbow mixture of tree bark brown, burnt carrot orange, egg yellow, and speckled hints of some dark herb.

"Before we eat," she said. "The announcement."

In the sitting room behind us, Mrs. Plaut's bird from hell began screeching.

"Ignore Jacob," Mrs. Plaut said.

Gunther and I looked at her.

"Great," I said.

"The changing of his name is not the announcement," she said. "My niece and Mr. Bidwell are officially engaged," Mrs. Plaut said.

Bidwell smiled. Emma blushed. He took her hand.

"Congratulations," said Gunther.

"Congratulations," I echoed.

"Nuptials on January 2 of the coming year," said Mrs. Plaut. "In the parlor. All invited. Gifts mandatory."

The doorbell was ringing. Mrs. Plaut didn't hear it.

"I will begin preparing the menu," Mrs. Plaut said. "You may eat now."

The doorbell rang again.

The omelet was damned good.

The doorbell kept ringing. Mrs. Plaut was obviously not wearing her hearing aid.

"The door, Aunt Irene," Emma said, standing.

"Of course," said Mrs. Plaut, a forkful of omelet moving toward her mouth.

Emma left the room and passed through the sitting room, sending Jacob into a new frenzy of screeches.

When she returned to the room, Harry Blackstone was at her side. He was wearing a dark suit and red tie. His hair was brushed back and he reminded me of Adolph Menjou.

"I'm sorry to intrude," he said.

"We are not in the market this morning for brushes, vacuum cleaners, knife sharpenings, or the like," Mrs. Plaut said, turning to him.

"This is Harry Blackstone," I said. "The magician."

My announcement brought a smile from Bidwell and Emma and a look of respect from Gunther. It also brought a strange look to the face of Mrs. Plaut, who did not turn to face him. I thought she hadn't heard me. I introduced everyone. When I got to Mrs. Plaut, she kept her back turned and held up a hand to acknowledge the magician's presence.

"Would you like to join us?" Emma asked.

"I've eaten, thank you," said Blackstone. "I must talk to Mr. Peters." And then, to me, he said, "Something new has come up."

"Let's go in the other room," I said, getting up.

Mrs. Plaut was still turned away. As I started to lead Blackstone out of the dining room, she made the mistake of turning her head to watch us.

Blackstone looked at her for an instant. She turned away and then he paused to look again.

"Irene Adaire," he said.

Mrs. Plaut concentrated on her Treet omelet.

"You are Irene Adaire," he said, looking at Mrs. Plaut.

We all looked at Mrs. Plaut.

"You're the widow of Simon Adaire," he said.

"I look nothing like her," Mrs. Plaut said, head down.

"I can't be mistaken," Blackstone said, moving around the table, standing between Bidwell and Emma to look at Mrs. Plaut. "The birthmark on the back of your hand is unmistakable."

Mrs. Plaut shifted the fork from her right to her left hand and put the right hand on her lap out of sight.

"I've been searching for her for forty years," Blackstone said, looking at me.

We all looked at Mrs. Plaut, who adjusted her glasses and continued to eat with a fury that made it clear she had a sudden attack of starvation, or else she was doing her best to hide behind the blend of carrots, Treet, and eggs.

Blackstone shook his head and smiled before looking at me.

"Simon Adaire was an amazing magician," he said. "I saw him in Chicago when I was about twelve years old. He performed an illusion, a brilliant trick, which no one has to this day been able to duplicate."

Mrs. Plaut was now gulping tepid coffee.

"He placed his wife," said Blackstone looking at Mrs. Plaut, "in a glass sphere about the size of an armchair. A steel mesh surrounded the sphere. And then . . ." Blackstone let his right hand lift toward the ceiling, "in full view and with his wife clearly visible, he had the sphere raised by a golden rope high above the audience. There was a drum roll and with a shout of 'Kabow' Irene Adaire disappeared."

"Kapow," Mrs. Plaut corrected. "Not 'Kabow'."

"Kapow, yes," Blackstone said. "An instant, no more than a heartbeat later, Simon Adaire called out 'Lights.' The house lights came on and he pointed to a spot in the audience. From a seat, not an aisle seat, Irene Adaire stood up wearing the same costume she had worn in the sphere. I waited at the stage door till the show was over," said Blackstone. "Adaire shook my hand and I told him I wanted to be a magician. His wife shook my hand. That's when I saw the small birthmark, the tiny purple star."

"It's not a birthmark," Mrs. Plaut said. "It's a tattoo."

We were all looking at Mrs. Plaut now.

"You were lovely," Blackstone said.

Did Mrs. Plaut blush? Maybe.

"Simon Adaire died two years or so later," Blackstone said. "My brother and I have tried for years to duplicate that piece of magic. We've come close, but never quite got it. Others have tried. Cheap and obvious imitations. Eventually, people began to think that the original Simon Adaire's Woman in the Sphere illusion had been one of those cheap imitations. But it wasn't. I was there."

"More coffee anyone?" Mrs. Plaut asked, rising with her cup and saucer in hand.

In the hundreds of pages of Mrs. Plaut's family history, there had not been a mention of anyone named Adaire, had not been a word about Adaire, whom she must have been married to before she married "The Mister" who had died about fifteen years ago.

"Amazing," said Blackstone. "The wonders of the world of magic are nothing compared to the tricks of fate that God plays on us. To find you after all this time, after all the hands of women I have looked at, all the . . . forgive me."

"I'm having more coffee," said Mrs. Plaut, moving toward the kitchen.

"Mrs. Adaire," Blackstone said. "You are almost certainly the only living person who knows the secret of the Woman in the Sphere."

"Drat," Mrs. Plaut said with a sigh, returning to her seat.

Blackstone laughed, a deep laugh showing even, white teeth.

"I thought when I found you I would beg you to tell me the secret, offer you whatever amount you wanted, tell you that I would forever attribute the illusion to Simon Adaire whenever I performed it," said Blackstone. "And now . . ."

"You don't want to know," said Mrs. Plaut.

"That's right," said Blackstone. "How did you . . . ?"

"That's just what Thurston said when he found me," she said. "He used a private detective named Richard Olin who charged him a sincere sum. Thurston never even asked me to tell him. Mr. Thurston said, 'Even magicians need some magic in their lives.' "

"*Especially* magicians," said Blackstone.

"I've written the secret in a letter," said Mrs. Plaut. "The letter is in the safe of my lawyer, Mr. Leib. When I depart this vale of woes, good food, and Eddie Cantor on the radio, Mr. Leib will give the letter to Mr. Peelers who can do with it as he believes best."

She looked at me and added "Accompanying the letter is a chapter of my family history about Simon. I have no more to say."

"And I have no more to ask," said Blackstone.

"Well, does anyone want more coffee or not?" she asked.

"I'll have some," said Bidwell.

"And I," said Gunther.

Mrs. Plaut nodded, looked at Blackstone and said, "You do the buzz saw better than Simon. You do it all better than Simon, except for the girl in the ball. That's all he really had."

Mrs. Plaut disappeared into the kitchen.

"Amazing," said Blackstone. "To find Irene Adaire on the same day . . . Mr. Peters, can we go in another room?"

We could and we did move into the parlor on the other side of the hall beyond Mrs. Plaut's rooms.

"I'm sorry I didn't wait till you got to your office, but I thought you or your brother should know immediately. You were closer to the hotel."

Phil lived in the Valley, North Hollywood, across the hills.

"I got a call at the hotel at five this morning," Blackstone said. "A man. He said that at the testimonial dinner for me tonight the audience would be watching the death of a magician. He said, his exact words, 'And that will be the finish of Harry Blackstone.' And then he hung up."

"Was it Ott?"

"Perhaps."

"Why would he warn you?" I asked.

"It wasn't a warning," said Blackstone. "It was a challenge, a challenge I intend to accept."

CHAPTER

Place two identical glass bottles on a table. Borrow a dollar. Put the dollar over the middle of the mouth of one of the bottles. Turn the other bottle upside down and balance it on the mouth of the other bottle with the dollar between them. Announce that you can remove the dollar without disturbing or even touching the bottles. Challenge your audience to do it. Let them try if they wish. Solution; When you place the dollar between the two bottles, do not put the bottles on the center of the bill. Take the long end of the bill, draw it taut. Holding the end of the bill, raise the other hand above the dollar. Hit it in the middle and out comes the dollar.

From the Blackstone, The Magic Detective *radio show*

"ARE WE READY?" Phil asked, running his thick palm over his short-cropped steel gray hair.

I knew Phil was controlling his lack of approval of the group of misfits who sat around the round conference table in the new office of the new firm of Pevsner and Peters.

The office was large, one of the largest in the building. It wasn't, however, a suite, just one big room whose last renter was now in prison.

Jeremy Butler, our landlord, was seated at the table, and had set up a blackboard against the wall. Phil rolled a fresh piece of chalk in his hand and looked at us before he began.

I sat on Phil's left. Next to me was Jeremy, large, bald, and serene. I was afraid he had written a poem for the occasion. I was reasonably sure he had or would. Jeremy, the ex-wrestler, was a poet for all seasons and reasons. I hoped he didn't decide to read his latest work for this more-or-less captive audience.

Next to Jeremy sat Gunther, nattily dressed, tiny, erect, dignified, and ready with pencil in hand and pad of paper in front of him.

On Gunther's left sat Shelly Minck, fidgeting with his thick glasses, wearing a fresh white dental smock, gnawing on an unlit cigar.

The last person at the table was the one neither Phil nor I wanted there. His name was Pancho Vanderhoff. Pancho was thin, old, wearing a long-sleeved purple shirt and what looked like a thin red scarf draped around his neck. Pancho's face was unlined, his badly dyed black hair thick.

Shelly had introduced Pancho as a screenwriter "with lots of great credits."

Shelly—now in the chips with money from a company that had bought one of his dental hygiene inventions, money from his recently dead wife Mildred, and money from the sale of his house at a hefty profit—had hired Pancho to write a movie about Shelly's life, a movie which Shelly would produce.

"Pancho's just going to observe," Shelly had told me in the hall when I told him about the meeting. "This will be a great chance for him to see me in action as a detective. That's what he's going to concentrate on. You know, respected dentist by day, fearless private investigator by night, and on weekends."

"You're not a private detective," I had reminded Shelly on the landing outside his office.

"I know. I know," he had said impatiently. "But we've worked together on so many cases. I've helped a lot. You know that, Toby. I've helped a lot."

That was true, but he had also nearly gotten me killed more than once, and I had been called upon at least five times to keep him from getting killed or sent to prison.

"Pancho's in your old office," Shelly had said earnestly.

I had rented a cubbyhole with a door and window in Shelly's office till Phil and I had become partners. The cubbyhole was big enough for a desk and two chairs, one behind the small desk, one in front of it.

"You'll love him," Shelly had assured me, thick hand on my shoulder. "I'm telling you. Have I ever led you wrong?"

"Always, Shel," I said.

"Well," he said, waving it away, "That was in the past. Pancho's worked with the best. He's Dutch."

"I see the connection," I said.

"Good," Shelly had said, adjusting his glasses.

I knew he had a patient in his dental chair, waiting. Even with the door to his office closed and the inner door shut, I could hear some poor victim gently moaning.

"You should get back to whoever's in there," I had said.

Shelly looked at his office door as if he had never seen it and then smiled sadly.

"Mrs. Shmpiks," he said, shaking his head. "Molars like rotten little rocks. A challenge. But I'm up to it."

"You always are," I said. "Pancho can stay in his office when we meet."

"Toby, please," Shelly said, putting his hands together. "I'm pleading with you. This is important to me. He'll be quiet."

"I don't think Phil will go for it," I said.

"He's your brother."

"Yeah."

"Toby, after all we've been through together," said Shelly.

There were actually tears in his eyes. The door to his office had opened and his receptionist, Violet Gonsenelli, who also took messages for me and Phil, stuck her head out and said flatly, "I think your patient is dying."

"She's not dying. She's not dying," Shelly said. "She's hurting. It's natural. She's fine."

"I think she's dying," Violet said.

Violet was young, brunette, pretty, and the wife of a promising middleweight whose climb in the ratings had been postponed by the war. Rocky was somewhere in the Pacific.

"Okay, Shel. I'll talk to Phil. Don't be late."

And now Pancho Vanderhoff sat at our conference table.

On the wall behind my desk in the corner were two things: a painting of a woman holding two babies, and a photograph of a young Phil, me, and our father with Phil's German shepherd, Kaiser Wilhelm, in front of us. Our father was wearing his grocer's apron. He had an arm around each of us. Young Phil didn't look any happier in the photograph than he did standing next to the blackboard. The painting was a genuine Salvador Dali, given to me by Dali in appreciation for a job I did for him. Only a few people knew knew it was a real Dali. Three of them—me, Gunther and Jeremy—were seated at the table.

There was coffee in large reinforced Dixie cups and three bags of tacos from Manny's down the street. All of this would go on Blackstone's bill.

Everyone but Gunther was working on a taco. Phil and Gunther also worked on their coffee. Pancho Vanderhoff had consumed three tacos by the time Phil said, "Okay, let's get started."

It was a few minutes after noon.

"Toby and I went to the hotel this morning to check out the space at the Roosevelt. The dining room, lobby, kitchen, toilets, exits," Phil said.

He turned to the blackboard and drew a rough but accurate sketch of the spaces. Then, in the box labeled "dining room," he drew a rectangle and then made eight circles in front of the rectangle, numbering them from one to eight. He said, "These are the tables. There'll be eight people at each table. Here. . . ."

He pointed at the rectangle.

"Here, on a three-inch high platform, Calvin Ott, also known as Marcus Keller, will be seated with Blackstone."

"Ott is the one we'll be watching," said Shelly with a knowing nod.

"No," said Phil. "Ott is the one Toby and I will be watching. Jeremy, you'll be at table four, near the kitchen. You watch the kitchen door, the people at your table and tables five and six and the exit door near the kitchen."

Jeremy nodded.

"Gunther, you'll be at table one, watching the entrance to the dining room, and tables one, two, and three."

"I understand," said Gunther.

"Minck, you'll be at seven, watching that table and eight plus the exit behind you."

"Why do I only get two tables?" Shelly asked. "The others get three."

I knew what Phil was thinking. He paused, held it in. He didn't want Shelly watching any tables, but we were running thin on free help.

"Those two tables are the most likely ones to have people who might want to hurt Blackstone," Phil lied.

He had been a cop for nearly thirty years. He was a better liar than I was, and I'm pretty damned good.

Shelly nudged Pancho Vanderhoff, who was working on his fourth taco. Pancho nodded.

"Toby?"

"Wear tuxes," I said. "If you don't own one, rent one. Blackstone will pay."

I knew Gunther had a tux. I knew Phil and I didn't. I didn't know about the others.

"Pancho will be there," said Shelly.

"This dinner is for magicians," Phil said.

"Something might happen," said Shelly. "It could be a big scene in *Dentist in Disguise*. I'll pay for his ticket and his tux."

"It is a dinner, isn't it?" asked Pancho, cheeks full.

"Yes," I said.

"Do you happen to know what will be on the menu?" asked Pancho.

"No," Phil said.

I knew he was close to throwing them all out. There was the voice of a demon ominously lurking behind his words. I got up.

"Other questions?" I asked.

"What do we do if we see something happen?" asked Gunther.

"Stop it," said Phil.

"Where will you and Toby be?" asked Jeremy.

"Here and here," said Phil, pointing to a spot next to the kitchen and another one at table six. This last was directly in front of the rectangle that marked the platform on which Ott and Blackstone would be sitting.

"We'll be watching Ott and Blackstone," he said.

"You'll have guns?" asked Pancho, sensing the meeting was almost over and pocketing a wrapped taco.

"You don't need to know that," said Phil.

We would be armed, though there was almost no chance that I would shoot with a room full of people. I'm not a bad shot, I'm a terrible one. I've accidentally shot myself twice on cases. Phil was a good shot, but he far preferred to use his hands and fists. Phil took crime very personally.

"We meet in the Roosevelt lobby at seven-thirty," Phil said. "Come earlier, if you like, but no later. That's it."

I took a final bite of the taco I had been working on and bit into something hard. I fished what looked like a small gray pebble from my mouth and dropped it in the wastebasket near the table.

Everyone rose. Shelly whispered to Pancho as they left. Gunther and Jeremy, as unlikely a pair as a man could imagine, left together.

When the door closed, I started to gather taco wrappers, bags, napkins, and coffee cups.

"If Cawelti gets wind of this, of me working with them . . ." Phil said, looking at the closed door and shaking his head.

"He'll make some stupid jokes," I said.

"If he does, I'll punch a hole in his stomach," said Phil, moving to his desk and sitting.

There were three small framed photographs on his desk facing his chair. One was of him, his dead wife Ruth, his two sons, and his baby daughter. The baby, Lucy, was in Ruth's arms. They were all smiling. There was a wedding photograph of Phil and Ruth and one more photograph he never explained to me. That last photograph which had turned a brownish color, showed three men in muddy uniforms looking down at a square box in a muddy field. All three men held helmets in their hands. Phil had been in the First World War. He had come back making it clear that he was not going to talk about what he had seen and done.

"You check the waiters, the kitchen staff for weapons," Phil said.

"Right."

"I'll be at the door to the dining room," he said. "I'll check the magicians for weapons."

I knew Phil had no intention of actually patting down the magicians, not because he was afraid of coming up with a rabbit or white pigeons, but because he knew they wouldn't stand for it. It didn't matter because Phil could tell with about a two percent margin of error if someone was carrying a gun. I had seen him do it with people whom I could have sworn were clean. He could spot the smallest bulge, the slightest abnormal motion that would signal a concealed weapon. He could also detect the hint of guilty sweat or overconfident swagger. My brother was a master of suspicion. Everyone was definitely guilty until he decided they were innocent.

I moved my tongue to the tooth that had bitten down on the pebble. It felt like something was stuck between the teeth. I felt with my finger. Nothing was stuck. A piece of my upper right molar was missing, leaving a jagged remnant. It didn't hurt. I knew I'd have to take care of it. I hadn't been to a dentist in at least twenty years, but I'd find one when I had time. Shelly was not an option.

My plan was to go to the hospital and talk to Gwen Knight. Phil's was to go home, spend the afternoon with his family, have dinner with them, and put on a tux.

We both had to wait. There was a knock at the door. Before we could answer Calvin Ott, a.k.a. Marcus Keller, stepped into the office and closed the door behind him.

CHAPTER

Put a dozen pennies, each with a different date, in a hat. Turn your back and tell someone to pick a coin, hold it to his forehead, and put it back in the hat. Have them shake the hat. Turn around. Take each penny and put it to your forehead until you come to the penny the person has selected. Show them the penny they have chosen. Solution: Chill all the pennies. The penny the person selects and puts to his or her forehead will be warmer than the others. Go through the pennies. The warm one you press to your forehead is the one selected. Note: The trick works best if you do it rather quickly so the coins do not have time to warm to room temperature.

—*From the* Blackstone, The Magic Detective *radio show*

OTT WAS WEARING DARK SLACKS, a blue blazer, a white shirt, and a red tie. He was also wearing a smile. In his right hand was a black pebble-leather satchel with a gold clasp.

"Good morning," he said cheerfully, placing his satchel on the conference table.

"You look like Calvin Ott," I said.

"Keller, Marcus Keller," he corrected, still smiling.

"But you don't sound like the Ott, excuse me, Keller we disagreed with last night," I said.

"It's a new day," he said, snapping the gold clasp and opening the satchel. "And I've come to present you with an offer."

"Get out," Phil said.

Phil did not like games. Phil did not like banter. Phil most definitely did not like Calvin Ott.

Ott paused and looked at Phil.

"I have a civilized offer," he said.

"You're a weasel," Phil answered, taking a step toward him.

I sat back down in the chair at the table where I had sat a few minutes earlier.

"Not very colorful," Ott said with a smile. "Not very creative. Weasel, weasel. How about marmoset? Or reptile. No, you should be more specific. Cobra?"

"To increase the possibility of your survival," I said as Phil took another step toward Ott, "I think you should close your bag, pick it up, go out the door, and call for an appointment."

"You don't want to hear my offer?" he said with less of a smile now that Phil was about four feet away from him and definitely not smiling.

"Not particularly," I said.

Actually, I did want to hear what he had to say. He was our prime suspect in a murder and an attempted murder. He was the one who had threatened our client and was planning a surprise party for Blackstone. He was the one with the big fat ego that might make him say something that would help us and hurt him.

Phil was now almost in Ott's face.

"Look," Ott said with something that was supposed to be a let-bygones-be-bygones little laugh. "I'm not a bad person. I've got a mother, a sister. I give to charity. I follow the war news. I read *Captain Easy* in the comics."

Phil said, "Out."

Phil's right hand was now around Ott's tie.

"When you tickle me," said Ott, "do I not laugh?"

"How the hell should I know?" said Phil.

"Well then, when I tickle you, do you not laugh?" asked Ott, trying to decide whether it would be a good idea to reach up and try to remove my brother's hand from the red tie.

"He doesn't laugh when you tickle him," I said. "Never did."

This was definitely not going the way the great Marcus Keller had planned. Good entrance. Nice bit with the satchel. Good line about an offer. But he had the wrong audience.

"When you torture him, does he not cry?" Ott said, looking into Phil's eyes.

"I doubt it," I said. "Now take me. You torture me and I make a funny sound. Something like uhh-uhh. Drawing in my breath. Not loud. Do you cry when you're tortured?"

"Ten thousand dollars," Ott said, looking at the satchel.

I reached over for the satchel and looked inside. It was filled with green bills in neatly wrapped bundles.

"Phil," I said. "Let's listen."

"It's some full-of-shit trick," said Phil, eyes fixed on Ott who must by now be thinking that he had made a very big mistake.

"Sure," I said. "But the money's real."

"He's trying to pay us off," Phil said.

"No," said Ott, his voice a little reedy like a clarinet played wrong. "May I speak?"

Phil removed his hand from Ott's tie. Ott adjusted the tie and said, "If you prevent me from doing what I have planned for the dinner tonight," he said. "I'll give you ten thousand dollars. This ten thousand dollars."

"If we stop you from killing Blackstone?" I said.

"I didn't say anything about killing Blackstone," said Ott.

"You threatened him," Phil said.

"No, I . . ."

"Why?" I asked.

"Why?" Ott repeated.

"Why do you want to give us all that money to stop you?" I said.

"I don't," said Ott. "I'm offering it. I'm confident you won't collect it. I intend to let every magician who will be at the dinner, every newspaper, every radio station know that I've made this challenge. But my goal isn't to pay you ten thousand dollars. My goal is to make that strutting, pompous Blackstone look like a fool. This offer will give the moment of his humiliation publicity and poignancy. He won't be able to live it down."

Ott was looking from me to Phil now, his eyes darting. He was smiling again. He was most definitely a little nuts.

"How do we know you'll pay if we stop you?" I asked.

"With all that publicity? I wouldn't dare not pay. I'll have this satchel with me. Stop me, and I'll present it in front of everyone in the hall."

"Deal," I said.

"Toby," Phil warned, looking at me.

I didn't say anything, but he knew what I was thinking. He had three kids, had just started a new career with a brother who lived on the edge of poverty. He shook his head and backed away from Ott.

Ott closed the satchel and snapped the gold clasp shut.

"Tonight," he said, satchel in hand.

With his free hand, he reached into the breast pocket of his jacket and pulled out his white handkerchief and waved it in the air. Then he snapped the handkerchief and a small bird flew out from under it. The bird flapped past Phil, made a small circle, and perched on my desk.

Ott nodded as if he were waiting for applause.

"How'd you like to see me pull a rabbit out of your ass?" Phil said, his face red moving back toward Ott.

"I don't have a . . ."

"Well we can just check to be sure," Phil said.

"Phil," I said, trying to keep my voice even, trying to sound like Lewis Stone as Judge Hardy telling Andy to curb his enthusiasm.

Phil paused just long enough for Ott to make it through the

door. The slam it made as he exited started the bird fluttering around the office over our heads.

"Open the window," Phil said, moving to his desk.

I got up and did as he asked.

"Tell the bird to get the hell out of here," he said as he sat down.

I chased the bird around the room two or three times before it found the open window and dived into the smog.

Phil got out of the chair, went to the window, and closed it. He turned to me.

"People are dying," he said. "Thousands of people. Kids. There's a war going on. And that grinning rich monkey in a fifty-dollar jacket is playing games with people's lives."

His fists were clenched.

"If he comes back . . ." Phil began and then changed his mind.

"He won't come back," I said. "He's saving his next trick for tonight."

"I'm going home," Phil said.

"I'll tell Blackstone what's been going on," I said.

"Do that," said Phil, heading for the door.

"See you at the Roosevelt," I said.

"Yeah."

"I've never seen you in a tux," I said.

"You're in for a treat," Phil said, slamming the door as he left.

When he was gone, I called the Pantages and found out from Pete Bouton that his brother had gone to the hospital to see Gwen.

I turned off the lights, went in the hall, locked the door, and listened to the late morning sounds of the Farraday: The muffled whimper of Shelly's patient. From above, the badly tuned piano of Irwin Duncan, "voice teacher to the stars," as he batted out *Rum and Coca Cola* and his latest off-key client tried to mimic Patty Andrews.

I took the stairs, hearing a typewriter clacking on the third floor, a drum beating on the second floor, and a floor polisher on the lobby floor. Jeremy was pushing the polisher gently and evenly. He saw me and flipped it off.

"I just saw Calvin Ott leaving," he said.

"Right."

"And Phillip was not far behind," Jeremy said, rubbing the side of his bald head with two fingers.

"Ott offered to pay out ten thousand dollars if we succeed in stopping him from doing whatever it is he plans to do to Blackstone tonight. Like a challenge."

"We'll stop him," said Jeremy confidently.

I tried to imagine Jeremy in a tuxedo. I couldn't.

"You have a moment?" he asked, reaching into his pocket.

I knew what was going to come out, but I really had no choice.

"Sure," I said. "A poem?"

"It isn't long," he said, unfolding the sheet. "It's called *Magic*."

The Farraday did not suddenly go silent, but the persistent clatter and clang didn't stop Jeremy Butler from his poem.

"It is not real magic we expect
but the illusion. We desire to be fooled,
are pleasured to know the miracle
we are about to witness is a trick
inside of which are hidden wheels.
'How did he do that?' we ask.
But do we really want to know?
In theater darkness, looking up,
we are transported to a Camelot
where belief is truth and truth belief.
A man told me he knew there was a God.
'Miracles prove this truth.'
'Today I believe there is no God," I said.

'How do you know there is no God?'
'I do not know, I tell you what I believe.
You tell me what you believe
and declare that it is truth.'
The magician asks us to believe
for only the space and time of illusion.
He does not ask for endless faith.
We need more magicians."

He folded the sheet of paper neatly and put it back in his pocket.

"We need more magicians," I said.

I didn't understand most of Jeremy's poems and this one was no exception.

"I have to revise it," he said, moving back to his floor polisher. "I fear there are too many magicians like Mr. Ott and they are not all on the theater stage. Many of them are on the stage of life."

"Yep," I said, feeling the rumble of forgotten taco in my stomach, the hole in my molar, the slight but distinct ache in my shoulder. "You going to publish it?"

"When I revise it," he said. "Perhaps it should rhyme."

"Good idea," I said. "You make it rhyme, and people know for sure that it's poetry. See you tonight."

I headed for the door. Behind me, the polisher rattled back to life.

"He's right." I heard a familiar voice say behind me as I stepped onto Hoover.

I turned my head to see Juanita.

"I heard the poem," she said. "He's right. At least about some of it."

Juanita was a seer. Born seventy years earlier in Brooklyn, she had grown up as a nice Jewish housewife with a solid husband, and, when he died, a second solid husband who also died. She had not chosen to have visions, but they had come—on her fiftieth birthday, to be exact. She had then migrated to Los Angeles, rented an office in the Farraday, and handed out little printed cards. Now she had a running clientele, mostly Mexicans and Eastern European refugees. Juanita could see into the future.

"It comes in little flashes, like waking dreams or just words," she had once told me. "I don't know."

The problem with Juanita's visions was that they almost never made sense till they had taken place, and, by then, it was too late to do anything about them.

"Gift, curse, who the hell knows, you know what I mean?"

Now overly made-up, gypsy dressed, with bangled earrings tinkling, the slightly pudgy Juanita stood at my side and looked at the passing parade of cars, servicemen on leave, people going out to late lunch. She sighed.

"I was looking for you," she said.

"Juanita," I almost pleaded.

She shrugged.

"You don't want to hear, you don't want to hear. Who's going to force you?"

"You are," I said.

"Force is too strong a word," she said.

"Okay," I said.

"He's going to be dead, but he isn't going to be dead, but he is going to be dead," she said, looking at me.

"What?"

"Soon," she said. "And the other guy. In what my first husband used to call a penguin suit."

"Tuxedo," I said.

"Whatever," she said with a dismissive wave of her heavily ringed and scarlet-nailed hand. "He's here. Darkness. Light. He's there. Darkness. Light. He's back over here again. You'll see. You'll be there. Lots of penguins. You're a penguin, too."

"Very helpful."

"My pleasure," she said. "No, my duty. Got no choice in the matter. I was heading to Manny's for a taco. I'll buy you one."

"Just ate a couple, thanks," I said.

"Suit yourself," said Juanita. "Just watch out for that dead penguin."

"Thanks," I said.

Juanita took a few steps toward Manny's and then turned around suddenly.

"Don't wait for the pain," she said earnestly.

"What pain?"

"I don't know," she said. "But you'll have warnings. You won't listen to them, but you'll have warnings."

"If I won't listen to them," I said, "why tell me not to wait for the pain?"

"You think I know?" she said with a shrug and a shake of her head. "I see it. I tell you. It happens. I'm a seer, not a magician."

"I know a magician," I said. "Maybe he can help me."

"You're kiddin' me Toby," she said, "but, kiddin' aside, your magician's got his own worries, let me tell you. I'm hungry like an ox."

This time she did move toward Manny's. I considered calling after her to be careful of pebbles in her taco, but decided she might think I was making fun of her.

I headed for the car and was at County Hospital about twelve minutes later.

Blackstone was standing next to Gwen's bed when I went through the door of her room. He was wearing a blue suit with a red bow tie. She was laughing. He was smiling. He held a rabbit in his hand. He handed it to her and she looked up at me.

"Look," she said, cuddling the white ball of nose-twitching fluff. "He's mine. He pulled him right out from under my pillow."

"We haven't given him a name yet," said Blackstone.

"I'll call him Tyrone," Gwen said. "After Tyrone Power."

She was sitting up, a little pale, but not the least like someone who had been shot the night before. She stroked the animal and rubbed her nose against his.

"We've been talking about what happened last night," Blackstone said. "Very curious."

"Very curious," I agreed.

The magician pursed his lips and looked at his hands before he said,

"The killer of Mr. Cunningham used a 9mm weapon, correct?"

"Correct," I said.

"But Gwen was shot at close range with a pellet gun," he went on. "As were you."

"Yes," I said.

"Which suggests that the killer switched guns and chose one unlikely to kill Gwen," he said.

"Or," I said, "there were two shooters."

"Working together?" he asked.

"Could be. Another thought," I threw in. "Our shooter only wanted to make it look like he was trying to kill the witness. He shot Gwen because it made sense to go for the one person who could identify him."

"But he didn't want to kill her," said Blackstone. "Suggesting that he wanted her alive to identify him. But why would he want to be . . ."

"You got it?"

"Got what?" Gwen asked looking up from the rabbit.

"Describe the man who shot you again," I said. "Was it the same man you saw shoot Cunningham in the dressing room?"

"Yes," she said. "Well, I think so. Tux, beard, turban."

"That's what you told the police?" I asked.

"Yes."

"And you saw him shoot Cunningham?" I asked. "You're sure."

"No," said Gwen. "I was on the landing. I heard a shot. I saw him come out of the dressing room."

"With a gun in his hand?"

"Yes, no. I think so," she said. "I turned and ran."

"Calvin Ott?" said Blackstone.

"But Ott couldn't have been the one who shot Gwen. He was at the Pantages talking to the police when Gwen was shot," I said.

"True. He made a scene," Blackstone said. "There was something definitely theatrical about it, but then again Ott is always theatrical."

"He wanted to establish an alibi while someone else was shooting Gwen," I said.

"But he still could have been the one who shot Cunningham in the dressing room," Blackstone said.

"Okay," I tried. "He shoots Cunningham. There's Gwen. He's out in the open now. Gwen runs. He follows. She runs out of the theater. He sends someone after her and goes into the theater to set up an alibi for when she gets shot by someone wearing the beard and turban."

"Assuming the police would decide that the person who shot Cunningham would also be the person who shot Gwen," said Blackstone.

"That's about it," I said. "That's why the pellet gun. Whoever shot Gwen wasn't trying to kill her. He was helping Ott set up an alibi."

"Maybe," said Blackstone.

"Maybe," I repeated.

"That's all very comforting," said Gwen, petting the rabbit and blowing gently on his ear. The ear twitched. So did the rabbit's pink nose.

"It's possible," said Blackstone. "But there's still something missing."

"There always is," I said. "I'd like to talk to your crew before tonight."

"We're going over the act this afternoon, around two," he said.

"I'll be there."

CHAPTER

Tell a person she or he will be hypnotized. Make a fist with your right and left hands. Put your fists on top of each other. Have the person looking into your eyes. Tell them they are hypnotized. Ask them to grab you by the wrists and pull your hands apart. They can't. Solution: When the person is looking into your eyes, move the thumb from your lower hand into the palm of your upper and grasp tightly. The bond is tight. The person will not be able to separate your hands. As the person loses eye contact with you, remove your thumb quickly, make fist and separate your hands showing that they are empty.

—*From the* Blackstone, The Magic Detective *radio show*

IT WAS LUNCH TIME AT MAX'S Drug Store on Melrose, but there was only one red-leather swivel stool open in the middle of the lunch counter. The others were occupied by women shoppers drinking coffee and yakking, salesmen on their lunch hour wolfing down egg salad sandwiches, and a sailor reading the newspaper.

Anita Maloney was alone behind the counter keeping up with orders, serving, preparing, brushing away dangling hairs with the back of her hand. She was a one-woman show: with one hand juggling orders, keeping coffee mugs full, slinging burgers, popping toast and scooping quarter tips into the front pocket of her peach-colored uniform while she piled the dirty cups and plates with the other.

Anita was the reason I was here. We had been seeing each other for about four months. It had started when I stopped in at Max's for a coffee and recognized the woman behind the counter was the girl I had taken to the senior prom at Glendale High more than thirty years before.

We had lost touch with each other. I had gone through a marriage and lost my wife Ann who wanted a husband and not a battered kid in his forties. Anita had also been through a divorce, one she didn't want to talk about it. Anita had a daughter, grown, living on her own in L.A. I had a cat named Dash living on his own in Hollywood backyards.

Anita saw me, gave me a small smile. Good teeth. White. Even. Anita was lean, energetic, and a little washed out when she was behind the counter, definitely pretty when she cleaned up after work. She wasn't a beauty like Ann, but we were more than just comfortable with each other.

She didn't ask me for my order, simply bringing me a Pepsi on ice and a slice of apple pie.

"End of the counter," she said, without moving her head. "He's been sitting there for the past twenty minutes watching the door. When you came in, he stopped watching and buried his head in the *Times*."

She handed me a fork and went down the line to a woman with a cracking voice who called, "Miss!"

I glanced up at the shining aluminum rectangle over the grill. The reflection was wavy like an image behind the August heat of a steamy street. But it was enough. At the far end of the counter, not far from the restrooms and the telephone on the wall sat a man in a purple shirt and a red scarf flung over his neck. Less than two hours earlier, I had seen someone like that attempt to beat the California taco eating record in my office.

Pancho Vanderhoff did not lift his head. I couldn't see him clearly, but I had the feeling his eyes were rolled upward watching me work on my pie.

The pie was good. Anita wouldn't steer me wrong. The good thing was that I felt no pain in my left shoulder. I was aware of where the pellet had gone in and then pulled out, but I couldn't call it pain. What I could call pain was the small, sharp jab in my chipped tooth. I stopped eating.

"Not going to finish?" Anita asked.

"Frank in?" I asked.

"Always," she said. "What's up?"

"Be right back," I said, getting off the stool.

Pancho glanced at me, trying not to let it show. He was bad at not letting it show. When it was clear that I wasn't headed for the door or the restroom but toward the pharmacy counter, Pancho went back to pretending to read the paper.

Frank stood reaching up to get a bottle on a high shelf behind the counter. The white pharmacist's jacket he wore strained as he stretched. His fingers managed to pull the glass bottle forward. It fell and he caught it deftly with a grin of relief.

"Haven't lost the touch," I said.

He put the bottle of white tablets on the counter, looked at his hands and said, "Once a catcher, always a catcher."

"Catcher?"

"Glendale High," he said.

Phil and I had gone to Glendale, but Frank the Pharmacist was definitely a decade younger than me, and, by the time he was in high school, Phil and I were long on our way—he to the war to end all wars and me to a life of poverty, confusion, heartbreak, a reasonable amount of fun and satisfaction. Not to mention the occasional pain, leading me to ask now, "What have you got for a toothache?"

"Advice," he said, picking up the pill bottle again. The pills rattled.

"Go see a dentist. You know a dentist?"

"Not one I'd want in my mouth," I said.

"My brother's a dentist," he said. "You want his number? Use my name. He'll take care of you. Wait."

He put down the pill bottle, reached for the pad of paper on the counter, pulled a push-pull click-click pen out of his pocket and wrote his brother's name and phone number. He handed the sheet of paper to me and picked up the bottle again. I pocketed the paper.

"Anything I can use till I see him?"

"Let's see the tooth."

I leaned over, pulled my upper lip back and he leaned forward.

"I've seen worse," he said, wrinkling his nose.

"That's comforting."

"Oil of cloves," he said. "It's what dentists use."

He handed me the bottle of pills and ducked behind the counter. I put the pills down as he came up with a bottle of green liquid with a screw top. He handed the bottle to me and said, "Just dab it on with your finger. A buck ten."

I fished out the money and handed it to him.

"See Fred," he said.

"Who?"

"My brother Fred, the dentist."

"I will," I said.

I could hear the pills rattling behind me as I headed back to the counter, pausing to open the screw-top bottle and use my finger to dab some oil of cloves on what remained of my tooth. The slight pain went away, replaced by the smell of something I recognized from a recent semimeat dish Mrs. Plaut had prepared a few days earlier.

"You okay?" Anita asked.

"Peachy," I said, sitting again.

She poured me more coffee. I drank it, avoiding the side of my mouth with the sore tooth. I'd respect it, if it would respect me, at least for a few days.

People left. Others came. Anita scrambled. She put in ten-hour shifts four days a week and sometimes she worked an extra day.

A contrast: If I said to Anita that we had to go on a high-speed chase in ten minutes in order to catch up with a guy who'd kidnapped Paul Muni, she'd say, "Sure." And she would mean it. If I had said the same thing to my ex-wife Ann, she would have said nothing, but she would have looked at me with a shake of her head, earrings dancing, breasts heaving, and turned away to deal with something serious.

I guess I still loved Ann. I know I liked Anita more than I liked my ex-wife. Anita knew how I felt about Ann. It didn't bother her. She wasn't looking for another husband.

At one, the lunch counter was almost empty. People had gone back to their buying or selling. The only ones left were me and Pancho who still pretended to read the *Times*.

Anita was cleaning up. Armed with my cup of coffee, I moved to the stool next to Vanderhoff.

"Henriot is dead," I said.

"Huh?" asked Pancho, looking up from his newspaper.

"Front page, bottom, right where you were looking. French patriots killed the Vichy Minister of Information and Propaganda, Phillippe Henriot, in his bed in Paris."

"Oh," he said, his right cheek twitching just a bit. "Yes, I see."

"And if you turn the page," I said, reaching over to do it for him as Anita placed a fresh piece of pie in front of me, "you'll see that Joe E. Brown presented a flag to the new Don E. Brown World War II American Legion Post 593. You know Brown's son was a captain, killed in a plane crash near Palm Springs a couple of years ago."

"I didn't know that," Pancho Vanderhoff said, turning pages.

I held out my hand to stop him.

"You want to talk?" I asked.

"I . . . well," he muttered, adjusting his red scarf.

"Question one," I said. "How did you know I would be coming here?"

"Miss Gonsenelli," he said.

"Mrs.," I corrected.

"She said you might be coming here. I told her I needed to talk to you about the script I'm working on for Dr. Minck."

"Okay, so you just answered my second question, why are you here? I'd like another answer. Would you like a slice of apple pie. On me. It's good. They don't have tacos."

"Well," said Pancho. "I wouldn't refuse."

I asked Anita for a slice of pie for my buddy Pancho, who looked decidedly older than he had in our office. His skin was still unlined but tight like a tom-tom. His hair was black, too black, with spots of the liquid that had made it so speckling his neck.

"I'm a bit of a fraud," he said with a sigh, finally looking straight at me. "I've never written a screenplay. I was a studio gopher for Edwin S. Porter. I brought him coffee and carried his bags. I met D. W. Griffith when Mr. Porter was shooting *Rescued from an Eagle's Nest*. I was in the picture. One of the townspeople who look up and see the eagle carrying the toddler away. Mr. Griffith was the star. Then I went to work for Mr. Griffith."

"Gopher?"

He nodded.

"The truth is, Mr. Peters, I have no talent. I'm an old man living in the back bedroom of my granddaughter's apartment. Closest I got to really being part of the movies was when I played a mute sinister butler in a Republic serial in 1937. Kane Richmond was the star. I was in four episodes. Dr. Minck is a godsend."

"And?"

"And you are his friend and a detective," he said with a sigh, digging into the pie. "This is good. I . . . I was afraid you'd find out that I'm a . . ."

"Fraud," I finished.

He shook his head "yes" again and took on a forkful of pie so big that it stood a good chance of choking him.

Anita was halfway down the counter cleaning the grill, looking over her shoulder at us. I knew she could hear.

"Can you write a script?" I asked.

"Of course," he said. "Probably a very bad one, but I certainly know the format."

"Then do it," I said. "Shelly can afford it."

He smiled at me gratefully, his left cheek full of pie. Then the smile faded.

"There's one more thing," he said. "When we finished our meeting in your office, I went back to my office to work. A man came in. He said he knew I had been at a meeting with you and the others and that it had something to do with the dinner tonight for Blackstone."

"The man have a name?" I asked.

"Everyone has a name," he said. "In Los Angeles, it is usually one that bears little resemblance to his or her given name. He didn't give me his."

"What did he look like?"

Pancho described Calvin Ott.

"What did he want?"

"He wanted me to tell him what went on in our meeting this morning," said Vanderhoff. "He had seen me come out of your door."

"And you told him?"

The thin old man looked at the ceiling. I could see then why he wore the scarf. The wrinkles on his neck made me add ten years to the seventy I had already credited him with.

"How much?"

"I sold my honor for a mere fifteen dollars," he said, pulling three fives from his pocket and placing two of them on the counter. "Filthy lucre, but I truly need it. I spent some of it on a cab to get here."

"Keep it," I said.

"I had to tell you," he said.

His pie was gone. I asked if he wanted another slice. He considered it and shook his head.

"You did the right thing," I said.

"And you won't tell Dr. Minck?"

"Write his screenplay," I said.

"I don't think he has a realistic idea about it," Vanderhoff said. "He's planning to produce this himself if he can't get studio backing. And he wants to approach Clark Gable to play him. Dr. Minck claims to be friends with people like Gary Grant, Gable, Joan Crawford, and Fred Astaire."

"He has met them," I said. "The word 'friends' is definitely pushing reality."

"I feel better," he said, standing and rewrapping his scarf. "Confession. Very cleansing."

"Hold on and I'll give you a ride back to the Farraday," I said.

"I almost forgot," Vanderhoff said. "The man who gave me the fifteen dollars said something peculiar just before he left. He told me not to tell it to anyone else. He told me to watch closely tonight at the dinner because the dead would rise."

That was pretty much what Juanita had told me. I didn't understand it any better coming from Pancho. I would, eventually—but "eventually" still was quite a few surprises away.

I placed a dollar on the counter and told Anita I would call her later. She gave Pancho a smile. He twitched one back at her.

I dropped off Pancho at the Farraday and headed for the Pantages where Blackstone had told me they would be rehearsing and making some changes to the show because of Gwen's absence and the damage to the buzz saw.

The old man at the stage door recognized me and waved me in with his pipe. I could hear voices coming from the stage beyond the heavy curtains, just out of sight.

"Catch him?" the old man said.

"Not yet."

He adjusted his suspenders with his thumbs, looked at his pipe over the top of his rimless glasses and then looked at me as if he were going to honor me with sage advice.

"Meat loaf sandwich for lunch," he said, touching his stomach. "Didn't agree with me."

"Sorry to hear it," I said. "Look . . ."

"Raymond," he said. "Raymond Ramutka."

He paused, his eyes wide, expecting a reaction. When I didn't respond, he rubbed his left hand on his thick wild mane of white hair.

"Before your time," he said with a sigh, looking toward the stage. "I was in the St. Louis and Chicago productions of *The Girl of the Golden West*. Played Jack. Had a voice. But you must hear stories like that all the time in your line of work."

"Some," said. "I know the police asked you, but can you tell me what you saw last night?"

"Saw? Let me think."

He rubbed his hair some more. It was now almost comically wild.

"Saw," he repeated. "Like what went on here?"

"Yes."

"Not things I saw earlier, on the way here after breakfast."

"No, before the shooting," I said.

"Let's see. People moving around in those costumes, moving that stuff, animals in cages. Everyone trying to be quiet 'cause the show was going on you know."

"I know."

He looked at his pipe again.

"Thinking back," he said. "Did see that one who got himself shot and killed. Talked to him. He was a talker. Asked questions. I had answers, but I don't think they were the ones he wanted. He went upstairs. Think maybe I saw him going into one of the doors up there, dressing rooms."

"You didn't hear the shot?"

"Who says?"

"I thought . . ."

"No, I didn't hear the shot. Nothing wrong with my hearing. I've got perfect pitch. Always did. Born with it. 'God's gift,' my mother used to say. 'God's curse,' my father said, because it got me into musical comedy, opera."

He was lost in reverie. I pulled him back.

"Gunshot."

"Never heard it. Buzz saw was going," he said. "Looked up some point. Not too many people backstage then. Saw the one, what's her name, long legs, little tiger costume."

"Gwen," I said.

"That's the one," he said with a nod. "She was about at the top of the stairs. Someone came out of the dressing room behind her. She turned and ran down the stairs, right past me, out that door there."

"The other person, the one who came out of the dressing room?"

"Nice suit, beard, one of those turban things on his head."

"What did he do?" I asked.

Raymond Ramutka was in no hurry. He played with the tobacco in his pipe with a stained thumb and hummed something.

"What did he do," he repeated. "Don't know. Don't think he came down the stairs. Don't know. I watched her go through the door."

"Thanks," I said.

About a minute later I saw Jimmy Clark, the freckled kid, carrying a wooden cage big enough for a cougar. There was a handle on top, and it took both his hands to carry it.

"Want a hand?" I asked.

"No place to grab except the handle," he said. "But thanks."

He put it down and looked at a spot behind the curtains, probably gauging how much further he had to go.

"The other night," I said. "What did you see?"

"Police asked me this," he said. "I'll tell you the same. I was standing about here. Even with the buzz saw, I heard the shot. I knew it was a shot. I've heard lots of shots."

"Army?" I asked.

"Yeah, a grunt. Infantry. Got this," he said, touching his leg, "getting off a landing barge on a little island near Guam. Didn't even make it out of the water. Jap shell hit about then yards away from me, went in, blew. Never got to the island."

He didn't look a minute older than eighteen.

"The shot," I reminded him.

"Oh yea. I heard it. "I was standing there with Meagan and Joyce. I looked up, saw Gwen running down. Saw this guy up there. Turban, beard. I think he had a gun in his hand."

"A pellet gun?' I asked.

"Don't think so," he said. "Looked bigger, heavier. Anyway, he came running down the stairs behind Gwen. I knew something bad had happened. Just had the feeling. Her tiger tail was wagging. You know?"

"I know."

"The man?"

"Stage right and gone," he said. "If I could run, I would have gone for him."

"He had a gun," I said.

"Yeah, right. Well maybe I wouldn't have gone for him but I like to think I would have."

"Did the guy with the beard look familiar?'

"Well maybe, yeah, sort of," he said plunging his hands into his pockets. But I can't place him."

"Keep trying," I said.

"I will," he said.

He rubbed his hands together, took in a breath and picked up the box again.

I found Pete Bouton standing in the wings to the right of the stage. His arms were folded and he was watching his brother slowly go over a number in the act, one that involved swords and a colorful big box that was about the size and shape of an outhouse.

"High," Pete said. "Anything?"

"Not yet," I said.

He looked out on the stage.

"Want to know the real trick?' he asked. The real skill?" He didn't wait for an answer. "Timing, practice, confidence, making it look easy. Don't let them see you sweat. We used to work together on stage, but I'm more comfortable making things work, watching from the wings."

"You were in the wings when Cunnningham died?"

"I was. I didn't hear the shot, but I did hear people talking behind me. I turned. There were four or five people. Joyce, Meagan, Al Grinker, looking toward the stairs leading up to the dressing room. They tell me Gwen ran down. They tell me a man in a beard and a turban came out of the dressing room with a gun."

"But you didn't see this?"

"Not from here," he said. "Just the people looking up."

I looked back. I could see the bottom of the steps but nothing of the upper landing where the dressing rooms were.

I looked at Bouton who was definitely worried.

"I don't like this dinner thing tonight," he said. "When Ott showed up here after the shooting, he was wild, threatened Harry. But my brother doesn't back away from a challenge."

"Ott's got some kind of surprise," I said.

"So has Harry," he said.

I talked to everyone I could find who had been there when Cunningham was shot. They all told pretty much the same story. The only difference, and it was a big one, was that some of them said they thought they saw the man with the beard and gun come down the stairs and either go into the shadows stage right, through the door to the outside, or saw him move the other way outside the dressing room. Some said he was holding a gun. Some said he wasn't.

I went up the stairs, passing a girl in blue tights. Her hair was pulled back and tied in a kind of tail. She reminded me of Ann Miller, which reminded me of Ann Preston who used to be Ann Peters.

"You looked cute in that costume the other night," she said as she passed.

"Cute is what I aim for," I said.

There were two doors beyond the dressing room where Cunningham had been killed. One was a closet with no windows. The other was a storage room with no windows. Around the corner was a dead-end alcove. The alcove was small. Over the railing were rungs fitted into the wall, a ladder down to the stage level and up to the roof.

I didn't bother to climb down. It would just take me where I had been. I went up, pushed the trapdoor open, climbed out, and looked around. Nothing much to see. I walked around the roof to see if there was some way onto it. There was—a fire escape. So, the guy in the turban could have climbed up the fire escape and through the trapdoor. I checked my watch. Useless. It had been my father's. It kept its own time. I had another stop I wanted to make but I wasn't sure I had time. I had a tuxedo to put on, shoes to polish, maybe a murder to stop.

I went back down the stairs, waved at Raymond Ramutka who leaned against the wall near the rear door, probably remembering the score of *Tosca*.

I decided to make a quick stop.

I checked the phone booth and found a listing for *The Pellegrino Agency, Robert Cunningham, confidential investigations.* The address was on San Vicente. When I got there, I walked into The Pellegrino Bar.

The Pellegrino Bar wasn't exactly a dump. The neighborhood was just good enough to keep it from getting a label like that. It was small, dark, clean, and smelled of beer, even when no one was drinking it. The dark windows were glowing with neon beer signs, one of which for Falstaff flickered in the first stages of death.

Early afternoon. One customer at the bar. None in the four booths to the right. Customer and barkeep looked over at me when I came in. The customer, short, round, and needing a shave, was about sixty. He was wearing a gray cap worn off to the side. He wasn't trying to be rakish. He looked as if he were about to burp. Both of his plump hands went to the glass of beer in front of him as if he were afraid I was going to snatch it from him.

The bartender was a woman. She was huge, sad of face, and did not look particularly happy to see another customer come in. A voice on the radio said the British had crossed the Odon River after beating back nine Nazi attacks. The bartender changed the station. The Dorsey brothers' band was halfway through *I Should Care*.

I went to the bar. The bartender moved slowly in front of me, hands on the bar. She was supposed to say, "What'll it be?"

But she didn't. She didn't say anything. Just glowered at me.

"Pepsi, ice," I said.

"And?" she asked.

"What makes you think there's an 'and'?"

"Three in the afternoon, weekday, you order a Pepsi," she said.

"Maybe I just came for the quiet surroundings and friendly atmosphere," I said. "Maybe I'm just thirsty."

"And maybe I'm standing back here waiting for Hal Wallis to come in and discover me," she said.

"Cunningham," I said. "Telephone book says this is his office."

"Back booth over there," she said. "Paid five bucks a month to sit there a few hours a week and for me to take messages. I answer the phone 'Pellegrino.'" If they asked for Cunningham, I let him know or took a message."

"You're using the past tense," I said.

"Because he's dead," she said.

"Cops have been here, right?" I asked.

She just looked at me. "One nasty son-of-a-bitch," was all she said.

"Red hair, bad skin," I guessed.

"That's the one."

"What did you tell him?"

"Okay," she said, leaning toward me over the bar. "Now I know what game we're playing. I'll get your Pepsi. You decide on the going rate for answers."

She moved down the bar. The pudgy drunk held up his hand for service. She ignored him. He burped loudly. He almost lost his cap.

"You're not a cop," she said.

"I'm not a cop," I agreed, reaching for the Pepsi. In spite of two cubes of ice, it was still warm.

"He left two wooden fruit crates full of stuff," she said.

"Did the cop look through them?"

"He did."

"He take them?"

"Nope."

"I'd like to look through them."

"Not a problem," she said, smiling a smile I did not like, a smile that was about to cost Harry Blackstone some money.

"Ten bucks."

"Forty," she said.

"Thirty," I countered.

"I've got no time for games," she said.

I looked at the drunk who was about to fall off his stool. I could see that she had a lot to do. I opened my wallet and counted out forty dollars, all tens. She took them, tucked them into a pocket and said, "The Pepsi's on me. Come on."

She went to the end of the bar and pointed at the rear booth, Cunningham's office. I sat in it with my Pepsi and faced the front door. The dark wooden table was a jumble of rings left by countless glasses and the burn marks of enough cigarettes to kill the population of Moscow, Idaho.

In less than a minute, she came from behind the bar with a crate in her hands. She placed it on the table in front of me and then went back for a second crate. Then she moved behind the bar again, leaving me looking at a full-color picture on the end of the crate of a smiling blonde with frizzy short hair and impossibly white teeth. The blonde was holding a glass of orange juice and above her head were the words, "Sun Drenched Direct From Florida."

I spent the next hour drinking warm Pepsi, watching the drunk, exchanging glances of less-than-love with the bartender, and discovering something interesting among the letters, notes, candy wrappers, and bills that were the legacy of Robert Cunningham.

I discovered that Cunningham had lots of bills that didn't look as if they had been paid. I also learned that he couldn't spell. Examples included: instatution, sirvalence, proseed, cab fair, and naturul.

If there was anything worth taking, Cawelti had probably taken it. But I kept looking. I almost missed it. A scrap of paper torn out of a notebook. It was unwrinkled and might have fallen to the bottom of the pile when Cawelti was going through the contents of the boxes. Cunningham's handwriting was as bad as his spelling, but I could make it out:

> A Thousand and One Nights, Wild, Thursday at eight.
> Culumbia.

Cunningham had said "Wild on Thursday" to Gwen before he died. Tomorrow was Thursday. I had a pretty good idea of what it meant, but I didn't have time now to check. I folded the sheet, put it in my wallet, finished my third Pepsi, made a trip to the gents' and waved good-bye to the barkeep and the drunk, who smiled.

I had a tuxedo to put on, a party to go to, and a magician to protect.

CHAPTER

10

A number of items are placed on the table. No limit to the number of items. You work with an accomplice who goes to the corner and covers his or her eyes or even goes in another room. The victim points to an object on the table. The accomplice returns. The magician points to each object saying nothing and pointing in the same way. The accomplice correctly identifies the object as the one selected when the magician points to it. Solution: Be sure there are objects of a number of colors, including black. Point to a black item as you go around only if the next item is the correct one. If the victim has chosen a black item, it makes no difference, just so the accomplice knows that the chosen object will be pointed to after the first item the magician points to.

—From the Blackstone, The Magic Detective *radio show*

"YOU LOOK ELEGANT," Anita said, stepping back.

We were in her apartment, and I was standing in front of her full-length mirror.

She was either blind or being kind.

The stiff in the mirror looked like the uncomfortable bodyguard for a mobster. The tux was black and pressed. The black bow tie had been tied perfectly by Anita. My shoes were shined. My hair was brushed back and glistening with Vitalis. It was my face that gave me away. It was the middle-aged face of an ex-boxer who had taken at least eight or ten too many blows to the face. I had never been a boxer, but I had lost more than my share of battles. My nose was flat. My cheeks were rough, and you didn't have to look too closely to see a small white scar over my right eye and another one just left of my chin. It was a good face for someone in my business.

"First time," I said, looking at myself.

"Not bad," said Anita, moving to her couch and reaching for the glass of iced tea she had left on the nearby table.

"Hard to breathe," I said.

"It's supposed to be tight," she said. "Sleek lines. Elegant. You planning to find a place for a gun under that jacket? It would show."

"No gun," I said.

Phil would have a gun. Phil could shoot. I owned a gun, a .38. I kept it in the glove compartment of the Crosley. I seldom carried it. The people I might try to protect were in as much danger from me as from some bad guy with a grudge.

"You're a scrapper, not a shooter," Shelly had once consoled me when I had been shot by my own gun. "Some of us are born with the knack," Shelly had said.

That was before Shelly had shot and killed his wife with a crossbow in a public park.

"You want to throw something on fast," I said, turning to her.

Anita sipped some iced tea and shook her head.

"I'm tired. I can't throw something on fast, and it's a little late to ask me," she said.

"Yeah," I agreed.

"And I thought you said it was for men only?"

"It is," I said, "but I have clout with all the wrong people."

"I pass," she said.

Anita was wearing a robe, green, maybe silk. I think it had belonged to her former husband. It was too big on her. I didn't ask.

"I'm going to listen to Baby Snooks and *The Aldrich Family* and get to bed early," she said. "Do me a favor Toby.' "

"What is it?"

She got up, walked over to me, put her arms around my neck, and kissed me. When we finished the kiss, she said, "Survive."

"That's my plan," I said.

I got to the Roosevelt just before six-thirty and parked half a block away on the street. Not much of a space, but enough for the Crosley, which is a little bit longer than a refrigerator lying on its side.

The lobby was bustling with men in tuxedoes, men and women in military uniforms, a few elegant young women with elegant older gentlemen of a comfortable ilk. My tux-clad group was in a corner behind a wall of low potted palms. The wall didn't protect us from glances and a few stares.

Phil looked uncomfortable, his thumb wrestling with his collar, his face pink and turning red. Shelly somehow managed to look rumpled, probably because his tux was a size or two too large. Pancho Vanderhoff, looking reasonably dapper, gave me a pleading look. Jeremy's tux made him look even larger than he was, but he seemed reasonably comfortable, as did Gunther. We had all, except for Gunther who owned his own, borrowed our tuxedoes from Hy's For Him. I had spent occasional nights alone in the dark aisles of Hy's lying in wait to catch occasional employees who snuck back in after hours to cart off merchandise. This entitled me to a discount and the loan of a suit from time to time, on the condition that I returned it without a spot so Hy could clean, press it, and sell it for new.

Jeremy and Gunther were sitting. The rest were standing.

"You're late," Phil said.

"I'm on time," I said.

"Let's go over it one more time," Phil said, tugging his collar.

We went through the plan, each of us saying where we'd be sitting and what was expected of us.

"Okay," said Phil. "Let's go in."

Phil had arranged for the door to the small ballroom to be locked. We walked down a corridor, made a right turn, moved down the hall and turned right into the kitchen. The temperature went up about twenty degrees. Cooks were cooking. Waiters were waiting. They paused to look at us as we marched single file past ovens and steel-topped tables with Phil in the lead.

The ballroom was empty. Phil checked to be sure the tables were where they were supposed to be. When he was satisfied, he turned his collar and moved to the small platform against the wall. There was a table with a set-up for two on top of a white tablecloth that hung to the floor. A wide solid dark wooden podium stood to the right of the table on the platform set back almost to the wall. There was a rectangle of blue cloth pinned to the front of the podium; it had gold trim and the words "Greater Los Angeles Association of Magicians" stitched onto it in matching gold. Phil checked the podium, checked under the tablecloth.

"Jeremy, no one comes through the kitchen but waiters," he said. "Understood?"

"Perfectly," Jeremy said.

"Look for bulges," Phil said. "Weapons."

Jeremy nodded.

"Everybody sit down," he said.

They went to their assigned seats. Phil and I went to the ballroom door. Phil checked his watch. We could hear voices on the other side of the door. A few people tried the handle.

"You'd think you'd find one magician out of the sixty out there who could open a locked door," I said.

Phil tugged his collar angrily, grunted, and opened the door. I stood on one side. He stood on the other. They came in one at a time, handing us their invitations. Phil and I checked for weapons. The magicians were of all ages, but mostly over fifty, and wore their tuxedoes as if they put one on every night, which some of them probably did. They were fat, thin, bushy-haired and bald. They had beards, mustaches, or were clean shaven. They chatted their way in, smiled as if they had a secret, and made their way to their tables. A few table-hopped. Some nodded across the room or held up a hand.

Ott, in a white tuxedo, didn't come in till everyone was seated. In his hand was the black satchel he had shown to me and Phil, the one containing ten thousand dollars. He was accompanied by his assistant, the little guy named Leo, who took Ott's black cape when Ott was sure that all eyes were on him. The cape came off with a swirl. There was a beat of silence as the assistant took a seat near the door and Ott marched to the platform without looking at any of his fellow magicians. He sat in one of the two chairs, placed the satchel on the floor next to his chair, and looked at the empty seat next to him, Blackstone's seat. Then Ott looked at the door.

Harry Blackstone's entrance was far less flamboyant than Ott's. He wore a black tux with a white tie and a white handkerchief in his pocket. He looked exactly the way he looked for every performance of his that I had seen. He walked, not marched, past tables, exchanging a word or two at each table, nodding at Phil, smiling at me. When he did get on the platform and sit, Ott turned to him and smiled, as false a smile as was inhumanly possible and passable.

When it was clear that no one else was coming, Ott rose as waiters moved from table to table with bowls of biscuits.

"Fellow prestidigitators," he said. "We are here to honor a man who truly needs no introduction."

Polite applause.

"Harry Blackstone is a legend," Ott said. "There are few true legends in our profession. And most of them fade into a mysterious cabinet called Time and are heard of no more. Many of them fall before their time because someone of imagination tests them, humbles them. None have yet been able to do that to the man we honor today. But, to make the evening one to remember, I have issued a friendly challenge to this man we so admire. There will be a surprise. But first, a few of our members have agreed to perform new feats of magical legerdemain. Wayne Dutton."

Polite applause.

A roly-poly man with a bushy head of hair and mustache rose from a table near the podium. He moved to the open space in front of Blackstone and Ott, turned to the roomful of magicians and pulled out a red ball tied to a piece of string about two feet long.

Someone groaned and whispered, "Not the dancing ball."

"The dancing ball," said Wayne Dutton in a very high voice that guaranteed he would never have a career in show business, at least not as a magician.

He held up his hands. His shirtsleeves were too long. He held the string and let the ball down in front of him. The ball quivered a little. Then it began to move from side-to-side and then suddenly the ball went straight up in the air and the string stiffened. The ball was balanced at the top of the string. Wayne Dutton smiled beneath his bushy mustache.

Polite applause again. One of the magicians at our table leaned over to me and said, "There's not a man in this room who couldn't do that when he was twelve, with the exception of old Wayne."

"How?" I asked.

"At least four different ways," the man said, continuing to applaud as the ball suddenly dropped and the string became a string again. "Wayne is Ott's number two sycophant, next to Leo."

Two other magicians presented tricks, one who kept plucking playing cards out of the air and another who made lighted cigarettes suddenly appear and disappear.

Ott stood when the applause stopped and said, "We'll have our dinner now, unless our honored guest wishes to entertain us with a feat of magic to start the evening, though it is obviously doubtful that he could top the marvel just performed by Wayne Dutton."

Blackstone shrugged, stood up, raised a hand and as he flicked his wrist, the lights went out. I started to get up, but the lights came back on almost instantly.

Blackstone was gone.

There was a snap of fingers at the ballroom door and there stood Blackstone, thirty feet from where he had been only a second earlier. All eyes were on him as he grinned and the lights went out again. Again it was an instant before the lights were back on again. Blackstone was no longer at the door. He was back on the platform standing behind the podium.

The applause was more than polite. A few people rose. Blackstone swept back his tuxedo tails and took his seat next to Ott, who forced himself to smile. He whispered something to Blackstone, but I was too far away to hear what it was.

Salad came and went. Tomato soup came and went. I kept my eyes on Ott who smiled, eyes darting around, looking very satisfied. The main course was served.

I was spearing a potato, my eyes on Ott who was leaning forward slightly, when the lights went out again. Again they came back almost instantly. We all looked for Blackstone on the platform, expecting a repeat of the trick he'd already done, or some variation on it. But there Blackstone sat exactly where he had been. Next to him Calvin Ott was slumped forward, his face pressed against his plate, eyes closed, a knife buried deeply in his neck.

"There!" someone shouted.

The ballroom door was open. Someone in a brown jacket stood in the doorway for a beat, turned and ran.

"Don't let him get away!" Sixty magicians, a dentist, a landlord, a tiny translator, a phony screenwriter, and two private detectives ran for the open door. I glanced back. The satchel was still next to the dead Ott's chair. Blackstone was hurrying toward us.

I pushed past four or five people and went through the door. I could see a man in a brown jacket running across the lobby. I ran ahead of the crowd and through the door to the street. The runner was going down the sidewalk, pushing people out of the way. I closed the distance between us, but he was younger than me and in better shape. A blur of black and white passed me, caught up with the runner, and jumped on his back.

I was panting when I caught up. Passersby stopped to watch. Magicians caught up with us. The young magician who had caught the man stood up. He had a thin mustache and wasn't breathing hard.

Phil caught up just as I was kneeling to double check the man in the brown jacket, who was lying on his back.

"Who the hell are you?" Phil asked, grabbing his neck.

The man wasn't even a man. He couldn't have been more than seventeen, and he was frightened.

"Nordman, Michael Nordman," he said. "It was a joke. My head hurts."

"A joke?" I asked.

"Or something. I don't know. A guy gave me fifteen dollars and told me to stand outside the door. I was supposed to watch under it, and, when the lights went out, open the door, stand there for a second or two, then run away as fast as I could."

"What guy?" asked Phil.

"I don't know his name," the kid said. "My head hurts. I was working down the street at Hudson's Restaurant yesterday. He came over to me and told me what he wanted. There was going to be an envelope with fifteen dollars for me at the hotel desk. It was there, so I did it."

Around us, magicians were shoving, talking, shouting. Phil

pulled the kid up by the arm, ripped his own collar off his neck, and started dragging Nordman back to the hotel.

Cars slowed down to watch us parade back through the lobby and into the ballroom. It was empty, except for Ott at the table facedown with a knife in his neck.

"That's him," said Nordman, pointing at Ott.

"The one who paid you to run away?" I asked.

"That's him. What happened to him?"

No one answered.

"Get them out of here," Phil said to Jeremy, nodding at the magicians. "Put them somewhere, but don't let any of them go."

Jeremy was next to me now. He heard what Phil had said and turned to wrestle the magicians back into the lobby.

"Can you handle it?" I asked.

Jeremy nodded calmly and began to herd the crowd away from the door. Phil moved quickly past the tables and stepped up on the platform.

The knife was deep in Ott's neck, with blood—a lot of it—seeping from the wound. We didn't have to check, but we did. No pulse. I wanted to lift Ott's face out of the plate, but I knew better.

We looked at each other thinking the same thing. One of us had to say it.

"Lights were out no more than a second."

"Only one person was close enough to do this," said Phil, looking at the dead magician.

"Unless he was a contortionist and killed himself," I said.

"Knife is straight down and deep," said Phil.

"Blackstone," I said.

"Blackstone," Phil agreed.

"Phil," I said. "The satchel's gone."

CHAPTER

11

Ask for a coin. In your hand is a handkerchief spread over the fingers of one hand. Ask someone to place the coin in the center of the handkerchief. Poke it down showing that the coin is still there. Reach over with the other hand, snap the handkerchief. The coin is gone. Show that both your hands are empty, wipe your brow with the handkerchief and put it in your pocket. Solution: Before you place the handkerchief over your fingers, put a rubber band around your thumb and first two fingers of the hand, which will hold the handkerchief. As you touch the end of the handkerchief, let the rubber band slip over the coin. Snap the handkerchief. Show your hands are empty.

—*from the* Blackstone, The Magic Detective *radio show*

"SIXTY WITNESSES," SAID CAWELTI, leaning back against the table, arms folded, smile on his pink face.

"Sixty-six," Gunther corrected. "Plus at least one waiter."

Cawelti glared at Gunther for a second, shook his head and looked at Blackstone who sat in front of him. The set-up was makeshift: two rows of chairs, four chairs in the first row, three in the second. It was a small meeting room in the hotel, rearranged quickly for Cawelti's show.

A huge cop named Brian Alexander stood at the door to the room. He was a good guy, considered the toughest man in the Wilshire station, and we all knew he was there for one reason, which was to protect Cawelti from my brother. Alexander didn't look comfortable.

It was Cawelti's show, and he was going to play it out, trying to make us all squirm. It was his moment of triumph. It would be a very short moment.

In the ballroom, police lab guys were looking at Ott's body. In another room, the magicians were being interviewed by four detectives. All of them were coming up with the same story that pointed to our client as a murderer.

Blackstone sat in the first row of chairs with me on one side of him and Phil on the other. Gunther sat next to me. In the second row sat Shelly, Pancho, and Jeremy.

"Ott threatened you," Cawelti said, pointing at Blackstone.

Blackstone nodded his agreement.

"You all heard the threat," Cawelti said, looking at each of us. "Right?"

We all nodded, except for Shelly who said, "right."

"So you killed him before he could nail you," said Cawelti, looking at Blackstone.

"Incorrect," said Blackstone.

"Come on," said Cawelti, folding his arms again. "No one was within twenty feet of the victim but you. Lights go off. Lights come back on. How long were they out? A second? Two?"

No one answered.

"Not enough time for anyone to stand, let alone get up on that stage and stab Ott," said Cawelti. "Not enough time for anyone to do it but you. Right?"

He pointed again at Blackstone, who was lost in thought.

"Pardon me," said Blackstone, looking up. "What did you say?"

"I said you killed Ott," Cawelti shouted.

"No," said Blackstone. "It was an illusion."

"It didn't happen," said Cawelti. "That what you're telling me? We walk back in that ballroom and Ott is alive? That what you're telling me?"

"No," said Blackstone. "He is dead. The ultimate trick designed to create the illusion that I was the only one who could have killed Ott."

Cawelti looked at the ceiling and then at the carpeted floor.

"If you'll give me a little time, I'll figure out how it was done," said the magician.

"Like Sherlock Holmes?" asked Cawelti.

"Something like that," said Blackstone, straightening the lapels on his jacket.

"And Cunningham, you didn't kill him in that dressing room?" Cawelti hammered.

"I was onstage before more than a thousand witnesses," Blackstone said. "I didn't know the man and there are witnesses who saw the real killer."

"You could have . . ." Cawelti began.

"Show's over," said Phil, standing.

Cawelti's eyes turned toward my brother and then to Alexander at the door.

"Charge him, book him, and tell the reporters you arrested him," said Phil. "And when we prove he didn't do it, we tell the reporters that you are a pisshead which they already know."

"I need to use the bathroom," Shelly said behind me.

"Suffer," said Cawelti, trying to stare Phil down.

"I am," whined Shelly.

"Something was different," said Gunther.

We all looked at him.

"Something was different?" Cawelti repeated, looking at Gunther. "What the hell does that mean?"

"The dead man," said Gunther. "He did not look the same when we came back after chasing that young man. Something had changed."

"What?" asked Cawelti.

"I'm not certain," said Gunther. "But I am certain that something was different."

"Very helpful," said Cawelti.

I looked at Blackstone. He was looking at Gunther and I could see that the magician was beginning to get an idea.

"I've got to pee, really, " said Shelly. "Now."

"Oh for Chrissake," said Cawelti with a sigh. "Go pee and get your ass back here in one minute flat."

Shelly got up. So did Pancho.

"Where the hell are you going?" Cawelti asked.

"With him," said Pancho.

"Sit down."

Pancho sat as Shelly waddled toward the door. Alexander took a step to one side to let him pass.

"John," I said.

"Detective Cawelti," he corrected.

"I thought we were friends," I said.

"Cut the shit Peters. Your client is burnt toast."

"Why would he turn out the lights-and kill Ott, knowing that when they came back on he'd be the only possible suspect?" I asked.

"He didn't know the lights would come back on so fast," said Cawelti. "He pulled the lights-off trick earlier to be sure it would work. This time it didn't work. Somebody turned the lights back on too fast."

"Somebody?" I asked. "Who?"

"What's the difference?" Cawelti said, looking at Blackstone again. "Who turned them out the first time, when you did that trick about getting across the room?"

"A young man in our show," said Blackstone.

"How did you get across the room and back in less than a second?" asked Cawelti.

"If I tell you, the illusion is spoiled."

"Fine," said Cawelti. "You can tell it to a jury if it gets that far."

"Unlikely," came a voice from the open door behind Alexander.

Martin Leib, the best lawyer money can buy, filled the doorway. Marty was immaculately dressed in the best suit his clients' money could buy.

Before Cawelti had shown up, I had called Marty's number. He hadn't been there, but his wife had taken the message and said she would find him.

Now Marty moved past Alexander gracefully, briefcase in hand, and said, "From what I've been able to gather, no one saw my client commit the crime."

"No one else could have," said Cawelti.

"That remains to be seen," said Marty, moving to the table against which Cawelti was leaning.

He placed his briefcase on the table, opened it, and pulled out a cigar box. He held the box up, opened it, showed it to Cawelti and to all of us, closed the box, and handed it to Cawelti.

I thought I heard Blackstone let out a small chuckle at my side, but he said nothing.

"Open it," said Marty.

"What the hell are you . . . ?"

"Indulge me," said Marty, adjusting his jacket.

Cawelti opened the cigar box. A white dove flew out and almost hit him in the face. The dove flapped its way around the room and came to rest on a small table at the back of the room.

"I can put you on the stand and make you swear the box was empty," said Marty. "But, given what you have just seen, all you could honestly say is that you thought the box was empty."

Marty looked at Blackstone, who nodded his approval.

"God, I've always wanted to do something like that," Marty said. "I'd almost take on this case for nothing for the pure satisfaction of this moment. Almost."

Gunther applauded. We joined him. Marty dropped his head in a near bow, and Cawelti turned bright red as Shelly came back through the door. The dentist was zipping his pants and pushing his glasses back on his nose.

"What did I miss?" he asked, looking around.

"Sit down!" Cawelti boomed.

Shelly hurried to sit, and Pancho whispered into his ear to explain what had happened.

"Would you like to see another one?" Marty asked.

"No," shot Calwelti.

"So," said Marty, "are you going to arrest my client? Put him in handcuffs? I'll give you a hundred dollars to your ten that he'd be out of them in less than eight seconds. Was my client wearing gloves when all this happened?"

"What?" asked Cawelti.

Marty looked at us.

We all shook our heads.

"Well," said Marty. "I've just been told by Joe Moark, one of your men, who's in the ballroom, that there are no fingerprints on the murder weapon."

"That son-of-a-bitch," said Cawelti. "Blackstone could have dumped the gloves."

"Where?" asked Marty. "Have you searched my client?"

Cawelti didn't answer.

I thought of some place Blackstone could have dumped a pair of gloves, plus the missing black satchel.

"I'll take that as a 'yes.'" Marty looked at Blackstone, who nodded. "And you've searched everyone in this room?"

We all nodded "yes."

"He dropped them somewhere in the confusion," said Cawelti.

"Let me know when you find them," Marty said, snapping closed the cigar box and returning it to his briefcase. He pulled a folded sheet of paper from the briefcase and held it up as if he were going to do another trick.

"Signed by Judge Froug," he said, handing it to Cawelti.

Cawelti didn't go down easily. He looked at the paper, refolded it, jammed it into his pocket, and said,

"In my office, tomorrow morning at nine."

In the lobby, Blackstone moved to Marty's side and said, "Marvin Morosco."

"Marvin Morosco is right," said Marty.

"Who's Marvin Morosco?" I asked.

"The dove in the cigar box," said Blackstone. "It's one of his."

"Ah, yes," said Marty. "I borrowed it from Mr. Morosco. I came across him in the lobby before the show I did for Detective Cawelti. It will go on your bill for my services, of course."

"Of course," said Blackstone. "And what would you have done if Detective Cawelti had taken you up on your offer of a second piece of magic?"

Marty shrugged his shoulders.

"I would have resorted to the last refuge of a gifted lawyer, verbal prestidigitation. Nine, tomorrow. My office."

He handed Blackstone a card and walked confidently away.

On the street in front of the hotel we formed a huddle, six mismatched penguins. If we had a tin cup and could carry a tune, we probably could have picked up some loose change singing *Carolina In The Morning* and doing a soft shoe with our hands in our pockets.

"There was definitely something about the dead Mr. Ott," said Gunther.

"What?" I asked.

"I don't know. But I will sit in my room this night in darkness and re-create the events of this evening," said Gunther.

"You do that," said Phil.

"We'll solve it," Shelly said, his face pink, a fresh cigar in the corner of his mouth.

He looked at Pancho who nodded, either in agreement or falling asleep. Shelly put a hand on Pancho's shoulder and ambled away saying, "Great material for the movie, huh?"

"I have a question," said Jeremy, who hadn't spoken for the past half hour. He looked at Blackstone and said, "Your brother."

Blackstone smiled.

"That's not a question," said Blackstone.

"Is it an answer?" said Jeremy.

"What the hell are you two talking about?" Phil asked impatiently.

"The illusion in the ballroom at dinner," said Jeremy.

"Yes," said Blackstone. "Would you like to explain how I did it?"

Jeremy looked up at the night sky. We all looked up wondering what he saw. There was nothing up there but stars.

"When the lights went out the first time," Jeremy said, "you hid."

"Under the podium," Blackstone supplied. "I came to the hotel this afternoon and with the help of my brother, switched podiums, placed the new, larger one closer to the wall and when the lights went out, I ducked behind and under the podium."

"And when the lights came on," said Jeremy, "it was Peter, your brother standing near the door, not you. He clapped so that everyone would look in his direction and not at the stage."

Blackstone nodded.

"And when the lights went out again, your brother went through the door and out and you stood up behind the podium."

"You have the eye of a true magician," said Blackstone.

"But neither the dexterity nor calling," said Jeremy.

"Hold it," I said. "Your alibi for the killing of Cunningham in the dressing room was that you were onstage. If Cawelti figures out how the trick in the ballroom was done, he might also figure that it was Pete onstage that night while you were killing Cunningham."

"How likely is it that one of those magicians," Phil said, nodding at the hotel entrance, "will figure out how you did the disappearing act in there?"

"At least six of them have already done so," said Blackstone.

"Marty's tomorrow at nine. I might be a little late," I said.

"Why?" asked Phil.

"I've got to see a wild man about a thousand and one nights," I said.

And I might have to see a dentist named Fred, I thought. My tooth definitely wanted me to know it was there and not happy. I reached into my pocket for the bottle of oil of cloves. It wasn't there. I had left it in my room.

Jeremy headed for the entrance of the hotel.

"Where is he going?" Phil asked.

"To rescue the bird," said Gunther.

CHAPTER

12

Place a hat on the floor. Drop a playing card. The card floats away, always. Invite others to drop a card. You take a card and drop it right into the hat. Solution: Hold the card shoulder high over the hat. Hold the card flat, level with the floor, with your thumb on one side and a single finger on the other side. Release the card. It will fall into the hat.

—From the Blackstone, The Magic Detective *radio show*

"SUSTENANCE," CAME MRS. PLAUT'S voice from the darkness.

I sat up on my mattress on the floor and blinked at the broom-thin shadow in the doorway. The overhead light came on and I looked into the face of Irene Plaut.

"You cannot go through a day such as you had yesterday without enough stick-to-the-ribs sustenance," she said. "Breakfast in fifteen minutes. You have left your bib and tucker in a heap."

She pointed at my tux on the floor near the door and started to turn.

"Was your husband really a magician?"

She either had her hearing aid turned off or chose not to answer. She turned right and walked away, leaving the door open. Leaving the door open guaranteed that I would have to get up to at least close it.

My shoulder where the pellet had hit felt fine. Well, "fine" was a little optimistic. In addition, my tongue told me that I hadn't lost any more of the tooth. The tooth told me that it would behave. I did not trust the tooth. I used the oil of cloves, got up, put on a reasonably clean pair of underpants and trousers and hurried to the bathroom to shower and shave before one of the other tenants beat me to it. I was sure Gunther had long since cleansed himself from toenails to the ends of the hairs on his head. It was Bidwell I tried to beat. He took about fifteen minutes in the bathroom, probably because he had only one hand to work with, though he seemed to be doing reasonably well with that one hand where Emma Simcox was concerned.

I was the first one at Mrs. Plaut's table, having passed the screeching bird whose name I no longer knew nor cared about. I had dropped my tux in a neat bundle near the front door.

"I have to hurry," I said as Mrs. Plaut came in with the coffee.

"We all have to hurry," she said. "It is the lot of man, the human condition. Breakfast today is Spam and egg casserole with loganberries."

"Sounds great," I said, picking up the coffee.

"I'll bring it out when all are assembled," she said.

"I'm really in a hurry."

"You'll not live a moment longer nor accomplish anything of true pith and moment by hurrying," she said, daintily picking up her coffee cup.

"Alright," I returned. "Was your husband really a magician and were you the famous Irene?"

She put down her cup, turned it so the handle pointed away, pursed her lips and said,

"Mr. Blackstone is illusional."

"Delusional," I corrected.

"That, too," she said. "I'll get the casserole."

Up she rose and ambled into the kitchen. Gunther arrived, and I told him where I was going before our morning meeting with Marty Leib. Gunther asked if I would like his company and I said I would.

Mrs. Plaut arrived with a steaming Pyrex container, which she held with two potholders. Gunther moved to place the bamboo mat on the table closer to her.

"There," she said, putting down the dish and standing back to admire her work as Bidwell and Emma came in and sat next to each other.

"Smells good," said Bidwell with his car salesman smile. If he had two hands, this is the moment he would have rubbed them together.

"The zesty, crusty topping has been recommended personally by Betty Crocker," said Mrs. Plaut.

I considered telling Mrs. Plaut that there was no Betty Crocker. I considered asking Mrs. Plaut again about her rumored career as a magician's wife. I considered finishing my coffee, motioning to Gunther and leaving without the pleasure of the savory casserole. The latter was not a serious consideration, not if I intended to remain a boarder in Mrs. Plaut's house of a thousand pleasures.

The casserole was good, strange but good. That was Mrs. Plaut's specialty: strange but good cooking, with an emphasis on the former. Bidwell always shook his head and ate with gusto, frequently adding comments on the brilliance of Mrs. Plaut's culinary skills. I think he meant it. The man survived on enthusiasm. I could take just so much of it. I ate, chewing only on the left side of my mouth.

I had seconds and then waited while Gunther finished. He did not eat quickly. When he finally placed his knife and fork neatly on his plate, I stood and said, "Sorry, we've got to run."

"With caution," said Mrs. Plaut. "Always with caution. The mister always said, 'If you don't look where you are stepping, someday, somewhere you will step into something that will be hard to clean off.'"

"Sage advice," I said, and we were off.

Gunther had brought his tux downstairs before he came to

breakfast. His was on a hanger and didn't look as if it had been worn. We gathered our uniforms and headed for my Crosley. On the way to Columbia, we dropped the clothes off at Pearson's Cleaners on Pico, which opened at dawn. They would have to be cleaned before I returned them to Hy's.

Ten minutes later, we were pulling into the parking lot at Columbia Pictures, where a uniformed attendant recognized me.

"Toby? Son-of-a-bitch," said Dave Crouch as I rolled down my window. "Last time I saw you was . . ."

"Burke Reilly's retirement party," I said.

"Five years?"

"Six or seven," I said.

Dave was a heavy man in his midfifties with clickety-clack false teeth and a constant smile. We had both been guards at Warner Brothers. Harry Warner personally had fired me when I'd taken a short right jab at a second-rate cowboy star after he'd tried to saddle a would-be kid starlet who wasn't interested. It wasn't so much that I had punched the cowboy, but that I had broken his nose, which set the picture he was working on off its shooting schedule for more than a week. Dave Crouch had simply traded the Warner brothers for Harry Conn and a few dollars more per week.

"You here looking for a job?" asked Dave, glancing at Gunther.

"Looking for a movie star," I said.

"Who?"

"Cornel Wilde. I hear he's shooting *A Thousand and One Nights*."

"That he is," said Dave. "Stage Two. He expecting you?"

"Would I be here at eight in the morning if he weren't?"

"Yes," said Dave. "You would, but who gives a damn, you know? I've had it up to here with Cohn and company. I'm thinking of moving down to San Diego, buying into my brother-in-law Sam's bar. Right near a shipyard. Goddamn gold mine.

Sam's got a liver thing, and my sister likes cooking for me. Seen Ann?"

"No, not for a while," I said. "Rose?"

"No," he said. "Go on in. If someone asks me, I'll say you showed me a pass. You got a pass right?"

"Right here in my pocket," I said.

"Good enough for me," said Dave.

I drove past the gate and headed for Stage Two.

"Rose is his former wife, I take it?" asked Gunther.

"She took it," I said. "Dave once had a house in Santa Monica."

Stage Two didn't look any different from the other sound stages on all the lots of all the studios. Maybe it was a little smaller. Maybe the outside brick walls weren't as clean, but a sound stage is a sound stage from the outside. On the inside, it can be anything from a crater on Mars to a battlefield in Germany to a Sultan's palace in fairy tale, which was what Stage Two was when Gunther and I went through the door. The green light was on, indicating that they were not shooting at the moment.

It was the Hollywood I had learned to love and distrust. Around the walls were ladders, lights, piles of electrical equipment, chunks of scenery leaning against other chunks of scenery. In the middle of the sound stage was what looked like the garden of a palace with a little fountain in a pool. Girls in colorful billowing costumes with veils pulled back were chatting in little groups, some of them smoking, some of them sipping coffee.

The garden was painted in bright colors, reds, blues, greens, golds, yellows, in contrast to the black and gray beyond what the camera would see.

In the middle of the garden stood two men. One man wore dark trousers and a white shirt with the sleeves pulled up. He was holding a script. His companion, in billowing purple pants and a white shirt with puffy sleeves, was looking at the script, nodding his head and saying something. The man in the costume, Cornel Wilde, was tall, handsome with dark curly hair and serious dark eyes.

Gunther and I started toward Wilde when a bald young man, wearing glasses that didn't quite go with his Scheherazade costume, said, "You guys lookin' for me?"

He had a cup of coffee in his hand.

"No," I said.

"No?" he asked. "You sure. Phil Silvers? You from Manny? I'm supposed to place a bet on the Fifth at Aqueduct. Dangerous Antics on the nose? Sure you're not from Manny? You look like you'd be from Manny."

"No," said Gunther.

Silvers pulled up his sleeve and looked at his watch.

"You're not bookies?" he asked.

"No," said Gunther.

"You wouldn't want to make a bet? A small wager on the race? Dangerous Antics is seven to one. I'll take six to one."

"We are not . . ."

"Five to one," said Silvers, shaking his head as if he were making a terrible mistake. "I'm a crazy man, but what can I do? I'm addicted. Four to one. Last offer. I'm breaking my heart here."

"You don't . . ." Gunther tried.

"He's joking Gunther," I said.

"Peters," Silvers said, taking my hand. "You could have given me a few more seconds of shtick. I had the little guy goin'."

"Very amusing," Gunther said soberly.

"Take a joke," Silvers said to Gunther, extending his hand. "It's free. Toby and I go way back. The Green Pussycat in, what was it, thirty-eight, thirty-nine?"

"Green Door, downtown," I said. "Thirty-seven."

"Right, right," said Silvers. "Guy gets a little snickered while I'm doing my act, see. Starts heckling. Big mistake. You heckle crooners. You heckle ventriloquists. You heckle magicians. You don't heckle comics. I was on that night. Right?"

Silvers beamed.

"You were on," I agreed.

"Made the guy look like the shmuck he was. Am I right?"

"You're right," I said.

"Big guy. Charges the stage."

Silvers demonstrated, taking a few lumbering steps toward Gunther with his shoulders down.

"Toby here is working nights at the Green Pussycat, see?"

"Green Door," I corrected.

"Yeah," said Silvers. "Whatever. Well he gets between the drunken bull and me. Bull rams Toby with his head. Toby rams Bull with his right or left. Down goes Bull. Audience applauds. I grin like this and go on with the act. I took two curtain calls and I wasn't even the headliner. That was Kenny Baker."

"And I took seven stitches," I said.

"Who's counting?" said Silvers with a shrug. "I'm not counting. You?"

"No," said Gunther, at whom the question was directed.

"I like this guy," said Silvers, looking at Gunther and grinning.

Gunther is not easy to confuse, but Phil Silvers was doing a good job.

"Phil . . . ," I began.

"You can call me Abdullah," he said. "That's my name in the picture. Classy, huh?" He winked at Gunther.

"Has anyone been around here this morning looking for Wilde?" I asked.

I didn't expect a "yes." I was sure the person who was supposed to meet Wilde was Robert Cunningham, who was stone cold dead.

"Yeah," said Silvers. "Blond guy. A few minutes ago. Couldn't hear what they were saying, but he was in Cornel's face. Not a good idea. Mr. Cornel Wilde is built better than Billy Conn on whom I lost . . . it doesn't matter."

Silvers looked around for the blond guy and didn't see him.

The man with the script backed away from Wilde, who waved to a man in black tights and a black shirt. The man had a sword in his right hand.

"Watch this," said Silvers, holding out his right arm to keep us back.

The crew stopped moving. The girls in costume stopped talking as the man in tights stepped onto the set. A young man stepped into the light and handed Wilde a sword.

Wilde and the man in black began to slowly duel with Wilde circling right and then left, up three stairs, and then a leap over the sword of the other man.

"Like that?" Wilde asked, looking at the man with the script.

"Perfect. Just speed it up a little."

Wilde nodded.

"Swords," said Silvers in a confidential whisper. "Wilde was a college champ. Olympic team. Good huh?"

"Very much so," said Gunther.

"You got class," said Silvers.

"Thank you," said Gunther.

"Gotta run," said Silvers again, using his confidential whisper. "A harem girl wants to share a ham sandwich with me behind the sultan's tent. See ya."

Silvers hurried away and Gunther said soberly,

"He is strangely amusing."

"That's a good way of putting it," I said, moving toward Wilde who was holding his sword out at arm's length.

"Mr. Wilde," I said.

He turned his head and looked first at me and then at Gunther.

"You won't remember me," I said. "I used to be a guard at Warner's. I met you one day on the set of *High Sierra*."

"I remember," he said with a smile. "You were talking to Humphrey Bogart."

"Right, I was a private investigator by then. You've got quite a memory."

"A gift and a curse," he said, tucking the sword under his arm.

"A little while ago," I said. "A man was here. You had words."

"Yes," said Wilde very seriously.

"Mind telling me what he wanted?"

"Five minutes," someone called from behind me.

Wilde nodded. Bright lights came on.

"He had made an appointment to see me this morning," Wilde said. "Said it would take no more than a minute or two and involved an old friend from college who was in trouble. He gave me the name of the friend. I agreed to see him."

"What did he want?"

"To blackmail me," he said. "He showed me photographs, all fakes, of me doing things I've never done with people I've never met."

"And?"

"I asked him if he could imagine what it felt like to have a very sharp blade pierce his stomach and come out through his back. He repeated his threat, said he could handle a saber. I told him that they were frauds, that he was a blackmailer and that I was going to call the police."

"He backed off?"

Wilde furrowed his forehead and said,

"Yes, but he gave up much too easily."

"Did he say anything else?"

"That he could always get back to me. His exact words were, 'I've got a much better fish to catch and a bigger hook.' "

"And he was gone?"

"They were gone," said Wilde.

"There was someone with him?"

"Yes."

"Did you get a good look at him?"

"No," he said. "The lights were on on the set, much as they are now, and he stayed back there in the shadows. But I did see his hands. I got a very good look at his hands. A fencer learns to look at his opponents' hands."

"Hands?"

"For scars, bruises, length of fingers, dexterity," he said. "The man who tried to blackmail me did have a fencer's hand, his right."

"You mean you'd recognize the other man if you saw his hands again?" Gunther asked.

Wilde looked down at him and said, "I'd recognize both of them."

"Let's get this shot," came a man's voice.

"Thanks," I said.

Gunther and I left the stage and went out the door into the morning. We had an hour to get to Marty Leib's office. Plenty of time. At least, there would have been plenty of time if a lean blonde guy in dark slacks and a white long-sleeved pullover shirt hadn't been standing outside the stage door, waiting for us with a gun in his hand.

"Missed you the other night," he said. "Won't make that mistake again."

He had nice teeth and a nice smile to go along with his big gun. It had to be the guy who shot Gwen and me with the pellet gun. I looked around for someone, anyone.

"It's bad luck to kill little people," he said, looking at Gunther, "but I'll just have to chance it."

The stage door opened behind us. The gunman looked over my shoulder at whoever was coming out the door. He lost his smile and then it came back again.

I turned my head and saw Wilde and the guy he had been sword fighting with. They were both carrying swords and talking. Wilde seemed to be demonstrating something he wanted the other man to do. It took them a beat to look up and see the man with the gun pointed at Gunther and me.

The blonde lost his smile. Gone were his flashing teeth. Two shootings, maybe. But four, including a movie star on a studio lot? Probably not.

Wilde looked decidedly angry as he stepped toward the blonde, who started to back away. The man Wilde had been dueling with on the sound stage matched Wilde stride for stride.

"Hold it there," said the blonde.

Wilde did not hold it. Sword in his right hand, he moved toward the gunman who looked over his shoulder and then back at Wilde. The blonde fired one shot into the air. No one came running. This was Columbia. People were shooting guns a good part of the day. The difference was that this gun had real bullets, one of which cracked into the brick wall of the sound stage.

Wilde grabbed the sword from the hand of the other actor and threw it to the blonde, who managed to catch it and move between Gunther and me.

"I think you said you knew how to use a saber," said Wilde with an undercurrent of anger I was glad was aimed at the blonde and not at me.

Wilde ignored the gun as he continued to move forward.

"Don't be crazy," said the blonde.

Wilde ignored him, now within ten feet of the man.

"Blackmail, guns, threats," said Wilde. "You're not very good with any of them. How are you with a sword?"

"You're crazy," the blonde said.

Wilde turned sideways and swished his sword, cutting the air and then hitting the blonde's arm with the flat of the blade. The gun flew and skittered on the concrete.

Wilde leaped forward with another swish of the sword and a thrust. The blonde decided it was a good time to defend himself. I don't know anything about fencing or sword fighting, but I'd seen plenty of it when I worked at Warner Brothers. My favorite at it was Basil Rathbone, who invariably died after a thrust by Errol Flynn, though Rathbone was the better fighter.

The blonde was pretty good.

The stage door opened again and Phil Silvers came out.

"What's up?" he shouted, adjusting his glasses to watch the battle. "Hey, they're not kiddin'. I'll give you six to one on Cornel."

The blonde was backing up and trying to keep away from Wilde's pointed jabs.

"The blades are not sharp?" asked Gunther.

"No," said the actor at our side. "But the points aren't blunt enough to keep them from doing a hell of a lot of damage."

Sword blades clanged just like in the movies. I'll give this to the blonde. He was almost holding his own.

"Ten to one," said Silvers. "Last offer."

Wilde lunged forward, swung his sword hard, and knocked the sword out of the blonde's hand. The blonde was only a few feet away from his gun now. He bent quickly and picked it up.

"That's it," he said, panic in his voice. "Stop there or so help me, I'll blow a hole in you."

Wilde, sword pointed at the man, stopped.

We all recognized the sound of desperation in the blonde's voice. He backed away, motioning for us to stay where we were. We stayed. He ducked around a building. Wilde started forward. The gunman, whom we couldn't see, fired off a shot.

We didn't follow.

"Is anyone hurt?" Wilde asked, turning to face us.

We were all fine. Wilde nodded, said "Good" and moved through us back toward the sound stage.

"Is he something, or is he something?" said Silvers, looking at Gunther.

"He is indeed something," said Gunther.

We asked Dave on the way out if he had seen a blonde guy leave the lot. He had. The blonde was driving a prewar black Ford and there was someone else in the car with him.

"Other guy was wearing a hat, pulled over his face, you know? Didn't get a good look at him. Sorry."

As we pulled away, Gunther said, "What have we learned?"

"We know what our killer looks like without the beard and turban."

"If he is the killer," Gunther said. "Which, if I am correct, is a reasonable supposition but not yet a certainty, in spite of our experience here. Remember, there was a second man."

"Point taken," I said. "Wilde can identify him."

"From his hands," said Gunther doubtfully.

"I think I trust Wilde on this one," I said.

"Our gunman displayed a definite lack of verve in his attempt to blackmail Mr. Wilde," Gunther added.

"He had bigger fish to fry."

"Blackstone?" asked Gunther.

"Maybe," I said.

"It seems we are gathering more reasons for Blackstone to have disposed of both Cunningham and Ott."

"Maybe," I said. "Let's find the blonde and that second man."

"A second man?" said Marty Leib, forty minutes later at the head of his conference table, his hands folded in front of him.

"That's right," I said.

"Promising," said Marty, looking around the table.

To his left sat me, Phil, and Gunther. To his right sat Jeremy, Shelly, and Pancho. At the other end of the table, with his back to the windows, sat Blackstone in dark slacks, a white long-sleeved turtle-necked sweater. His brother Peter wore a white shirt and tie. Peter was shorter. Their hair was combed differently, Harry's straight back and flat and Pete's parted on the left. They did look alike from a distance and made up for the parts, but next to each other the differences were clear.

"I've . . ." Marty began and then pointed at Pancho who was writing on a lined spiral pad. "Would you stop taking notes?"

Pancho looked up, startled.

"He needs it for the movie," said Shelly, looking ill-matched in a plaid shirt and red sweater.

"Alright," Marty said with a sigh. "I'll rephrase. It was not a question. It was an order."

"But . . ." Shelly tried.

Marty shook his head "no," and Phil said, "Shelly" in his best cut-the-crap voice.

Shelly responded by reaching under his sweater and pulling a cigar out of his shirt pocket.

"No," said Marty as Shelly searched for a match.

"Where are we, Germany?" asked Shelly.

"Minck," said Phil. "I think my son Nate has whooping cough. I've been up most of the night so my sister-in-law could get some sleep. I am in a very bad mood. Do you understand?"

Shelly pushed his glasses back on his nose and looked as if he were going to speak, then changed his mind and sagged back in his chair.

"I've talked to the District Attorney's office," Marty said. "I told them that if Mr. Blackstone were arrested for murder without airtight evidence, his reputation would be severely damaged and Mr. Blackstone would bring suit for one million three hundred and sixty dollars."

"How did you come up with that figure?" asked Pancho.

"Mr. Blackstone and I roughly calculated lost income," said Marty. "Roughly. The result was that there will be no arrest yet but there will be an investigation. My best estimation is that the brothers Bouton might well be arrested within the next week if we do not come up with the person or persons who killed Cunningham and Ott. And that is the job of the brothers Pevsner."

Marty looked at my brother and me. So did everyone else at the table.

"Would you gentlemen like to ask some questions?" Marty asked.

"Is Blackstone on the clock?" I asked.

Marty shrugged.

"I think we'll ask our questions in our office where we're not going at thirty dollars an hour."

"Forty-five dollars an hour," said Blackstone.

"This case will consume all my time till you come up with the killer," said Marty. "I'll tell you what. To show my good faith, you are off the clock until I inform you otherwise."

Phil and I looked at each other. Phil rubbed his thick right palm across his short gray hair. He looked tired.

"Who turned off the lights last night?" he asked looking at the Boutons.

"Jimmy," said Pete. "Jimmy Clark."

"The kid with the limp?" Phil asked.

Pete and Harry both nodded.

"The light switch is behind the curtains near the door. Jimmy was behind the curtain two hours before the doors were opened. He waited for the cue from me," said Harry. "Turned off the lights. Counted to three. Turned on the lights. Pete clapped to draw everyone's attention while Jimmy counted to five and turned off the lights again for a count of two before he turned the lights on again."

"We rehearsed it in the ballroom yesterday morning for more than an hour," said Blackstone. "Timing and misdirection are crucial ingredients in a successful illusion."

"Right," said Phil. "But who turned off the lights and did pretty much the same trick when Ott was stabbed?"

"I don't know," said Peter.

Harry shrugged.

"Maybe Jimmy saw someone by the lights," I said.

"Let's ask him," said Phil.

Marty remained stone silent, looking at his manicured thumbnails.

"It was deeper," said Gunther.

Everyone, including Marty, looked at Gunther.

"Deeper than what?" I asked.

"The knife," said Gunther. "When the lights came on and Ott was on his face, the knife was in so deep."

He demonstrated with his small fingers.

"When we returned after chasing that young man, the knife was in like so."

Gunther demonstrated again.

"So," said Phil. "You're telling us that, after Ott was killed, someone snuck back in and pushed the knife in deeper just to make sure?"

"I don't know," said Gunther. "But it was deeper. Of that I am certain."

"Why take the chance?" asked Phil.

"I do not know," said Gunther. "I am only reporting to you what I observed."

The Bouton brothers were whispering at the end of the table. Pete said something. Harry nodded and whispered back. It was Pete's turn to nod.

"What?" asked Phil.

"We may have an idea," said Harry.

"About what?" asked Phil.

"About how Calvin Ott was murdered," said Peter.

"Well?" asked Phil.

"We'll have to work it out before we say anything more," said Harry, touching his mustache. "We're not certain."

"Are we finished?" asked Marty, looking at his many-jeweled watch. "Anyone have anything more to say."

"Did you rescue the bird?" asked Gunther, looking at Jeremy.

"The bird is fine," said Jeremy. "I've returned it to Mr. Leib."

"And I've told my secretary to get it back to the magician I bought it from," said Marty. "Now I suggest that you . . ." he looked at me and Phil, "find that second man who was with Cunningham and talk to this Jimmy Clark about what or who, if anything or anyone, he saw behind that curtain."

"And you?" I asked.

"I," said Marty, "shall be making the life of Detective John Cawelti miserable and the District Attorney of this great county of Los Angeles angry and miserable. In short, I'll be stalling and earning my fee. Gentlemen. . . ."

Marty rose heavily, adjusted the white flower in his lapel, nodded, and waited while we all left his office.

As soon as we hit the landing, Shelly lit a cigar and said, "You get all that?" to Pancho, who nodded.

"Guys," said Shelly, examining his cigar and pausing dramatically. "Pancho is a very gifted writer, a man of great talent, but his imagination can't be stifled by the dull facts."

We all looked at Pancho, who pulled his scarf around his neck as if a cold front had leaped over a bunch of states from Canada and landed on his skinny body.

"So?" I asked.

"I believe Dr. Minck is informing us that Mr. Vanderhoff plans to take liberties with the truth," said Gunther.

"The truth," said Shelly with a wave of his hand that shifted a cloud of smoke and disposed of the need for facts. "My role in ongoing events will be . . ."

"Enhanced," said Pancho.

"We're going," said Harry Blackstone. "We have some things to do and then we'll be at the theater for tonight's performance."

"Let's go talk to Jimmy the Kid and ask some people about this blonde guy Cunningham was working with," I said.

Phil nodded.

"And how can we be of service?" Gunther said.

"Jeremy," I said. "If you can spare the time, you might keep an eye on Blackstone's back. Whoever killed Cunningham and Ott might be looking for number three, our client."

"I shall," said Jeremy solemnly.

"Whertham," said Phil. "Think you could do some leg work on Ott, see who he hung out with, or who hung onto his wallet? Might be a few people out there who didn't like him."

"He did not appear to be a likable individual," said Gunther. "I shall begin immediately.

"Our office, tomorrow, nine?" I asked.

"Nine-thirty," said Shelly. "I've got Mrs. Odell coming in for an impacted wisdom tooth."

I could almost swear I saw a Mona Lisa smile on the face of one round rich little dentist as he imagined Mrs. Odell, whoever the hell she was, in his chair. My tooth began to ache.

CHAPTER

13

Take out two packs of cards. Give one pack to one person and the other to another. Have them shuffle the cards. Tell them to reach into their deck, pull out a card, look at it and insert it in the other person's deck. Have them shuffle their decks again. Take the first deck and flip through it with the faces of the cards toward you. Do the same with the other. Take the two decks and shuffle them together. Cut the thick deck and let each person shuffle the cards as much as they like. Have them look at the cards to be sure that it is indeed two shuffled decks. Spread the cards faceup and point to the two that were chosen. Solution: The initial deck you gave the first person contained only black cards. The deck you gave the other person contained only red cards. When you flipped through the decks after the cards were reinserted, you could see which red one was among the blacks and which black among the reds. When the two decks were thoroughly shuffled, they could be turned faceup. They would look quite normal and you would pluck out the right cards.

—*From the* Blackstone, The Magic Detective *radio show*

JIMMY CLARK WAS BACKSTAGE AT the Pantages tightening a screw on a brightly painted red and green wooden box about the size and shape of a hatbox. He was the only one working.

"Have to get this fixed," he explained, brushing a lock of hair from his face. "Darned thing's snafued, won't play ball."

A small Arvin radio with a plaid cloth cover sat on the workbench next to him.

"The British forces . . ." the deeply serious voice on the radio was saying when Jimmy turned it off.

"Sorry, you were saying?" he asked, wiping his hands on his work pants.

"Guy on the radio was going to say the British crossed the Odon River and beat back nine Nazi attacks," I said. "We heard it on the radio on the way here."

"Great," he said, beaming and looking at us. "War's almost over, you think?"

Phil nodded.

"Looks that way," I said.

"My brothers are out there," he said, looking over his shoulder. "Terry's in Germany somewhere. Connie's in the Pacific. I'd still be if it wasn't for this."

He tapped his game leg.

"Mom says it was God's way of being sure she had one son safe. But . . . I'm sorry. You wanted to talk about last night, right?"

"Right," I said.

Phil just stood there, hands behind his back, feet apart looking less than happy.

"Nothing much to tell," said Jimmy. "Got to the hotel early, sat behind the curtain under a table with a big white tablecloth hanging over to cover me. People went by you know. Then, when the dinner started, I crawled out, waited for the cue from Mr. Blackstone, hit the light switch, out went the lights, made the count, hit the switch, on came the lights, make the count, lights out again and like that. Then back under the table."

"And you stayed there?" I asked.

"Didn't move," he said, playing with the screwdriver and looking at the box as if he wanted to get back to it.

"The lights went out again," I said.

"Yep. That's when Mr. Ott got killed."

"You see who turned the lights on and off? You were how far from the switch?"

"Few feet. Didn't see who did it. I stayed under the table."

"Didn't see anything?"

"Saw his shoes," Jimmy said. "And socks."

"Small feet? Big feet?"

"Regular feet."

"Black shoes?"

"Yeah, tuxedo pants. One thing funny though."

"What was that?" I asked.

"Socks were red. I mean the guy who turned the lights out. His socks were red," said Jimmy. "Why would someone be wearing red socks with a tuxedo?"

"I don't know," I went on. "Could you tell if he was big, little, young, old?"

Jimmy shrugged.

"Red. You're sure?"

"Positive."

"Thanks," I said.

"Mr. Blackstone going to be alright?" he asked as Phil and I moved toward the stage door.

"He'll be fine," I said.

"I'd do anything for Mr. Blackstone and Pete," he said. "I was doing dishes for food and a few dollars a week when they found me in Detroit, asked me if I wanted a job with them. I'm learning the business. I'm not just a gimp farm kid or a dish jockey."

"We'll let you know," I said. "Red socks?"

"Red," he said.

The radio came back on behind us as we headed for the door and the voice behind us said, "This is the N.B.C. Red Network."

Raymond Ramutka, the old man at the stage door, sat on a wooden chair smoking his pipe and playing with his suspenders. He looked up from his newspaper and said,

"The boy help any?"

"Maybe, a little," I said.

"Word is Blackstone is in some kind of trouble," said Ramutka, ruffling his bushy white hair.

"Where'd the word come from?" I asked.

"Here, there, the boy. The police don't really think Blackstone had anything to do with killing that big spender in the dressing room do they?"

He pointed his pipe stem up the metal steps toward the dressing rooms.

"Not Harry Blackstone," he went on before we could answer. "Wouldn't hurt an ant. I've been at this door for eleven years and before that at the Squire in Baltimore. Never met a performer as nice as Blackstone. Well, maybe Beatrice Kay or Eddie Cantor. Did I tell you I used to be a singer?"

"You did," Phil said impatiently.

"Girl of the Golden West," Ramutka reminisced.

"You said," said Phil.

"Did I? Well . . ." he shrugged, put his pipe back between his teeth and looked down at his newspaper as we went out the door.

I looked at Phil. He looked at me.

"What?" he said.

"You could have been nicer to the old man," I said.

"Oh crap. You want me to go back in and ask him to sing me an aria?"

"Too late," I said.

"Fine. Let's go find a magician with red socks."

We stopped at a Rexall Drug Store where I called Mrs. Plaut's while Phil had a cup of coffee and a pair of donuts. Mrs. Plaut answered.

"Can I speak to Gunther?" I said. "This is Toby Peters."

"Of course you can speak to him," she said. "I do not make a habit of keeping telephone calls from people who reside in my abode."

"May I speak to him?" I tried.

"You are capable of speech," she said. "Therefore you can speak to him. And I just told you you don't need my permission."

"How should I say it?" I asked.

"Please get Mr. Gunther on the telephone," she said.

"Please get Mr. Gunther on the telephone," I repeated.

I heard the phone drop on the cord and bang into the wall. While I waited, I looked at Phil. In one month, he had lost his wife and his job and gone into business with me, and business was not looking as good as we would like. And now his son had whooping cough, and I could see that he was thinking that he had another son and daughter who could also get it. My brother did not look happy. This was a dangerous time for the world. When Phil wasn't happy, it was best to keep a reasonably safe football field length between you and him.

"Toby?" came Gunther's voice.

I could picture him standing on the small stool next to the phone on the second floor landing.

"Yes, anything yet?"

"I've been most fortunate," he said. "Following the autopsy of the unfortunate Calvin Ott, there will be a funeral at Horskey's Funeral Home in Sherman Oaks not far from the late Mr. Ott's home."

I knew Horskey's. One of my ex-wife Anne's ex-husbands had funeraled there.

"It seems the funeral arrangements are being made by a group called the Torch Bearers of Dranabadur," said Gunther.

It was the group that had been meeting the night Phil and I had gone to Ott's house. I was sure I had seen some if not all of them at the Blackstone dinner. I didn't remember any of them being blonde. Ott had given their names. I couldn't remember any of them but Leo.

"Can you get their full names and addresses?"

"I will endeavor to do so," Gunther said.

"I'll call you back."

We hung up, and I went to sit next to Phil, who was working on his second donut and second cup of coffee. There was a mug steaming for me and two sinkers.

"Gunther's got a line on the guy's who were at Ott's house the other night," I said.

Phil grunted and looked at what was left of his donut, probably considering whether he would go for a third.

"He's trying to find out their names and where they live," I said. "We can find out if they wear red socks."

Phil grunted again, reached into his jacket pocket, came out with the same notebook he used when he was a cop, flipped it open, and read:

"Wayne Dutton, Paul Steele, Walter Masonick, Milton Beckstall, Steven Freemont, William Teel, Richard Karkette, and Leo Benz."

He handed me the notebook. Each name had an address next to it.

Phil ordered another donut.

"Checked them out this morning. Ott had given us the first names. They were all registered with that magicians group. Took ten bucks to a secretary to get it."

"We'll put it on Blackstone's bill," I said. "I better call Gunther and tell him we don't need the names and addresses."

"I'm having someone in the department checking to see if any of our Dranabadurians have arrest records," said Phil.

"You're a treasure," I said, leaning toward him as the waitress leaned forward to refill our cups.

"Kiss me on the head and I'll break your face."

"It's okay," I told the waitress. "He's my brother."

I ordered another donut and called Mrs. Plaut's back, praying that Gunther would answer the phone. He did.

"Gunther, forget about tracking down those names and addresses. We've got them."

"Then what task shall I perform?"

"How about going back to Columbia Pictures and seeing if someone working on the picture when Cunningham showed up can give you a better description of the person who was with him when he talked to Wilde?"

"I would prefer not to talk to that Phil Silvers person."

"Then don't."

"I shall leave immediately," Gunther said.

I went back to Phil and said, "Let's go find a magician with red socks."

Being trained investigators with a combined total of more than thirty years of police work, we quickly figured out that we didn't have to talk to all of the Dranabadurians on our list. We just had to find one who could tell us which of his friends wore red socks.

We could work alphabetically or by distance from the drugstore. We went to the closest address. It was in Hollywood, on Vine, not far from Mrs. Plaut's. The address, a doorway wedged between a small bakery and an even smaller shoemaker's, was called Karkette's Gags & Tricks. We rang the bell in the doorway and waited. No answer. Rang again. No answer. No conference was necessary. We entered the shop and were greeted by a five-foot-high cardboard cartoon cutout of Adolph Hitler looking over his shoulder at us with his bare behind in the air just below eye level. Adolph looked as if we had surprised him getting off the toilet. We were definitely not in anyone's idea of a high class establishment.

Before we could pass Adolph, he passed air. I could tell by Phil's tightened jaw that he didn't find Hitler farting funny. I didn't either. Richard Karkette, however, clearly did.

He appeared from behind the cutout and said, "Funny, huh?"

I didn't recognize him from Ott's or the Roosevelt ballroom, but that may have been because he wasn't wearing a tux but a pair of tan trousers and a light green shirt with dark green buttons.

He was about my height, my age, and thin with a little belly that made him look like a pregnant stork. He was bald and grinning.

"Can I help you with . . . ?"

He stopped, looked at us both with recognition and went on, "You were at Marcus's house the other night and the ballroom last night."

He wasn't grinning anymore.

"I can see you're all broken up about Calvin Ott's murder," said Phil, moving to within a foot of the man's face.

"An act," Karkette said. "I've got a business to run, a living to make. I'm grinning on the outside, see."

He grinned, showing large, not very white teeth.

"But inside," he went on, touching his heart underneath a green button, "I'm mourning. Marcus was a great friend, a mentor."

"And a good customer?"

"The best," said Karkette. "What do you want?"

"Pull up your pants legs," Phil said.

"Huh?"

"Pull 'em up," Phil repeated, louder. "Now."

Karkette pulled up his pants legs. He looked like he was going to do a dainty dance. His socks were red. Had we got lucky on our first shot?

"Were you wearing red socks like those last night?" Phil said.

"Yes, sure. Can I put my pants down now?"

"Yeah."

"Did you turn off the lights when Ott was killed?" asked Phil.

"Did I . . . I was sitting at the table. Table Four. Ask anybody."

"Was he sitting at Table Four?" Phil asked me.

"I don't know," I said.

"When I said 'anybody,' I didn't mean 'anybody,'" said Karkette. "I meant the people at the table."

"Someone saw you turn off the lights," I said.

"They couldn't have."

Phil and I had fallen into our Ernest Hemingway *The Killers* act. We made a formidable pair. Karkette was most definitely intimidated from his toe of his red socks to his top green button.

"Red socks are a giveaway," I said.

"Red . . . We were all wearing red socks," Karkette said, looking from Phil to me and trying to decide which of us might be more reasonable.

"All?" I asked.

"The Dranabadurians," he said. "We wear red socks in honor of Dranabadur. Red socks were his trademark. He'd make a move sort of like this."

Karkette made a little turn.

"See, the socks sort of grab your attention," he said. "He'd do it when he wanted that split part of a second to help draw attention from whatever trick he was performing."

"You were all wearing red socks," I repeated.

"All, even Marcus."

"Okay," said Phil wearily, pulling out his notebook. "The names of everyone at your table last night."

"You're going to ask them if I turned out the lights?" he said.

"We are," I said. "And you're going to tell us who was sitting at the table when the lights went out."

"I see," he said. "Elimination. Like Sherlock Holmes said, 'When everything else is eliminated, whatever remains must be the answer.' "

"That's stupid," Phil said. "You never eliminate everything else. The names."

Karkette thought for a moment and then gave us the names of Dutton, Steele, Masonick, and Beckstall.

"What about Freemont, Teel, and Benz?" Phil asked, looking at his list.

"They were at another table," said Karkette as the door opened and two sailors who looked like they were about twelve walked in.

"Customers," said Karkette, wedging his way between Phil and me.

Karkette made Hitler pass air. The sailor kids thought it was funny. But they were only twelve.

We went back out on Vine. Phil went over the list again and flipped his notebook closed.

"Unless we're dealing with a conspiracy," I said. "One of these guys is going to turn up missing from his seat when the lights went out."

"Maybe," said Phil with a familiar sigh, "but what will that give us? If he was switching the lights on and off, he couldn't be killing Ott. He'll have to give up whoever he was working with, whoever killed Ott."

"Which we know wasn't our client," I said.

"Which we assume wasn't our client," said Phil. "Let's get started."

And start we did. We went to three apartments, a citrus warehouse, two offices, a golf club, and a bar before we made our way to the last person on our list, Leo Benz. Not one person on the list was a professional full-time magician. As Steele told us, there were only about sixty magicians in the entire country making a living from magic; most of them did kids' birthdays or Kiwanis Club and Rotary Club dinners or dish nights at the local movie house.

"Best for last," I said.

I rang the bell at the small freshly painted white house on a quiet side street in Van Nuys. We had chosen Leo Benz for last because he was closest to Phil's house in North Hollywood.

"Just a minute. Just a minute," came a woman's voice. "Hurrying, hurrying."

The door opened and a little heavy-set woman in her sixties stood before us. Her dyed blonde hair was wrapped in curlers and her blue dress covered with little yellow circles hung almost to the floor.

"You're not the mail lady," she said.

"We are not," I agreed. "We'd like to talk to Leo Benz."

"Why?"

"We have some questions," Phil said.

"What questions?"

"Is he here?" I tried.

"I can answer whatever questions you've got," she said.

"Not these," I said before Phil could explode. "It's about last night."

Phil took a step forward. She put her rotund body between him and the inside.

"Last night Leo was at the movies," she said. "He saw that new movie with Pat O'Brien. *Marine Raiders*. You want to know about the movie, ask me. I saw it."

"Last night Leo was at a dinner at the Roosevelt Hotel," I said. "A man was murdered. Your husband is a witness."

"He's my son," she said. "And he . . . that lying little son-of-a-bitch. Are you cops?"

We didn't answer.

She turned her head over her shoulder and screamed, "Leo, get your behind down here, you lying little twerp. The police are here."

Someone whined something inside the house. I couldn't tell what it was.

"He didn't kill anybody," she said. "Leo's not capable. If he could kill someone, he would have killed me years ago."

She turned her head again and screamed even louder, "L-E-0."

And behind her came the clap of feet.

Leo Benz, in all his lack of glory, stood revealed when his mother stepped back from the door. He was barefoot, wearing white boxer shorts and an undershirt. He needed a shave.

"I know you," he said, pointing at us and stepping behind his mother.

"Leo, we've got questions," Phil said.

"I don't have any answers," he said.

Leo's mother turned and thumped her son on the head with the palm of her right hand.

"Answer their questions," she said. "And then you'll answer to me."

Leo Benz, sans tux, beard, and shoes, looked like the kind of fat kid other kids like to poke in the stomach in the schoolyard.

Phil and I walked in the house and Leo's mother closed the door behind us.

Leo backed into the living room, his mother moving ahead of him to sit in a faded red padded chair with her arms folded. There wasn't much furniture, just a few chairs like the one Leo's mom was in and a sagging couch covered in what looked like blue fur with patches worn down to the skin surface of the imaginary animal it had been taken from.

Leo backed against the couch and sat. Phil and I stood over him.

"I didn't do it," he said.

"Do what?" I asked.

"Turn off the lights, kill Keller," Leo bleated, looking at his mother for a mercy she had no intention of granting.

"Who did?" Phil asked.

"I don't know," Leo almost wept.

"You killed somebody?" Leo's mother asked.

"Mrs. . . ." I said.

"Call me Cornelia," she said.

"Cornelia," I said. "Let us ask our questions. You'll get your crack at junior when we leave."

"That you don't have to tell me," she said, fixing her glare at Leo who looked away.

"I'm besieged," he said. "All sides. This isn't fair."

"Do a trick," said Phil. "Make us disappear."

"What do you want?"

"One of you Dranabadurians got up before the lights went out," I said. "Which one?"

I expected him to repeat the party line, say that everyone had been nailed to his seat when Ott was killed. Juanita's warning came back to me. The man in the penguin suit. The lights on and off.

"He wasn't sitting down," Leo said.

"Who?" asked Phil.

"Melvin Rand."

There was no Melvin Rand on Phil's list.

"Who is Melvin Rand?" Phil asked.

Leo bit his lip. Cornelia shouted the same question loud enough to make me nearly jump. I think Leo did jump.

"He's not really a Dranabadurian," said Leo. "Believe me. Not yet. He's new. Keller introduced him at the last meeting."

"And he was at the Blackstone party last night?" I asked.

"Yes."

"Where was he sitting?" asked Phil

"He wasn't," said Leo.

"What was he doing, crawling around on the floor like you're going to be doing?" Cornelia screamed.

Leo quivered and looked up to Phil and me for protection, which probably gives you an idea of who really scared him in this room.

"He was a waiter," Leo said. "It was part of Keller's plan I guess. He didn't tell us. I just looked up when he brought the bread to the table and he winked at me. Like this. He was wearing a black wig and a fake mustache, but I recognized him."

"Did the others at your table recognize him?" I asked.

"I don't know."

Leo slumped back.

"Where was Rand when the lights went out?" I asked.

"Don't know," Leo whispered.

"Was he wearing red socks?" asked Phil.

"No. I looked," Leo whispered even more quietly.

"Speak up," Cornelia shouted.

"No," Leo shouted back.

"Without the wig and the mustache is he blonde, thin?" I asked.

"That's him," said Leo.

"He was the waiter standing near the door who got us running after the kid," Phil said.

Which meant he was nowhere near the table where Ott lay dead with a knife in his neck.

"Any idea of where we might find Melvin Rand?" I asked.

Leo shook his head "no."

"Pathetic," snorted Cornelia, getting up from her chair, arms still folded. She walked over to the couch as Leo slid away from her. She unfolded her arms and gently put his head against her ample chest. "Leo Benz, you are a pathetic creature."

Phil and I left.

"Hotel Roosevelt?" I asked as we headed for the car.

"Stop at my house first," Phil said.

We were only fifteen minutes from Phil's. I parked on the street and started to get out.

"You've never had whooping cough," he said, putting his hand on my arm. "Stay here."

I stayed, tried to figure out what had happened when the lights went out last night, failed miserably and turned on the radio.

After I learned that Dewey had accepted the Republican nomination for President, Bing Crosby and I sang *Don't Fence Me In.* Jo Stafford followed with *Close As Pages In A Book*, but I couldn't keep up with her. Portia was about to face life when Phil came back and got in the car.

"Dave and Nate both have it," he said.

"Lucy?"

"She seems alright. Becky's trying to keep her out of their bedroom. I told her to stay away from her brothers, but she's five, takes after me more than Ruth."

"What's the doctor say?"

"Doc Hodgdon'll be here in about an hour."

Doc Hodgdon was eighty, retired, and working on a book. Phil had met him through me. We played handball regularly at the Downtown Y. The doc was slow, steady, straight-backed, and sure of hand. I rarely beat him.

I put the Crosley in gear and Phil said, "Stop."

I stopped. He opened the door.

"Call me later," he said getting out. "I'll meet you. I'll make some calls."

He closed the door and started back toward the house without looking back at me. I shifted into first and made a U-turn.

CHAPTER

14

Show your victim three cards: a 6 of clubs, 8 of diamonds, and a 10 of spades. Ask them to pick one and not tell you which one they have chosen. Put the cards in your pocket, close your eyes and concentrate, and then pull out two cards and place them facedown on the table. Ask your victim to tell which card he or she had chosen. Reach into your pocket and pull out that card. Announce that you'll gladly do the trick again. Solution: Arrange the three cards in order 6, 8, 10. You can use any three cards as long as they are numerical and increase in number. Put the three cards in your pocket where you already have two other cards. Pull out those two other cards and place them on the table facedown. When the victim tells you what card was chosen, simply reach into your pocket and pull it out knowing that the 10 is on top, the 8 in the middle, and the six on the bottom. You can do the trick again because you still have two extra cards in your pocket.

—*From the* Blackstone, The Magic Detective *radio show*

"RAND, RAND, RAND, RAND," said the young woman in the serious suit and large glasses.

Her name was Miss Sandford. It said so on the pin over her right jacket pocket. Her hair was dark and pinned back. She was, young, pretty, and all business. She pointed her sharpened pencil at a name on the sheet of paper on the clipboard in her hand.

We were standing in the lobby of the Roosevelt. The only reason she was talking to me was that I had worked from time to time filling in for the regular night house detective when he was on vacation or got sick.

"Here he is," she said. "I remember him. Mr. Ott insisted that we use him, told us we wouldn't have to pay him. Carlos, the head-waiter, didn't much like the idea but Mr. Ott was paying the bill for the evening and . . ."

"Did Ott say why he wanted Rand working last night?"

"Said it was part of a surprise for Blackstone's party," she said.

"The surprise was Ott skewered on a platter," I said.

"That's not really funny," she said.

"Guess not," I agreed. "Got an address for Rand?"

"Of course," she said. "We wouldn't let him work, even for one meal, if we didn't have his address and full identification. Board of Health."

She gave me the address. I wrote it in my notebook.

"Thanks," I said. "You related to Tony Sanford?"

"My father," she said.

Tony was the regular night house detective I filled in for. Tony and I were about the same age. No, I was a few years older. I looked at his daughter and felt old, very old.

"Anything else I can help you with?" she asked.

"No," I said.

"You're working for Mr. Blackstone, right?" she asked.

"Right," I said.

"He and his brother are in the ballroom now," she said, looking toward the ballroom door.

I tapped my notebook on the back of my hand, pocketed it, said "thanks" and headed for the ballroom, almost bumping into a laughing young couple.

"Sorry, sir," the girl said.

They moved on. So did I.

Inside the ballroom, Blackstone stood on the platform. The table and podium were just where they had been the night before. Blackstone had his right hand on his chin and was saying "Once more" as I stepped in.

The lights went out.

Blackstone counted "One, two, three, and then said", "Now."

The lights came back on. Peter Bouton came out from behind the drapes to my left, nodded at me, and looked across the room at his brother.

"Door," called Blackstone.

Peter moved past me, opened the door I had come through. On the platform, Blackstone began counting again as he strode toward me, nodded, and went out the door closing it behind him. A beat later the door opened and the brothers Bouton came back in.

"I was the last one out of here," Harry said, looking at me with his arms crossed. "I saw no one behind me but Ott facedown. It took no more than twenty seconds to clear the room. We've timed the whole thing eight times."

"Which means?" I asked.

"We think we're close," said Pete.

"There's no event in here tonight," said Blackstone. "I've reserved the room for a reenactment that we'll conduct after our show at the Pantages. We've got the guest list, and everyone on it is being called now and urged to return for the event."

I told them about what Jimmy Clark had seen, about Rand the waiter.

He told me that Gwen was out of the hospital and ready to do the show that night.

"We told her 'no,' " said Blackstone, "but I did ask her to come here tonight."

"If we're ready," said Pete.

"If we're ready," Harry agreed.

"We have to reenact it?" I asked.

"An impossible murder," Harry said. "The police are baffled. An audience of magicians expecting a solution from Blackstone. I'll never have another moment like this. I've invited that policeman with the red face and hair."

"Cawelti," I said. "You think you'll be able to tell us who killed Ott?"

"We'll be able to show you how it was done," Harry said. "As for who did it, I think we can guarantee the revelation of at least one guilty party."

The Bouton brothers looked at each other with satisfaction.

"No formal wear required tonight," said Blackstone.

"Good," I said.

"Back to work," said Harry, heading back to the platform.

"Back to work," I agreed and went through the door and back across the lobby.

I made what I thought was going to be a quick stop at our office, which was only a few blocks from the hotel.

Mistake.

Alice Pallas Butler was sitting at the conference table with her arms folded across her more than ample chest. Jeremy was a very big man. Alice was a match for him. Before they were married, Alice had run a very soft-core pornographic printing operation out of her office in the Farraday. In moments of trouble—meaning a possible visit from the police—Alice had been known to pick up the small printing press, which weighed something in the vicinity of two hundred plus pounds and take it out the window and up the fire escape to the roof.

Jeremy had won her over to the beauty of poetry instead of pornography and she had taken to it, printing Jeremy's poems for about a year before taking to Jeremy, as well, and marrying him.

They had a daughter, Natasha, who was just starting to walk and was definitely talking. Natasha looked nothing like either parent. She had a beautiful round face with big brown eyes, a great smile, and no sign that she was going to grow into someone with the size and strength of either of her parents.

"Where's Natasha?" I asked.

"Upstairs with her father," Alice said. "She's taking a nap. I think she's going to start reading soon."

I didn't sit.

"She's not even two," I said.

"Her father is a genius," Alice said seriously.

I could have contested that having been subject to Jeremy's poetry for a lot longer than Alice, but I just nodded in agreement.

"I have something to say," she said.

"I know," I said.

"No, you don't."

"I don't?"

I thought she was going to say I had my last warning about involving her husband in one of my cases, that she knew someone had been murdered, that she wanted me to tell him to stay home. We were past the "or else" stage. She had given that to me two cases ago.

"My husband is almost sixty-three," she said. "I think he should be taking care of this building, his family, and himself."

So far, it sounded like what I expected to hear.

"You want me to tell him that I don't need his help," I said. "And if I don't you will do me bodily harm."

"No," she said. "If he wants to work with you on these things, I've decided I don't have the right to try to stop him. I can only let him know how I feel. Jeremy needs to be needed. He would never admit it. He values your friendship. God knows why."

"Thanks," I said.

"He's a poet."

"I know."

"And he's also the strongest man I've ever known."

"Me, too."

"So, I won't ask him to stop anymore," she said, still sitting.

"But if any harm comes to him when he is working with you, you'll deal with Alice Pallas Butler. Is that clear?"

"Perfectly," I said.

"You don't want to deal with Alice Pallas Butler."

"I do not," I said.

"He told me about what you're doing tonight, the Blackstone business. I want to be there with Jeremy."

"My ballroom is your ballroom," I said.

She got up now and walked to the door.

"I left some photographs of Natasha on your desk," she said.

"Thanks."

"Her father is in some of them."

"And you?"

"I'm behind the camera watching," she said. "I'm a watcher."

"I'll remember that."

And she was gone. I went to my desk. The four photographs, all black and white, were lined up so I could sit at my desk and look at them. The kid was cute, bright, smiling. Jeremy holding her. He wasn't so cute. I piled the photographs and put them in my top drawer. Alice had a point.

Melvin Rand's address was off of San Vicente, a street of three-story apartment buildings with courtyards and signs in front saying that you were looking at the Reseda Palms Apartments, or the Mexicali Arms, or, in Rand's case, Caliente Fountain Court.

The fountain was small, in the center of the courtyard, and needed a good cleaning. Green algae turning black lined the stone sides of the round pool into which the fountain trickled. There were pennies on the bottom of the pool, not many. Most of them were green, too. I threw one in and made a wish as I headed for the entrance to the right at the rear.

The names of the tenants were on little cards slid into slots. The cards were different colors, some typed, some scrawled. Rand's was typed.

I didn't ring the bell. There wasn't any, just an apartment number and a stairway I didn't have to walk up, because Rand's number was six which was at ground level.

The blinds were down on Apartment Six. I knocked. It was definitely past my lunchtime. Mrs. Plaut's Spam casserole and the two donuts I had with Phil at the drugstore were holding me together, but I decided that if Rand didn't answer, I'd find someplace to get a fried egg sandwich and come back. I knocked again. Nothing. I looked around. No one was in sight, and all I could hear was the trickling of the fountain behind me.

I tried the door. It wasn't locked. I considered not going in. People locked their doors in Los Angeles. There was a war going on. Wars made people a little crazy. Some of them, particularly gangs of young guys facing the draft and willing to take some chances, would consider an unlocked door an invitation and a locked one a challenge.

I went in, found the light switch on the wall to my right, hit it, and closed the door behind him.

Melvin Rand did not make me look for him. He lay on the floor in the middle of the small living room into which I had stepped. He was definitely the same guy Wilde had sent running at Columbia. He was wearing nothing except for a pair of shorts and a bright yellow short-sleeved shirt opened to reveal a not very neat hole in his chest right about where one might expect to find his heart. In his right hand was a gun. In his left hand, a sheet of paper. His arms were sprawled at his sides.

I pulled out my handkerchief, wiped the light switch where I had touched it, and moved to the body. There wasn't much blood, but what there was was enough.

I touched the body. The room was warm. So was the former Melvin Rand. He hadn't been dead long. I angled my head to see if I could read what was on the sheet of paper in his hand without touching it. I could. It was written in block letters in ink and unsigned.

> I KILLED CUNNINGHAM. I KILLED OTT. I AM SORRY.
> BLACKSTONE IS INNOCENT.

That was it. It was probably the most unconvincing murder made to look like a suicide I'd ever seen. Now, for most people, a statement like that wouldn't mean much, but I had, in my nearly half century of existence, witnessed four fake suicides.

Using my handkerchief, which I carried less for my allergies and more for occasions like this, I searched the apartment as quickly as I could. There wasn't much to it, just two rooms and a kitchenette. The bedroom was small. The room where Rand lay looking at the ceiling wasn't much larger.

I found one Waterman pen. I unscrewed the top and touched the point. It was dry. It hadn't been used to write the note in Rand's hand. I looked for paper and found some sheets on a table near the bed. They didn't come close to matching the one in Rand's hand.

I looked at the note again. If someone was trying to clear Blackstone of two murders, he, she, or they had made him look more guilty. Plus, now they had added a third murder to the list.

Cawelti was a vindictive, petty, grudge-carrying hothead, but there were some things he was not. He was not corrupt, and he was not congenitally stupid. He would come to the same conclusion I had, and then Blackstone would be in even worse trouble than he had been when Rand had still been breathing.

I finished looking around. No address book. No checkbook, no notes. There was a black chest in the bedroom closet. I opened it. Magic tricks. No black satchel full of money. I snapped it shut and got out of the apartment, closing the door with my handkerchief-covered hand.

"He in?" a man's voice said behind me.

I didn't know when he had crept up on me. I lifted my hand and knocked at the door I had just closed.

"Doesn't seem to be there," I said, turning to face an old man with stoop shoulders, a little shorter than me with bright blue eyes in a very craggy face. He was wearing overalls and a gray work shirt.

"You a friend?" he asked.

"No," I said. "Greater California and Arizona Life Insurance Company. Harvey Cortez. Got a call from Mr. Rand, but . . ." I shrugged. "It happens in my line of work. They tell you to come and they're not there."

"You weren't in there just now?" the old man said.

"Nope," I said.

"Mrs. Gatstonsen next door said she heard a noise from in there a little while back," the man said. "Like something breaking, someone falling down."

"Seems quiet in there now," I said.

"Mrs. Gatstonsen is always hearing noises," he said. "She's a widow."

"That explains it," I said. "You think she might be interested in insurance?"

"Ask her," he said. "Your risk. She'll give you coffee and an earful, and I doubt she'll buy the time of day for a penny—but it's your time."

"I guess I'll skip Mrs. Gatstonsen," I said.

"Briefcase," the old man said.

"Briefcase?"

"Where's your briefcase, Mr. Harvey Cortez?" he asked. "Insurance man without a briefcase."

"In my car," I said, pointing at the street. "Wanted to be sure Mr. Rand was home. It's heavy and I've got a sore arm. Handball."

He stood there for a few seconds, sizing me up. I smiled. I don't think he liked what he saw and he would certainly remember me, but there was nothing I could do about it.

"I've got no time for games," he said. "Never did."

"I'm not playing . . ."

"Handball is for people who can't fill their time with what's worthwhile," he said.

"You're a man of strong convictions," I said. "I respect that."

"Then vote for Dewey," he said.

"I will," I lied. "Better get going."

I looked at my father's watch on my wrist. I didn't pay attention to the time. It was never right. I didn't wear it to know what time it was.

I stepped past the old man, knowing he was watching me over his shoulder. I walked at what I considered the normal pace for an insurance salesman who had clients to see and a living to make.

It wouldn't take long for the old man to try the door of Rand's apartment. It wouldn't take long for him to reach for the phone and call the police. It wouldn't take long for John Cawelti to come looking for me.

The lunch crowd was gone, so Anita took her time serving me a tuna on toast, fries, and a Pepsi. I could have gone back to the Faraday, picked up a few tacos from Manny's, sat at my desk, and waited for Cawelti to come for me.

My tooth was most definitely bothering me, creating a constant heavy pressure that I still didn't want to call pain. I used the oil of cloves. I also needed a dose of common sense, a remedy I generally was a little short on. I told Anita what had happened at Rand's apartment.

"So?" I asked, washing down a French fry with a drink of Pepsi.

She brushed a wisp of hair from her forehead and said. "So, I think you should pull out a nickel, put it in the phone, call Phil and tell him what happened."

"Makes sense," I said. "But he's got sick kids and . . ."

"He's a big boy," said Anita, taking my now-empty plate and walking over to put it in the bin of dirty dishes under the counter.

"Very big," I said.

"Got a nickel?" I asked.

"It can be arranged. How's that tooth?"

"Playful," I said.

She reached into her uniform pocket, came up with a nickel and flipped it to me. I caught it in my palm and closed my fist on it.

"Just like in the movies," she said with a smile.

I went to the phone in the back of the drugstore near the washrooms and called Phil's house. Phil's sister-in-law Becky answered.

"Me," I said. "How's everyone?"

"Doctor Hodgdon said we'll all survive." Her voice dropped. "How's Phil been behaving?"

"Like Phil," I said. "Well, not exactly."

"Right," Becky repeated. "Not exactly. He's going through the motions, Toby. You have some good news for him?"

"Not exactly," I said.

"I'll put him on."

I looked over my shoulder toward the counter. Anita was serving coffee to a guy in a brown delivery uniform. He was leaning forward and grinning. Anita was smiling. I was jealous.

"Toby," came Phil's voice.

I told him about Melvin Rand, my tap dance with the old guy Mrs. Gatstonsen had called.

"Where are you?"

I told him.

"Stay there."

He hung up, and so did I. I went back to the counter. The delivery guy was a few years younger than me, a few pounds lighter and definitely better looking. He looked over at me and raised his cup of coffee. When he put it down, Anita refilled it. He winked at her. She looked at me and gave a shrug so small that only a trained detective or a half-blind bus driver could see it.

"How's it going?" the delivery guy asked me.

"I'm waiting to be picked up by the police," I said.

"That a fact?" he said, winking at Anita to let her know he knew a joke when he heard one, even a bad one. "Maybe I'll just hang around and watch. Don't have to make the next delivery for an hour and change."

"Be my guest," I said. "What do you deliver?"

"Appliances. The May Company," he said. "Who'd you kill?" Another wink.

"You mean in my lifetime, or just today?"

"Let's stick with today. Who do the cops think you killed?"

He was obviously enjoying himself. I wasn't.

"A magician," I said. "No, make that a waiter."

"A magician? Hey, he do any tricks?"

"He plays dead," I said.

The appliance delivery man looked at his watch and then at Anita. He kept looking, drinking coffee, and checking his watch. After about ten minutes of banter and a full bladder, he headed for the men's room.

"You did the right thing, Toby," Anita said. "Calling Phil."

"Depends on who comes through that door," I answered.

When a lone, lean man with slumped shoulders and a fedora pulled down over his eyes came in, I felt a little better.

Steve Seidman saw me, walked over, and sat. Anita brought him a cup of coffee. Seidman added three spoons of sugar and a lot of cream.

Steve was my brother's former partner, and still a cop. The best thing about him was that he wasn't Cawelti.

The delivery man came out of the men's room tightening his belt.

"Hey, fella," he called to Seidman. "Don't sit too close to him. The police are coming to arrest him for murdering a waiter."

Steve put down his coffee mug, reached into his jacket pocket, came out with his wallet, flipped it open and displayed his well-polished badge to the delivery guy.

The fellow dropped two quarters on the counter and left without looking at Anita.

"How's Phil?" he asked.

"Could be better," I said.

"You play it too cute, Toby," he said, reaching for the sugar.

"It's the imp in me," I said. "Phil told you the story?"

"Officially, I haven't talked to Phil," he said. "You called me about an hour ago, said you went to see this guy Rand and found him dead. You were being a good citizen."

"The old man," I said. "The janitor."

"I'll talk to him," Seidman said.

"Cawelti?"

"It's my case," Seidman said. "You called me. You might even wind up with the mayor giving you a good citizenship medal. Finish up and we'll go take a look at the body, and you can fill me in on what this is all about."

"It's a long story, with two other dead guys," I said, sighing.

"Is it interesting?" asked Seidman.

"I think so," I said. I sighed again.

"Make it a short story."

We both finished our coffees, left what we owed, and got up. I waved to Anita, who waved back, and we headed back to the Caliente Fountain Apartments. We went in Seidman's unmarked car, and I kept the story short.

The old man was nowhere in sight when we stood in front of Apartment Six. Seidman turned the knob. The door was still unlocked. We stepped inside. Everything looked the way I had left it, except for one thing. But it was an important thing: Melvin Rand's body wasn't lying there looking up at the ceiling.

"Maybe he wasn't dead," said Seidman.

"He was dead."

We looked in the bedroom, under the bed, in the closet. No Rand. No gun. No note.

"He was here," I said.

Seidman was about to say something when the phone started to ring. We were standing in the living room. The telephone was on a small coffee table with a scratched top.

Seidman picked it up and said, "Hello."

He listened for a moment, then held it out.

"It's for you."

"Phil?"

"No," said Seidman.

I took the phone and said, "Hello."

"I'm sorry," the person on the other end said. The voice sounded high, maybe falsetto, filtered through a towel or a piece of cloth.

Seidman had already moved to the window and parted the blinds enough to get a look outside. Whoever was calling must have seen us come into the apartment, must have gone for a nearby phone. He or she couldn't be more than a few minutes away.

"Where's Rand's body?" I asked.

Seidman nodded and mouthed, "Keep him talking."

Then he went out the door and closed it behind him.

"Where it belongs," the caller said, almost weeping. He seemed genuinely upset.

"And where is that?"

"Keller's house."

"Why there?"

"It's where he belongs," said the caller. "I didn't think you'd find the body."

"You saw me come in here earlier?"

"I followed you. I wanted to tell you to stay away, but how

could I? Then you'd know I killed him. And then after that old man showed up . . . I had to move him."

"And nobody saw you?"

"I put him in a trunk and . . . it doesn't matter. I already called the police and told them to go to Mr. Ott's. They'll find the body and the note and the gun and it will all be over."

"I don't . . ." I began, but he cut in.

"I've got to go."

"Wait," I said. "You were with Rand at Columbia, weren't you?"

"I had no choice," the caller said.

"You always have a choice."

"Yes." There was a pause. "But sometimes the choice is a very, very bad one."

"Just one more question."

He hung up, and so did I. I went out the door and ran toward the street where I stopped and looked both ways. There was a phone booth about two blocks to my left. I could see Seidman running toward it. I started after him.

"Missed him," he said. "He saw me coming, didn't even have to run, just got out of the booth, walked to the corner, and turned. When I got there, there was no one."

"Get a good look?" I asked.

"No," he said. "Dark coat, collar pulled up. It could have been a woman. It could have been Myrna Loy."

Seidman was a sucker for Myrna Loy.

"I know where Rand is," I said.

"Lead on," he said, and we went back to his car.

CHAPTER

15

Hold up a handkerchief. Show it is plain and white. Hold up a wooden kitchen match. Wrap the match in the handkerchief. Tell the victim to break the match. They break the match. You hand the handkerchief to another person who you ask to shake the match loose. The match is no longer broken. Solution: Slide a match into the hem of the handkerchief before you do the trick. When you have the second matchstick in the handkerchief, hold the handkerchief so that the person breaks the one in the hem. Then, when you shake the handkerchief, the whole match will fall out.

—*From the* Blackstone, The Magic Detective *radio show*

THERE WERE TWO MARKED POLICE cars in front of Ott's house in Sherman Oaks. Seidman pulled in behind them, and we went to the door where a uniformed cop stood guard.

The uniformed cop was an old-timer named Ginty. Ginty had seen it all, including us. He didn't have to see Seidman's badge. We went in and down the hall of posters to the living room.

Rand wasn't on the floor. He was seated in an armchair, note in one hand, gun in the other. Cawelti and a uniformed cop I didn't know were standing over him.

Cawelti turned and said,

"You got him," Cawelti said.

"What are you talking about?" said Seidman.

"Peters," he said, pointing at me. "He set up this phony suicide to protect his client."

"Suicide," Seidman repeated.

"Phony," said Cawelti, looking at Rand who looked at me. "He couldn't shoot himself in the heart at that angle. No blood on the floor. Note's not signed. Phony. What are you doing here?"

"Called in," Seidman lied. "Desk said you were here. I was having coffee with Peters at a drugstore."

"Just pals," said Cawelti with as perfect a smirk as man could create.

"Talking about Phil," Seidman said.

"Won't wash," said Cawelti.

"Calling me a liar?" said Seidman flatly.

Maybe there'd be a shoot-out at the Calvin Ott corral. Cop against cop. With the uniformed guy, me, and Rand as witnesses.

"Bullshit," said Cawelti.

"You have some evidence or just bluff?" asked Seidman. "Seems to me if Peters did this he'd do a hell of a better job. This looks sloppy, amateur."

"Then it was Blackstone," said Cawelti. "Phony note to clear him of a murder he can't squirm out of."

"Can't we all be friends?" I said.

Cawelti glared.

"You aren't funny, Peters. Never were."

"You need a sophisticated sense of humor to appreciate my droll wit," I said.

"Why does Blackstone want me at the Roosevelt tonight?" he asked.

"Come and see," I said.

"Message said he would show how Ott was murdered," Cawelti said. "Maybe he can explain about this guy and Cunningham, too."

"Be there and find out," I said. "Should be a good show."

"Let's go," said Seidman.

"I've got more questions," said Cawelti.

"I've got a good lawyer, remember?" I said.

"You going to hold him for something?" Seidman asked.

Cawelti clenched his fists and looked at the uniformed cop, who was trying to be invisible.

"Okay, then we're going," said Seidman.

On the way down the hall I expected Cawelti to call out something, probably an echo of some old movie, like "You haven't heard the last of this, Peters." Or, "We'll see who has the last laugh" or "You'll never get away with this one."

He said nothing.

I started thinking of that other man, the one who had been with Rand at Columbia, the one Cornel Wilde said he could identify from his hands, the one who had maybe killed Rand, called me at Rand's apartment, and moved the body to Ott's living room. I was wondering who and why.

When I got back to the office, Phil was at his desk.

"Kids okay?" I asked.

He nodded. I told him what had happened and then got on the phone. I couldn't reach Wilde on the Columbia lot, and I didn't have a home phone for him. I asked Phil if he could get one for me. He got on the phone and, two minutes later, hung it up and gave me a number.

I called it. A woman answered, and I asked for Wilde, who came on almost immediately.

"This is Peters," I said.

"I remember you."

"The man you crossed blades with at Columbia. He's dead."

"I'm sorry."

"He was murdered," I said. "Maybe by that guy who was with him when he came to blackmail you. Still think you could identify him from his hands?"

"I'm certain."

I asked him if he could be at the Roosevelt for Blackstone's party later. He said he would make it.

I hung up and looked at my brother.

"I think I know who it is," he said.

"The other guy?"

He told me. I said, "We'll see in a few hours."

I started to reach for the telephone to call Gunther, and then it hit me. It hit me violently in my tooth, like the stab of a long needle. I think I made a less than manly sound and closed my eyes.

"What the hell's the matter with you?" Phil asked.

My eyes were watering. I reached into my pocket for the oil of cloves and pointed at my mouth. I couldn't talk. Phil watched as I dabbed the liquid onto my tooth with my finger. The pain was still there, sharp, and getting sharper.

"Toothache?" asked Phil, getting out of his chair.

I nodded.

"Open your mouth," he said, coming over to me.

I opened my mouth. It wasn't easy.

"What the hell did you do?" Phil asked.

"Taco," I managed.

He didn't ask me to explain.

"You need a dentist," he said. "I've got one."

I pulled the slip of paper with Frank the pharmacist's brother's name and number out of my pocket. My hand was shaking.

Phil dialed his dentist's number. I groaned.

"When did this happen?" Phil asked.

I pointed over my shoulder to indicate that it had been a while. He's my brother. He understood. He shook his head.

He held the phone to his ear and waited.

"Is Doctor Clough in? I've got an emergency. . . . Okay."

He hung up.

"Clough is in Denver."

I handed him the slip of paper with Frank's brother's phone number. He looked at it and dialed.

"Tell him I'm a friend of Frank," I managed to get out, putting my head forward, wondering if what was left of the bottle of oil of cloves would knock me out if I drank it or if it would just kill me. I would have settled for either one.

Phil dialed and waited.

"Dr. Block? "

Phil listened and then said, "When?"

Phil hung up.

"He'll be back in a few hours."

I lifted my head and met Phil's eyes.

"No," I said.

"How much does it hurt?"

I rolled my eyes to the ceiling.

"You see a choice here?" he asked.

Defenestration seemed a reasonable solution, but I shook my head.

"You want me to help you?" he asked as I started to get up, steadying myself with my hands on the desk.

I shook my head "no" and managed to stagger toward the door. Phil got there first and opened it.

In the hall, I took a step back, but the pain got me. Phil put a hand on my shoulder, guiding me where I didn't want to go, to the door of Sheldon Minck, the devil's dentist.

My brother opened the door, and Violet looked up from the telephone. She hung up the phone and said,

"What happened?"

Violet is a dark beauty who regularly took my money on bets I made with her about a variety of sporting events, mostly boxing. Until I met Violet, I had thought I was a near expert on the fight game.

"Someone in there with Minck?" Phil asked.

"No," said Violet. "Tooth?"

"Yeah," said Phil, moving to the inner door.

"You sure you want to see Dr. Minck?" she said.

"Emergency," said Phil.

"It'd have to be," said Violet.

We went in. Shelly was sitting in his chair, listening to the radio. Something classical was playing, and Shelly was eating a sandwich with his left hand and conducting the orchestra on the radio with his right, which also held a half-finished cigar.

He looked up, got up, and Phil put me in the chair.

"What happened?" Shelly asked.

"Tooth," said Phil. "Fix him up enough so we can get him to a real dentist."

"I am a . . ." Shelly began indignantly.

"Fix him," said Phil softly, looking at Shelly who nodded.

"Get rid of the sandwich," said Phil. "Get rid of the cigar. Go wash your hands."

Shelly adjusted his glasses and waddled over to the sink where he dropped the sandwich and cigar in the trash.

"Soap," said Phil.

Shelly turned on the water and picked up a bar of soap, showing it to Phil.

I think I groaned. The door was about ten feet away. I knew I could make it that far. I didn't know how much further. I closed my eyes and heard the water running.

"Those instruments clean?" Phil asked.

"Violet cleaned them this morning," Shelly said, his voice quivering.

"Move," said Phil.

I considered opening my eyes and decided not to. I could smell garlic and tobacco as Shelly leaned over me.

"Open your mouth, Toby," he said.

I refused.

"Open up," Phil said.

I opened and felt Shelly's pudgy fingers entering where I thought they would never enter.

"Wow," he said. "That must hurt like hell."

It was a great diagnosis.

"I've got to give you a shot," he said.

How many screams had I heard from this chair when I sat in the little office a few feet away where Pancho the phantom screenwriter was probably now seated pencil in hand searching for something creative to say about the man who was about to do mortal damage to my mouth?

I closed my mouth. Phil told me to open it. I considered defying him. Then I remembered the last time I had defied my brother when he was close enough to reach out and grab me. I opened my mouth.

"Don't hum," I whispered.

"Huh?" said Shelly.

"Don't hum. Don't sing," I managed to get out.

"Okay," he said. "Keep your mouth open. This is going to hurt a little, maybe."

My mouth already hurt more than a little, and there was no "maybe" about it.

"There," Shelly said.

I opened my eyes.

"You okay?" Shelly asked.

"Didn't feel it," I said.

Shelly was sweating. Shelly was smiling. He leaned over his tray of tools of torture, squinting at them through the super-thick lenses of his glasses. He started to hum.

"No," I said.

He stopped humming. I looked at Phil who stood with his arms folded.

"Open wide," Shelly said.

He had something in his hand. I didn't want to look at it. Then I heard the familiar sound of the drill. I think I passed out.

I had a dream. Violet was sitting in my lap. She smelled like oil of cloves. She was putting five-dollar bills in my pockets and smiling as she said, Zale, Galento, Louis, Tenn Hoff. In the background, Vaughn Monroe was singing *I'll Walk Alone.* I was afraid Violet's husband Rocky would come through the door in uniform, drop his duffle bag when he saw his wife in my lap, and then kill me. I hoped that death didn't come from a right to my molar.

No one came through the door. Vaughn Monroe kept crooning. Violet kept putting money in my pockets and then there was darkness.

"Toby?" I heard a definitely worried voice. "You there?"

I tried to open my eyes. They refused.

"Toby," came a different voice. My brother's. "Come out of it."

I forced my eyes open and saw Shelly. His cheek was twitching. Behind him stood Phil.

"Are you alright?" asked Shelly. "How does it feel?"

I felt my tooth with my tongue. It was smooth, no piece missing.

"I got rid of the decay and gave you a gold filling," said Shelly.

"Tobias," said Phil.

"Feels fine," I said, still running my tongue over my tooth.

I looked at Shelly, who was blinking madly and wiping sweat from his face with his sleeve.

"You're kidding?" he said.

"No," I said. "Feels fine."

I sat up. I was a little weak, but there was no pain, no throbbing, nothing but normal feeling.

I stood.

"Can I smoke now?" Shelly asked.

"Go ahead," said Phil hand on my arm.

"I'll be damned," I said.

"Eventually," said Phil.

"I feel fine," I said. "It didn't hurt."

I looked at Shelly. He was fishing in the pocket of his jacket, which was on a hanger near the door to what had been my office. Shelly beamed at me.

"What do we owe you?" Phil asked.

Shelly found a cigar and waved his arm.

"No charge," he said. "Anytime."

"Thanks Shel," I said.

"Nothing," he said, sticking a fresh cigar in his mouth. "See you at the Roosevelt later."

Phil and I moved into the reception area where Violet sat waiting for us.

"You're alright?" Violet asked.

"Perfect," I said.

Violet looked at Shelly's door and then at us.

"That's the first time since I've been working here," she said.

"We've got work to do," I said to Phil.

"We've got work to do," I agreed.

CHAPTER

16

Two hats are upside-down on the table. Next to them spread out a deck of cards facedown. Have your victim pick two cards and show them to others while you put the rest of the deck in one hat and cover it with the other hat. Have the person who selected the cards slide them between the two hats. Shake the hats together to mix the cards or have someone else shake them. Reach into the hats and pull out the two cards selected. Solution: When the victim picks the two cards and shows them, you put the rest of the pack in the hats bending the entire deck. When the two selected cards are put back in the hat, you'll easily be able to reach into the hats even after the cards have been shaken and pick the two unbent cards, which you can show.

From the Blackstone, The Magic Detective *radio show*

ALICE PALLAS BUTLER AND HER HUSBAND were standing just inside the ballroom door when Phil and I arrived. Jeremy wore dark slacks, a white shirt, and a tie. I wondered, and not for the first time, what his collar size was. It wasn't much larger than his wife's. Alice wore a black dress that covered her ample arms, went down to her ankles, and left just enough room at the neck for a string of pearls.

They were talking to Jimmy Clark, who wore what looked like the same flannel shirt and dark slacks I had always seen him in.

There was no one else in the room.

Phil nodded and began his search of the room, which, except for the lack of table settings, looked exactly the way it had when Calvin Ott had been killed.

"Toby," said Jeremy. "How is your tooth?"

"Do you believe in miracles?" I asked.

"Yes," Jeremy answered.

"Me, too," said Jimmy.

Alice didn't answer. I had a feeling she didn't believe in miracles. She believed in Alice and Jeremy.

"Shelly fixed it," I said.

"Fixed . . ." asked Jeremy.

"My tooth," I said, opening my mouth and pointing.

No one looked.

"It's perfect," I said. "If you've got a very broad definition of 'perfect.'"

"Once in a lifetime," said Alice.

"Did you know there was once—and only once—a perfectly symmetrical major league baseball game?" asked Jeremy.

I knew Jeremy had played baseball when he was about forty years younger. He'd been a first baseman. He had even read me a couple of poems he'd written about the game.

"No, I didn't," I said.

"I was there," said Jeremy. "Some called it a miracle. August 13, 1910, the Pirates and Dodgers played an 8-8 tie. Each team had 38 at bats, 13 hits, 12 assists, 5 strikeouts, 3 walks, 2 errors, 1 hit batsman, and 1 passed ball."

"A tie?"

"Darkness," said Jeremy. "God or the Fates chose that day and that game and said 'it shall end in a perfect tie.'"

"Amen," I said.

"And like so many miracles," Jeremy went on. "No one watching was aware of it till the next day when someone looked at the statistics."

"I saw a miracle once," said Jimmy Clark. "Back home in Decatur. We were . . ."

He was interrupted by the arrival of the Bouton brothers. Pete, wearing a gray sports jacket and no tie, beckoned to Jimmy who said, "Excuse me" and moved toward the brothers who had paused at the door.

Harry was wearing a dark suit and a white turtleneck sweater. No tux. After I introduced him to Alice, he moved to the platform against the wall with Pete, who was carrying a black satchel very much like the one filled with money that Ott had shown us.

"Who's watching Natasha?" I asked while Harry took the satchel, placed it on the table, and looked inside, checking whatever it was he needed.

"Violet for a while," said Alice, her eyes on the activity.

Pete pointed to the curtain near the door and spoke to Jimmy. We couldn't hear what they were saying, but Jimmy nodded.

Gunther and Shelly arrived together. Gunther, as usual, had dressed for the occasion, in a suit, vest, and perfectly Windsor-knotted tie. Shelly, in a yellow sweater bunched awkwardly at the waist, wore a grin as large as his biggest cigar.

"How's my patient?" he asked, coming up to me and adjusting his glasses for a better look.

"Fine," I said.

"Open," Shelly said.

"I'm fine," I repeated.

"Open, open," he said, head tilted to one side.

I opened my mouth, hoping he wouldn't put his fingers inside. He leaned forward and peered.

"Yep," he said, backing away and actually rubbing his hands together. "Yep. You tell them?"

"I told them," I said.

"Yep," Shelly repeated.

"You wish us to go where we were when Calvin Ott was murdered?" Gunther asked.

"Yep," I said.

"Toby, tell Blackstone," said Shelly as Gunther guided him away. "About your tooth."

Phil went through the door to the kitchen. Harry, Peter, and Jimmy bustled. Magicians, dressed as somberly as they thought the occasion required, began to arrive at the open door.

Alice and Jeremy, as we had arranged, had the job of preventing them from entering. Unless they could levitate, which a few of them did indeed claim, they would not get by the Butlers.

Phil came out of the kitchen and looked at Harry, who was adjusting his tie, hands folded in front of him.

A minute or two passed and the magicians in the hall had started to grow restless. I moved between Jeremy and Alice and announced that we were waiting for a special guest who would be here in a minute or two.

They grumbled. The magicians in Ott's circle were all there. Leo Benz hunched down, hoping Phil and I wouldn't see him.

From the rear of the pack, someone began making his way forward, apologizing as he came. Their backs were turned to him, so there was no recognition till Cornel Wilde was at the ballroom door, shaking my hand and smiling.

"Sorry I'm late," he said.

"I'm Alice Pallas Butler," Alice said with what could almost have passed as a shy smile.

Wilde took her hand and said, "A pleasure to meet you."

Alice stepped back and looked at Jeremy with a wider smile.

"You want me to . . . ?" Wilde said.

"Just stand here as we let them in one at a time," I said. "We told them we had a guest. You're it. You can shake their hands to get a good look."

Wilde nodded and Phil told Jeremy and Alice to let the magicians in one at a time. Wilde smiled with very white teeth as they moved past him. He held a few of the hands longer than others, didn't seem to look at them, and let each person pass.

Phil and I watched Wilde for a sign of recognition, something to show that he had spotted the person who had been with Melvin Rand at Columbia.

They filed in, and, at the urging of Gunther and Shelly took their seats, looking up at Blackstone, who smiled like a man who had a secret.

When everyone was seated, I glanced toward Wilde. He shook his head, indicating that the person we were looking for hadn't come through the door.

"I'm sorry," he said.

"Eliminates a room full of people," said Phil, eyes scanning the crowd.

"If it's alright with you," said Wilde. "I'll just stand by the door."

Phil nodded, and Wilde moved to the door next to Alice and Jeremy. The room was full. I motioned to the Butlers, who started to close the door. John Cawelti held up his hand and entered just as the doors were closing. He looked around, saw Phil and me and did a cross between a sneer and a smirk. Then he moved to the back wall, not far from Wilde, leaned against it and crossed his arms.

Pete Bouton sat at a table near the door. Jimmy wasn't anywhere in sight. I knew he was behind the curtain, where he had been the night Ott was murdered.

"Gentlemen and lady," Blackstone said, closing his eyes and dipping his head toward Alice. "This will not take long. I begin with a statement. I did not kill Calvin Ott, but I know how he was killed. If any of you would prefer to be the one to explain how it was done, I will relinquish the podium to you."

He looked around the room. Magicians looked at each other. No one raised a hand.

"Very good," said Blackstone. "Now if Mr. Peters will step up here."

I wasn't prepared for this. The last time I had been part of Blackstone's act, I had almost been sliced in half wearing a chocolate soldier uniform. I moved to the podium.

"Mr. Peters shall play me," said Blackstone, positioning me where he had stood when Ott had died. "And I shall play the late Calvin Ott."

Blackstone moved to the table and sat where Ott had sat, with the black satchel now on the floor beside him.

"Question," said Blackstone. "Why did Calvin Ott arrange a testimonial dinner in my honor? He'd never made any attempt to hide his jealousy. He said he had a surprise. But, obviously, this surprise was designed to embarrass me and to bring him applause. But what could it be?"

Blackstone's hands were now folded.

I stood a few feet away from Blackstone, watching him.

"Ah," he said. "I have it."

The lights went out.

Someone gasped. The lights came back on.

Blackstone was slumped over, face on the table, knife sticking out of his neck.

"There he goes," Pete Bouton shouted. "He killed my brother!"

The ballroom door was open. Someone ran out. Pete ran for the door shouting, "Don't let him get away!"

People started to rise. Pete stopped at the door, turned, and held up a hand to keep the first pursuers from exiting.

I took four quick steps to Blackstone, who suddenly sat up and said, "The illusion is complete. Please return to your seats."

Blackstone reached up, pulled down the collar of his sweater. He snapped a white band and pulled it off of his neck and held it in front of him. A knife handle and an inch or two of blade were attached to the band. Blackstone placed the device on the table.

"When the lights went out the other night," said Blackstone,

"Calvin Ott pulled something very like this from his satchel, snapped it on his neck, and put his head on the table just as I did now."

Phil and I looked at each other. Ott had come to our office not to make a sincere bet but because he wanted to establish why he would be carrying the black satchel at the testimonial dinner.

Blackstone looked around the room and continued, "I think he planned to be sitting here when we all returned from our wild goose chase. I think he had something ready to say about having fooled me with his illusion, but . . . someone else had the perfect conclusion to Calvin Ott's illusion.

"The killer, who was part of Ott's scheme, came to the podium as he was supposed to do, stood behind Ott, and when the device was removed, stabbed Ott in the neck. The victim had inadvertently participated in his own murder. The killer dropped the device with the fake knife into the satchel and ran."

"Where?" asked one of the magicians. "Who is he?"

"Some of you know Melvin Rand," said Blackstone.

There were murmurs around the room.

"Melvin Rand was a waiter that night," said Blackstone, looking at the ballroom door.

Jimmy Clark, who had turned out the lights at Blackstone's cue and then run through the door, came back into the ballroom. Blackstone smiled and nodded at him. Jeremy said something, and then Jimmy went back out the door.

"Rand killed Ott?" asked someone.

"And Rand is now dead. There was a suicide note, a confession," said Blackstone, looking at Cawelti who stood impassively, arms still folded. "The case appears to be closed. The illusion revealed. The show is over."

The magicians applauded and rose. Some headed for the door, including Leo Benz. Others went up to congratulate Blackstone.

"Too easy," I heard one lean man say.

"Best illusions always are when you find out how they're done," said the tall man to whom he was talking.

The congratulating of Blackstone went on for about ten minutes. Cornel Wilde also made his way to Blackstone, who reached out to shake the actor's hand.

When almost everyone had cleared the room, Cawelti shook his head, went through the door, and disappeared. Phil, the Butlers, Shelly, Gunther, and I stood in a half circle in front of Blackstone and his brother.

"Something is missing," said Blackstone. "Something doesn't feel right, but. . . ."

Blackstone shrugged and picked up the satchel. I went with Wilde to the door.

"Thanks for coming," I said.

"I enjoyed it," said Wilde.

"Well," I said. "Too bad he wasn't here, the man who was with Rand at Columbia."

"He was," said Wilde.

"Wait," I said. "When everyone was inside the room and the doors were closed, you let me know he wasn't here."

"He didn't come through the door," Wilde said.

Besides Blackstone and his brother no one had been in the room except. . . .

"Jimmy?" I said.

"The young man with the limp," said Wilde. "That's Jimmy?"

"Yes," I said.

"It was him," said Wilde, looking at his watch. "I've got to hurry. As I said, I enjoyed it."

He shook my hand and was gone. I hurried over to Phil to tell him what Wilde had said. I then turned to Pete Bouton and asked, "Do you know where Jimmy is?"

Before he could answer, Jeremy said, "I do."

Phil and I looked at him.

"He's babysitting Natasha," said Alice.

"I thought you said Violet was watching Natasha," I said.

"Until Jimmy could relieve her," said Jeremy. "She had to catch the last red car home at nine."

Okay. I had choices to make and fast. Did I just turn and run the three blocks to the Farraday Building? Did I tell Jeremy and Alice what was happening? Maybe nothing was happening. Did I have time to explain it to Phil?

I motioned to my brother as I moved fast across the floor and out the door. The phones were in the lobby on a wall to the right near the registration desk. I fished for a nickel as I reached for the phone.

"What's going on?" Phil asked behind me.

I held up a hand for him to wait while I called Jeremy's apartment.

"Toby?" Phil insisted. "What the hell's wrong with you?"

The phone rang.

"Jimmy Clark was with Rand when he went to Columbia to try to blackmail Cornel Wilde," I said.

The phone rang.

"Jimmy was backstage when Cunningham was murdered," I said. "Jimmy was handling the lights here when Ott was murdered. Jimmy . . ."

Someone picked up the phone and said, "Hello."

"Why the hell . . . ?" Phil started, but I said,

"Juanita?"

"Toby?"

"What are you doing there?" I asked.

"I was working late," she said. "The Scoufas sisters wanted an emergency session, get in touch with their dead brother, you know. So I said to myself, they're good Greek ladies. How can it hurt if I give them a little support, though, in truth, I can no more talk to the dead than I can turn myself into Rita Hayworth or . . ."

"Juanita, is Natasha there? Is a kid named Jimmy Clark there? He's supposed to be sitting with Natasha."

"Nice kid," Juanita said. "He saw me going down the elevator and asked if I could sit with Natasha for a little while. He had to do something. How do you say no? Know what I mean?"

"Where did he go?" I asked, looking at Phil who stood with his fists clenched and his feet apart.

"Who knows? Am I a mind reader?" Juanita snapped, with a distinct return of her New York City roots.

"Yes, you are," I said.

"No, I'm a seer, a clairvoyant, I beg your pardon. I don't know what people are thinking," she said. "I've told you all this before. There was something I felt about that young man. Something was heavy on his mind. You didn't need special gifts to see that."

"Where's Natasha?" I asked.

"Asleep in bed I guess," Juanita said.

"You guess? You haven't seen her?"

"No, I'm sitting here listening to *Big Town* on the radio, playing a little solitaire."

"Juanita," I said calmly. "Go look at Natasha and come back on the phone and tell me she's alright."

Something in my voice got through to Juanita. She said "Sure," clunking the phone down on the wooden coffee table in the Butler apartment as she went to check.

"Where's Clark staying? What hotel?" Phil asked.

I told him, and then Juanita came back on.

"Toby, she's not there!"

CHAPTER

17

Take a piece of paper. Fold it evenly in thirds. Write the name of three people in the room on each third. Tear the paper along the creases. Have someone fold the sheets in half and drop them into a hat. Have someone say one of the names in the hat. Reach in, pull out a folded sheet, open it, and show the name chosen. Solution: Simply remember where the paper is torn. If the piece with the name on it is the centerpiece, it will be torn on top and bottom. For the other two, be sure that when you make the tear on one that you very slightly nip it off in a corner so that you can feel where you made the nip.
—*From the* Blackstone, The Magic Detective *radio show*

PHIL BARRELED ACROSS THE LOBBY and out the door. I went back in the ballroom, took a deep breath, and went to the place on the platform where Blackstone had stood.

"Listen," I said.

Jeremy and Alice were near the door talking to Gunther. Shelly and Pancho were a few feet in front of me, talking to Blackstone and his brother.

"When you smile," said Shelly, pointing at Blackstone's mouth. "I can see a little turn, a twist in your upper right . . . that one there."

"I've never noticed it," said Blackstone.

"Trust me," said Shelly. "Come and see me tomorrow. I'll take care of it. No charge. I'll throw in a cleaning and exam. All I ask is that if I do a good job you let me do an ad with your picture.

And, right under your picture, it'll say, 'Sheldon Minck Will Do Magic With Your Teeth.'"

"Listen," I repeated loudly.

Everyone stopped talking and looked at me.

"We just got some information that gives us pretty good reason for thinking that Jimmy Clark knows something about what's been happening."

"What?" shouted Alice.

"Phil's on his way to your apartment to try to find him," I said.

"Try to . . . ," Alice said. "He's there with Natasha."

I shook my head and started to explain, but Jeremy and Alice were out the door and gone before I got two words out.

"Jimmy Clark?" said Pete Bouton. "I can't believe it."

Everyone began talking, and I raised my voice. "Hold it! Hold it!"

Nobody listened. Blackstone moved to my side and said quietly, "Listen."

They all stopped talking. Blackstone turned to me, indicating the floor was mine.

"I'll call the police," I said. "Gunther, go to the hotel where people in the show are staying. Shelly, you and Pancho get back to the Farraday and wait by your phone."

I looked at Blackstone and his brother and said, "Does Clark know anyone in Los Angeles?"

"No relatives, no friends," said Pete. "Just the people in the show. So far as I know."

"We'll get back to the theater," Blackstone said. "We'll check with everyone in the show about where Jimmy might be. You say he has a child with him?"

"Looks that way," I said.

Blackstone grabbed the satchel and hurried across the room and out the door with his brother.

"Let's move," I said.

I called the Wilshire Station from the Roosevelt lobby and was unlucky enough to find that Cawelti was still there. When he came on the line, he said, "Make it fast, Peters. I don't want to talk to you."

I explained what had happened. He was quiet. When I finished, a Cawelti voice I had never heard before said, "Spell the kid's name."

I did.

"You say he's from Decatur, Illinois?" he asked.

"Yes."

"Tell me everything you know about him," said Cawelti.

I told him. It wasn't much.

"Let me know if Blackstone has his photograph," he said when I finished. "I know what he looks like so I'll put out a description."

"Don't forget the limp," I said.

"I won't. Photograph of the girl?"

"I've got one," I said.

"I'll send someone to the Butler's apartment to pick it up. How old is she?"

"Two," I said.

Cawelti was silent.

"Two," he repeated softly. "Where can I reach you?"

"Shelly's in his office. I'll check in with him."

"Tell Butler . . . ," he began. "No, I'll go over to the Farraday and talk to him and his wife. It goes APB as soon as I hang up the phone."

He hung up the phone.

I probably could have gotten to the Farraday faster by running, but I might need the car later. It was parked half a block down in front of the Roosevelt.

When I got to the Farraday and through the front door, I could hear voices echoing from above. Voices at night in the cavern of a lobby were always indistinct and a little ghostly. The elevator was up on another level. I didn't want it, anyway. I went up the stairs as fast as I could and tried not to pant when I went through the door of the Butler apartment.

Juanita was the only one sitting.

"He called," Phil said. "Jeremy talked to him."

"What'd he say?"

"Natasha is alright," said Jeremy, his arm around his wife's ample shoulder. "He hasn't hurt her, will not hurt her. He saw you talking to Wilde before he left to come here. He knew by Wilde's face that he'd recognized him."

"He was right," I said.

"What does he want?"

"Time," said Phil.

"Time," said Jeremy. "Which is what we all want. He said he needs time to decide. I don't think he'll hurt her."

"I agree," I said, not mentioning that the freckled young fellow with the big grin and touching limp may well have murdered three men in the last three days.

Alice turned away to face the window and then turned back. "If he touches her or even frightens her, if he . . . I'll. . . ."

No one in the room, including her husband, doubted that she would make Jimmy Clark a very sorry young man if she ever got within reach of his neck.

"And you," she said, pointing at me. "I've warned you. Jeremy got involved with all this because of you. He met Jimmy Clark because of you."

I doubted if the combined efforts of Jeremy and my brother could have stopped her from getting to me if she had decided to tear off any part of my anatomy. She took one step toward me and stopped. Juanita had said something.

"High," Juanita said.

She was sitting in a straight-back wooden chair.

"High," she repeated. "He's some place high, looking up at the stars, crying. Natasha is sleeping in his arms."

There was nothing eerie, distant, or ghostly in Juanita's words. She had her head turned a little to the right, and she held up a single finger of her right hand. She was trying to see something. She gently bit her lower lip.

"You'll run and run and look," she said. "In darkness and light, searching for a secret where there isn't a secret. It's all simple."

"What's simple?" I asked.

"Huh?" asked Juanita.

"What's simple?" I repeated.

"Whatever you're all making complicated," she said, waving her bangle-covered left arm.

"We'll find her," came a voice from the open door behind me.

I turned. It was Cawelti. He looked at Phil. Neither man spoke, but something passed between them—a truce.

"He needs a photograph of Natasha," I said. "I've got one downstairs."

"Wait," said Jeremy.

He moved to the door to the bedroom on his right. The rest of us stood: Alice looking at me, me looking at Juanita, Juanita looking at her hand, pursing her lips and then getting up.

Juanita moved to Alice and touched her shoulder gently.

"Tea, I could use some tea. You got some?"

Alice didn't want to stop looking at me.

"Tea?" Juanita repeated. "I'll make it myself if you tell me where it is."

Alice turned toward the smaller woman and said, "It's in the cupboard over the sink. I'll get it."

As Alice moved toward the kitchen, Juanita stage-whispered to me, "I hate tea. My husband, Sol, loved the stuff. Never has any taste as far as I'm concerned."

Jeremy came out of the bedroom with a photograph in his hand about the size of a book. He handed it to Cawelti who repeated, "We'll find her."

"It's odd," Jeremy said. "The only poetry that comes to mind is that of Poe, and it gives me no solace. There are times when even poetry will not suffice or comfort."

After a last glance at Phil, Cawelti was out the door and gone.

I started to look at the watch on my wrist, my father's watch, the watch that never had the right time, that lived in a time world of its own. I've heard people say that even a stopped watch was right twice a day. But my father's watch just kept on ticking as long as it was kept wound and it kept on turning at its own pace.

"It's a little after ten," Phil said, looking sadly at his own watch, a birthday gift from Ruth.

It was going to be a long night.

And it was.

Phil went down to our office to call home. I went to Shelly's office. In the small reception room, Shelly was seated behind Violet's desk, phone to his ear. Pancho was in the one chair of the cramped space, an old *Look* magazine in his lap.

Shelly removed the cigar from his mouth, crinkled his nose in the hope of pushing his glasses up without touching them, nodded at me, and said, "Yeah. He just walked in. Here."

Shelly handed me the phone.

"Toby," said Gunther. "I am at the hotel. I have spoken with all members of the Blackstone troupe I could locate. None of them knows where Jimmy Clark might go. All they can say is that he's a friendly, helpful young man who appears to be completely devoted to Blackstone. One young woman says that he told her he would give his life for Blackstone."

"Why?"

"No one seems to know. They all say that Gwen knew him best. Perhaps I should go and talk to her."

"Okay. You know where she is right?"

"Yes, at her sister's apartment."

"Call in if you get something from her, anything."

"I shall," said Gunther.

He hung up.

"How's the tooth?" asked Shelly.

"Perfect, I said.

"When we find Natasha, we should make an appointment to do complete x-rays and see what else is going on."

"I'll think about it, Shel."

"Pancho's working on the script," he said.

I looked at Pancho who was dozing. The *Look* magazine was slipping from his lap.

"I see," I said.

"Now he needs rest," said Shel, smiling at Pancho. "Creativity is draining. He needs lots of food and rest. I'm learning a lot about the screenwriting game."

"Great," I said, turning to the door.

"Dentist in Disguise," said Shelly.

"What?"

I turned.

"The name of the script about me," he said. "Remember, I told you before."

Pancho was snoring now. Shelly looked at him benevolently and pointed at the little man with the stub of his cigar.

"Bad alignment," he said. "I've got a device that can take care of that, eliminate snoring. I'll just get a cast of his teeth and make one for him."

"Great," I said, going through the door.

The Farraday was dark and quiet, except for my footsteps. I went to our office and found Phil looking at the photograph of me, our dad, Phil, and Phil's German Shepherd, Kaiser Wilhelm. His back was to me.

"Anything?" I asked.

"Kids are getting better," he said, not turning to look at me. "Becky told me not to worry. I'm going to worry."

I went to my desk and sat. Phil was a few feet from me now.

"Becky's a lot like Ruth," he said, still not looking at me, really talking to himself.

"Yeah," I said.

"But she's not Ruth," he went on with a sigh.

Now he turned, went to his desk, and said, "Let's find the baby."

Phil looked at me now. I had the feeling he wanted me to say something, but I didn't know what to say. He looked older than usual, maybe because the first hint of nighttime stubble was starting to show on his chin and cheeks. The stubble was definitely gray like his hair.

"Gunther's going . . ."

The phone rang. I started to reach for the one on my desk, but Phil picked up the one on his first.

"Yeah," he said, nodding at me to pick up my phone.

"Just got off the phone with the police chief in Decatur," said Cawelti. "Jimmy Clark is William Tracy Carson. The chief recognized the description. The limp was the tip-off. Carson's got a history. Went into the army when he was seventeen. Action in the Pacific, got hit by shrapnel when he took out a Jap machine gun nest on Tarawa. Got all kinds of awards and medals. Came home a hero. Parade down Main Street, parties."

"Family?" asked Phil.

"Mother and father are here and well," said Cawelti. "I talked to them. William is their only son. Father's a welder. Mother's a ticket clerk at a movie house. William left home about four months ago. Said he had something to do and would stay in touch."

"Did he?" I said.

"Stay in touch? Yeah. He writes, calls. Doesn't say much."

"You ask them if he knows anyone in Los Angeles?" asked Phil.

"So far as they know, he doesn't," Cawelti said. "Maybe some old army buddies, but they don't have names."

"That it?" I asked.

Cawelti hesitated.

"No," he said. "William Tracy Carson spent four months in an army mental hospital before he came home from the war. Battle fatigue."

I looked at Phil. Phil had spent about a week in an army hospital after the last war. They had called it shell shock. When he came home, he had put a little distance between himself and the world. He had never been easy, but he was even touchier after the things he'd seen. Marrying Ruth and having the kids had given him a reason to live. What was William Tracy Carson's reason to live?

"Anything else?" asked Phil.

"No," said Cawelti. "We're getting copies of the photographs of Carson and the baby made up. It'll take another hour, maybe, and then we'll get them out to all cars."

"Make it a twelve-twelve," said Phil.

I wasn't sure what a twelve-twelve was, but it had to be some kind of special priority.

"Already have," said Cawelti. "I'll call you if we get any leads or find them."

One of us had to say it, and I could see Phil wasn't the one.

"Thanks," I said.

"For what?" said Cawelti. "It's my job. I'm not doing this for you. The only thing I'd do for you is throw the switch if you were sitting in the hot seat on your brother's lap."

"Ah," I said. "The John Cawelti we know and love."

He slammed the phone down.

"Love that guy," I said.

Phil grunted.

"Well?" I asked. "Got any ideas?"

He didn't. We sat staring at the phone for half an hour before it rang. I beat Phil to it, picked up the phone and said, "Yeah."

"I'm at the Pantages," said Blackstone. "I think it might be a good idea for you to come over here. There's someone you should talk to."

"We'll be right there," I said.

I hung up. So did Phil.

"Your car or mine?" I asked.

"I'm not getting in that tin box," he said, getting up. "We take mine."

It was after eleven. There wasn't much traffic. The blackout didn't make it much fun to be on the streets. When we got into Phil's car, he said, "A guy on foot with a limp and a little girl. They should be able to find him unless he's holed up somewhere."

I didn't say anything. When Phil made a U-turn, I reached for the radio. He slapped my hand away. I knew why. He was in no mood for music, the news, or drama. He had enough drama in his life, no room for music, and the thought of more bad news was more than he wanted.

Parking at the Pantages at this hour was no problem. We found Blackstone and his brother talking to Raymond Ramutka, the stage door man who sat behind his little desk drinking coffee. I wondered if he lived here. Harry and Pete stood in from of him.

There wasn't much light. A shaded lamp on the desk. An enclosed bulb over the door. A few bulbs glowing from behind the curtains of the stage and a single light at the top of the stairway where the dressing rooms were.

Ramutka, the stage door man from central casting, looked over the top of his glasses at us, put down his mug, and picked up his pipe.

"Raymond says he got to know Jimmy reasonably well in the last few days," Blackstone told us.

"Nice boy," said Ramutka. "Nice boy. Gave him some of my pain pills that first night. His leg, you know."

We knew.

"Raymond says Jimmy liked to be alone," said Blackstone.

"Yes," said Ramutka, looking at the stem of his pipe. "Liked to go up on the roof and look at the stars all by himself. Helped him to think. I got the feeling that boy did a lot more feeling than thinking."

"The roof," I said.

Ramutka pointed his pipe up at the ceiling high above us.

"You see him tonight?" Phil asked.

"No," Ramutka, said shaking his head.

"Could he get to the roof without your seeing him?" asked Blackstone.

"Sure," the old man said. "Lots of ways, if you know them. Through a window on the other side of the stage if there was one open or up the fire escape if he climbed up on something and . . . lots of ways, if you know them," he repeated.

"How can we get up there?" Phil said.

Ramutka pointed with his pipe again.

"Up the stairs, round the corner, past the storage room, and up the rungs."

He started to say something else, but we had all turned and were headed to the metal staircase in single file. Phil was first. I was second. Harry and Pete behind. We rattled past the dressing rooms into the shadows.

We turned the corner and saw the rungs to the roof jutting out of the brick wall.

"Hold it," said Phil, turning to us. "We're making too damn much noise. I'll go up. You wait here."

"I could talk to him," Blackstone whispered.

"Harry can be very persuasive," whispered Pete.

"So can I," said Phil.

Even with his face in shadow, I recognized the look on my brother's face. I didn't argue. Neither did Blackstone or his brother.

Phil went slowly and quietly up the ladder and was quickly lost in the darkness above us. We could hear his feet touch each rung and then a square opened above us and we could see stars and then, half a beat later, the bulk of my brother's body blocked the stars and went onto the roof.

We waited listening, looking at each other. A radio came on below us and out of sight. We waited. Nothing. And then Phil's body filled the square of stars and started down to us. He was making no effort to be quiet.

"Not there," he said when he got back to the landing, wiped his hands on his pants, and turned to us.

"The wrong roof."

We turned to Harry Blackstone who said, "I think I know what roof he's on."

Then I remembered what Juanita had said. It was simple. We had made it complicated.

"He's on the roof of the Farraday," I said.

Harry Blackstone nodded.

CHAPTER

18

Place a glass of water almost full on a table. Drop an ice cube into the water. Rest a piece of string over the ice cube with the ends of the string dangling over two sides of the glass. Challenge audience member to remove ice cube with string without touching the ice cube. When they give up, perform the trick. Solution: Pour salt on the ice cube and string. The salt melts the ice. The string sinks in and the ice hardens again when the effect of the salt wears off. The string is now frozen into the ice cube that can simply be removed by holding both ends of the string and lifting.

From the Blackstone, The Magic Detective *radio show*

WE CLATTERED DOWN THE STEPS and past Raymond Ramutka, who was listening to classical music on the radio on his little table.

"Not there?" he asked.

"Not there," Blackstone said.

Ramutka was going to ask another question, but he was too slow. We piled into Phil's car and he did a wild U-turn, heading back toward our office. I was in the front passenger seat. Phil ran two red lights and, amazingly, avoided a collision with a truck. His jaw was set as if it was he who now had a toothache. I considered talking about what we were going to do when we got to the Farraday, but Phil was in a don't-mess-with-me mood so I shut up.

"If he's there . . ." Pete said from the backseat.

"He's there," I said, or, rather, hoped.

I didn't pray. I don't pray, not for show, not to feel better. I don't know if there's a God or gods out there. I don't think about it much or often. It wasn't that I didn't believe. I just thought if there was a God and he wanted to get involved, he was watching. He could do what he wanted. What could I promise him that would make a difference? Why should he do something for me just because I asked him?

That's about the extent of what I think about religion. What I did think about now was a pretty, smiling little girl and a young man who had killed people—Japanese soldiers—about a year or two ago, and maybe three more men in the last few days.

"If he's there," said Blackstone behind us, "I want to talk to him."

If Phil had driven like a lunatic on the way to the Pantages, he drove like a man possessed on the way back to the Farraday. When we got there, he didn't bother to find a legal parking space. He just pulled up on the sidewalk in front of Manny's Taco Shop.

We decided not to stop at Jeremy and Alice's apartment for two reasons. First, we might be wrong and didn't want to give them hope and then find out Jimmy and Natasha weren't on the roof. Second, there was no way Jeremy and Alice would agree to stay behind, and, if they came with us, there was no way of knowing what they might do.

We walked up the stairs to the top floor, turned right, away from the Butler apartment, and made our way to the door to the narrow stairwell that led to the roof. I'd been up there a few times. I couldn't remember why.

"He's there," Phil said, pausing at a door on our left.

The sign on the door said it was the office of The Puccini Locksmith Company. Albert Puccini, a quiet little old man, would be his own client in the morning. His door was slightly open and shorn at the level of the lock.

"He made that call to the Butler apartment from here," said Phil. "He never left the building."

My gun was safely in the glove compartment of my Crosley. Phil had his tucked under his jacket in a leather holster he kept oiled and clean.

The door to the stairwell was closed but no longer locked. That meant more work for Albert Puccini in the morning. Phil led the way up the narrow, dark stairs to the door at the top. His gun was in his right hand. He opened the door with his left and stepped onto the roof. We followed.

The sky was bright with stars and almost a whole moon. Maybe it was the blackout or the fact that we were on a roof, but it was lighter up there than it was inside the Farraday.

We couldn't see Jimmy. There were four vents dotting the roof and a little wooden storage shack to our right. Then we saw him.

Jimmy was sitting on the two-foot wide concrete edge of the building. Natasha was in his arms sleeping, her chest moving slowly in and out, her mouth a peaceful pout. In his right hand, Jimmy held a gun. It was aimed at us.

"Jimmy," Blackstone said softly. "What are you doing?"

"Right now?" Jimmy said, glancing up at the stars. "I'm remembering."

We inched forward. Jimmy didn't pay any special attention to Phil's gun.

"Remembering what?" asked Blackstone calmly.

"An island," said Jimmy. "Don't remember which one. You think the sky is bright tonight? There wasn't any light out there. You'd lay on your back and look up and see, I don't know, millions of stars. Some nights it looked as if the sky was all stars and no dark. You know?"

"Yes," said Blackstone, moving ahead of us closer to Jimmy, motioning for us to stay where we were.

"Then in the morning the sky went flashing bright with the sun and we started to get incoming mail," said Jimmy. "Mortar fire mostly. They died around me. Mosberg, Tighe, Huang, Donaldberg. Donaldberg was from Detroit."

"I'm sorry," said Blackstone.

Jimmy bit his lower lip and looked down at the face of the sleeping child. He shook his head.

"I don't know," he said. "My friends got killed. I killed. You know?"

"I think so," Blackstone said. "Is it alright if I take the girl?"

"I don't know," he said. "I just want to get away. It's all over."

"It's all over," said Blackstone.

Phil moved slowly, very slowly to his right, his eyes on Jimmy, his gun waist level.

"May I sit here?" asked Blackstone.

"You don't need my okay," said Jimmy.

Blackstone sat on the concrete edge of the roof about six feet from Jimmy. "What happened?" he asked him.

"Tonight? I could see that Wilde recognized me," he said. "I'd stayed back when Cunningham and me went to the studio to see him, but I could see he recognized me. I don't know how. I was supposed to come here and sit with Natasha, so I came here and got her."

"Lovely child," said Blackstone with a smile.

Jimmy looked at her.

"Smart, too," he said.

"Why did you kill Calvin Ott?" Blackstone asked.

"Same reason I killed Mr. Cunningham and Mr. Rand," he said. "To protect you."

"Me? I don't understand."

"Mr. Cunningham was going out with Gwen," Jimmy said. "He talked to me a few times. Then just last week he asked me if I wanted to make a lot of money. I don't need a lot of money, but he said it funny. Kinda like it was a secret. So, I said 'yes' to find out what he was going to say."

Natasha made a soft sound and moved a little. Jimmy rocked her gently, the gun in his hand aimed in my general direction.

"Go on," coaxed Blackstone.

"He said he and some friends had good reasons for wanting to hurt you. He wanted me to help him do things, make the illusions mess up, help him come up with things they could blackmail you with. Said one of his friends was rich and would give me two thousand dollars."

"Ott?" asked Blackstone.

"Ott," Jimmy confirmed. "The other night, when the buzz saw had a problem, I went up to the dressing room and shot Cunningham. I waited till the buzz saw was making lots of noise. Then I came back down and sort of waited for someone to find the body. Mr. Rand was backstage in a turban and stuff. He went up to the dressing room and found the body. I was watching. Gwen saw him coming out of her dressing room with the gun. He ran down the stairs. She found the body and screamed. Then she ran down the stairs and out the stage door. Or maybe it was the other way around. Yes, it was. Gwen ran down first, and Rand followed her."

"Why?" asked Blackstone.

"I think because she saw him coming out of the dressing room, and he figured she would tell the police," said Jimmy. "But he didn't have a real gun, just the pellet gun we use in the bursting red balloon illusion."

"And then?" Blackstone prompted.

"Mr. Ott was there, in the theater. He came to watch the show come apart."

"And you killed Ott," Blackstone said.

Phil had edged a good six feet over now. He might, if he had to, have a shot at Jimmy. I knew he wouldn't take it unless he had to, because of Natasha.

"Yes," he said.

"And Rand knew?"

"Yes, he was there when I did it," said Jimmy. "I just walked past him to where Mr. Ott was sitting and laughing. I think he thought I was going to help him hide the fake knife. I had my own knife in my belt. I stabbed him while he was laughing about the look that was going to be on your face when you came back and found him alive and holding up a glass of wine to toast his making you look bad."

"But he didn't get the chance," said Blackstone.

"Didn't get the chance," Jimmy agreed. "Mr. Rand looked at me, looked real scared. He was right. I would have killed him there, too, but he ran."

"Jimmy, you could have told me and . . ."

"No," said Jimmy with a sigh. "Nothing you can do with people like that but kill them. War is going on. American soldiers are getting killed and twisted all up every day and they do stuff like this. They needed killing, Mr. Blackstone. You needed protecting."

Natasha definitely stirred and squirmed and looked like she was about to wake up. Jimmy looked over his shoulder and down at the street six floors below him. Phil raised his gun a few inches.

"Why should you kill three people to protect me?" asked Blackstone.

"Why? Because you saved my life and my mom's life," he said.

"I did? When?"

"Decatur two years ago, just a week before I went into the army," said Jimmy. "The theater fire. I was at the show. My mom was in the ticket booth when you brought us all out on the street. You got her to come out of the booth. The fire came flying out the door and cracked right through the booth. I don't forget. People shouldn't forget, you know?"

"I know," said Blackstone. "She's waking up."

Jimmy looked at Natasha, who definitely was about to wake up. He started to get up with her in his arms. Phil's gun hand was at waist level now.

"Jimmy," Blackstone said. "Please hand her to me."

"I wasn't going to hurt her," Jimmy said, holding the little girl out to the magician.

Blackstone rose and took her from him. Phil's gun was shoulder level and aimed at Jimmy.

Blackstone backed away and said,

"Thank you, Jimmy. Now, if you just put the gun down we can help you."

"Where's the satchel?" I asked.

"I threw it in the garbage," Jimmy said. "There was no money in it, just folded newspapers."

Jimmy looked at the gun in his hand as if he had forgotten it was there. Then he looked over at Pete Bouton and me and then turned his head toward Phil. He saw the gun aimed at him.

"Jimmy," Blackstone repeated. "Look."

Jimmy turned his eyes toward the magician, who was handing the child to his brother.

Blackstone held up both of his arms, clapped his hands and a flash of light appeared between them. When the flash ended, Blackstone was holding a duck in his hands. The duck quacked, and Phil fired.

Jimmy staggered back and looked as if he were about to topple over the roof. I ran toward him, grabbed his arm, and pulled him toward me away from the edge. He fell on his side, the gun sliding across the roof away from him.

Phil stepped forward, gun at the ready.

"How is he?" Phil asked.

"Hole in his thigh," I said. "Bleeding a lot."

"I'll call for an ambulance," Pete said, moving to the stairwell with a groggy Natasha in his arms looking over his shoulder at Jimmy. She looked as if she were going to cry.

"I wouldn't have hurt her," Jimmy said, not seeming to feel any pain.

"I know," said Blackstone.

"All those months," Jimmy said, looking at me. "Never got shot, just the shrapnel in my leg. Now I'm here, and I get shot. Funny, huh?"

"Yeah," I said. "Funny."

CHAPTER

19

Place two wooden kitchen matches side by side on a table about four inches apart. Place a quarter on the table just above the opening between the matches. Tell your audience that the coin will repel the matches. Let someone do it. Nothing will happen as they slide the coin between the matches. Then you do it. Lean forward and concentrate. Close your eyes. Move the coin between the matches as you blow gently on the coin without moving your lips. Blow slowly, easily. The matches roll away. Practice. Always practice.

From the Blackstone, The Magic Detective *radio show*

THE NEXT MORNING GUNTHER CAME to my room after Mrs. Plaut had given me her usual wake-up call. This morning we were having broccoli and cauliflower whipped egg delight. I was putting my pants on.

We had gotten to bed around three in the morning, and it was now a little after seven. I gave serious thought to coming back to bed after breakfast.

"Gwen is a very nice young woman," Gunther said, adjusting his tie. "And smart, very smart. Her family is French, did you know?"

"No," I said.

"Yes," said Gunther. "French. She speaks it quite well."

"So you got along?"

"Splendidly," he said. "We are having lunch together, if you would like to join us."

"You need a chaperone?"

"No."

"Good."

Jimmy had been taken to County Hospital where they pulled Phil's bullet from his leg. Cawelti was there to arrest him.

"Nothing's different between us," Cawelti had said to Phil and me when we saw him at the hospital. "Don't expect anything different."

"Wouldn't have it any other way," I said.

Phil didn't say anything.

"Come by the station in the morning. Someone will take your statement," he said. "I won't be there."

"We'll miss you," I said.

His face was red now, almost as red as his hair.

"Don't worry," he said. "I'll be seeing you soon."

His eyes met Phil's. They held for a few seconds. Then he turned and moved toward the room where Jimmy was being guarded by a uniformed cop.

"Back to his lovable self," I had said.

Phil only said "Good night" and went home.

At the breakfast table, Emma Simcox and Ben Bidwell were now officially holding hands. Mrs. Plaut came in with a steaming casserole dish, put it down and said,

"There are two announcements this a.m. One," she said looking at Gunther and me. "Mr. Bidwell and Emma will be wed on August 16 here. Wine for the occasion will be Virginia Dare. Rhubarb batter pudding will be the dessert. I have yet to decide which of the following patriotic main entrees would best suit the occasion, breaded fried tripe, liver and bacon rolls, individual liver loaves, brains in croustades, or heart patties. All are *Woman's Day* recipes. Your input will be duly considered as the blessed day draws nigh. Two," she went on, meeting my eyes. "I *was* in a magical act with the late mister. His secrets will not be revealed while I trod the earth and its environs. When I have gone to my reward or punishment, the mister's notebooks will be forwarded to Mr. Harry Blackstone. Emma will take care of that."

Emma Simcox smiled.

"Now eat."

We ate. It was good. The coffee was hot and strong. The bird in the parlor squawked "Kilroy" over and over. The bird was in his cage. All was right with the world.

I was in the office less than an hour later. I didn't meet any tenants on the way in, and I was relieved that I didn't run into Alice Pallas Butler. Phil wasn't in. He had said he was taking the day off to be with his family but that I could reach him at home if I needed him.

The phone was ringing when I unlocked the door.

"Toby," said Marty Leib on the other end. "I thought I'd best tell you that I have been retained to represent William Tracy Carson, who is resting comfortably in his hospital bed."

"He doesn't have any money," I said.

"His parents do," said Marty. "His father has a very successful welding shop in Decatur, Illinois. The war has been kind to him."

"Thanks for telling me," I said, knowing there was more.

"Temporary insanity," Marty said.

"Three times?"

"Why not? War wounds, mental trauma, a hero who worshiped a much-beloved magician. I would like your help in doing some investigation on this. You know the background, and I expect you will be testifying at the trial—if it comes to a trial, which I seriously doubt."

"Our fees have gone up," I said.

"How much?"

"You don't bill us for what you've done for us over the past three days and we don't charge you."

"A counter suggestion," said Marty. "You, or Blackstone, pays my bill, which will be in the mail today, and I do not sue your brother and your firm for excessive and unnecessary violence in shooting my client."

"That won't work," I said.

"But it is a nuisance," Marty said with a sigh.

"You win, Marty," I said.

"I always win," said Marty. "That's why I charge what I do."

He hung up. I hung my jacket on the coatrack and went to my desk. I didn't have to look up when the door opened. I knew who would be there.

Alice stood blocking the doorway.

"Good morning," I said, opening the letter on the top of a small pile on my desk. It was an offer to buy two suits at Hy's For Him for the price of one. "How's Natasha?"

"Fine," she said from the doorway.

I went to letter number two. It was from someone in Pasadena. I couldn't make out the name, but there was a phone number. If I read the scrawl right, she wanted to talk to us about finding her lost amoeba or ambulance or amulet.

I half expected Alice to come behind me, yank me from my chair, and hurl me across the room if I was lucky, out the window if I wasn't. She didn't move.

"Thank you," she said.

"You're welcome."

"For finding Natasha so fast last night," she added. "She doesn't remember any of it, but she asked about the man who told her a story."

"Great," I said, putting down my letter opener and looking at her with my best lopsided smile. "So we're friends now?"

"Yes," she said. "I still don't like your getting Jeremy involved in your work, but he's a grown man."

He's at least two grown men, I thought. But I just nodded. Alice left.

I called Anita and told her what had happened the night before. We agreed to go out for dinner and a movie after she finished work. Before I got off the phone, there was a knock at the door. I didn't have time to say "come in." Shelly entered, followed by Pancho. I hung up the phone.

"Is this great, or is this great?" said Shelly, holding some sheets of paper up to show me the typing on them.

"What?"

"The start of the script, *Dentist in Disguise*," Shelly said. "Pancho here is a brilliant genius. Look."

He placed the pages neatly on my desk and stepped back, chewing on his morning cigar. He looked at Pancho, who let a small smile twitch his thin lips.

"He worked most of the night on it," added Shelly. "Did I say he is a brilliant genius?"

"Your exact words."

"We're thinking of Walter Pidgeon to play me. Or Errol Flynn. He has the touch."

"Light touch," said Pancho.

"Let me know what you think," Shelly said and left the office with Pancho still behind him.

I flipped the title page over on its face and read the neatly typed pages:

INTERIOR, DAY. OFFICE OF SHELDON PEVSNER
Phone rings. SHELDON PEVSNER in clean freshly starched
whites is working on a bicuspid filling of a beautiful
BLONDE who looks at him with the complete confidence
he clearly deserves.

SHELLY

Excuse me.

He touches her shoulder gently, reassuringly, and answers
the phone on the wall.

Dr. Pevsner.

SPLIT SCREEN. SHELDON PEVSNER on right. TOBY PETERS on left.

PETERS

Sheldon, I need your help again.

SHELLY

I've got a patient. I'll come to your office in half an hour. What's the problem?

PETERS

I think someone is trying to kill my client, Blackstone the Magician. It's got me stumped. Please come as soon as you can.

SHELLY

Haven't I always been there to pull your cases from the jaws of disaster? As the Bard said,
"Take heed dear heart, of this large privilege;
The hardest knife ill used doth lose its edge."

PETERS

And thanks again for saving my tooth.

SHELLY

It's what I do.
SHELLY hangs up. TOBY disappears. We are only in SHELLY'S office. SHELLY walks to patient, smiles. She smiles back.

SHELLY

You are complete.
SHELLY helps her from the chair.

BLONDE

That was Shakespeare wasn't it?

Their faces are inches apart.

SHELLY

On the phone?

BLONDE laughs at his wit.

I should really observe that first bite of your renewed smile. Dinner tonight?

BLONDE blushes. SHELLY kisses her hand.

BLONDE

Oh, yes.

SHELLY leads her to the door. BLONDE exits. SHELLY turns on the radio, finds classical music, and cleans his instruments. The door suddenly opens. A MAN dressed like a sea captain, his cap pulled forward over his eyes, staggers in. Under his arm is a bundle about the size of a large ham. It is wrapped in brown paper and tied with a thin rope. MAN tries to say something, hands the package to SHELLY and then collapses. SHELLY touches the man's neck to be sure he is dead and then SHELLY puts the package down on his instrument table, unwraps it, and discovers a foot-high white statue of an owl.

It ended there. I looked at the door waiting for the knock I was reasonably sure would come. It did.

"Come in."

Pancho Vanderhoff came timidly in, his yellow scarf wrapped around his neck.

"You read it?"

"I did," I said, holding the few pages out for him to take.

"You're not angry? I mean about the way I depicted you?"

I smiled.

"Change the name," I said. "Or I'll break both your arms."

"But Dr. Minck wants real names," he said, taking the few pages of script.

"He'll have to make an exception in this case," I said.

"But he wants to say this movie is based on a true story."

"Pancho, you took the last page right out of *The Maltese Falcon*."

"It's a white owl, not a black falcon," he said.

I didn't answer. He clutched the few script pages to his thin breast.

"I ran out of ideas," he said. "And Dr. Minck likes it. He wants to know what comes next."

"Peter Lorre walks in with a gun and tells him to please put up his hands."

"I'm desperate," Pancho said. "I'm bereft of ideas."

"You'll come up with something," I said. "Steal from Shakespeare."

A light went on in Pancho's eyes, a dim light but definitely a light.

"MacBeth," he said. "Witches, magic, ghosts. A floating dagger like Blackstone's floating lightbulb."

"My goal in life is to inspire," I said.

He thanked me and hurried away.

I called my brother's house. His sister-in-law Becky answered.

"It's me, Toby. Everyone alright."

"Fine," she said.

"Mind if I drop by?"

"Come over for lunch," she said.

"I'll be there."

I finished opening my mail and started to make out the bill for Blackstone. Knock at the door. The magician appeared holding a package in his hands.

"We're leaving for San Diego tomorrow afternoon," he said. "We've got two shows to do there, for the troops sailing out. If you have your bill ready by this evening before six, bring it to the hotel, and I'll give you a check."

He placed the package on the desk in front of me.

"Care to guess what's inside?" he asked.

"The Maltese Falcon."

"Open it."

I did and pulled out an ornate Chinese box about the size of two cigar boxes. I reached over to lift the cover.

"Stop."

I stopped.

"Open it when I'm gone," he said.

He touched his right hand to his forehead in a salute like the one James Cagney gave in *The Public Enemy.* Then he was gone.

I opened the box slowly, half expecting white pigeons to come flying in my face, or a rabbit to peek over the side twitching its nose in my direction.

There was nothing in the blue velvet lined box, nothing but a lightbulb. The lightbulb, though, wasn't lying on the bottom of the box. It was floating. And then it turned on.